ALONG THE STARS

A Novel

ANTHONY MCDONALD

Anchor Mill Publishing

Anthony McDonald

www.anthonymcdonald.co.uk

First published in Kindle edition 2012 by BIGfib Books

Anchor Mill Publishing

4/04 Anchor Mill

Paisley PA1 1JR

SCOTLAND

anchormillpublishing@gmail.com

Cover design: Successful gay hook-up in public park. © istockphoto © Nicolas McComber

For Tony as always

Acknowledgements

Grateful thanks to Juan Carmona and James Simpson, who answered my many questions about Spain, and To Will Tatters, who furnished me with much information about the world of airlines. In this connection I also owe a debt to a book: *Flying the Big Jets* by Captain Stanley Stewart.

Time and Place

Spain, England, and the airspace in between.

ONE

You couldn't go straight home from Málaga. There were mountains. Even if you took off on the northerly runway you had to turn east across the city's outskirts and follow the hills along the coast. Only when you'd gained a safety margin of altitude could you head north across the sierras towards Britain. This added about two minutes to the flight time, though this hardly mattered to the co-pilot on this midday flight to Manchester, Senior First Officer Borja Alcorlo Silva. Slightly more concerning was his suspicion that his captain fancied him.

Borja liked Captain Amanda Symons. He had not often flown with a female captain; there weren't many of them yet. And he had no problem in principle with taking orders from a woman. He thought that men who said they did were being disingenuous. It could hardly be a new experience for any of them: every man on the planet had had a mother.

The direction-finder needle showed their track about to intersect the Hinojosa radial, the next leg of their pre-set route to England. It was time to make that sharp turn inland. Borja, who was flying the sector, moved the control column himself; the autopilot would not be engaged until they reached ten thousand feet. The plane banked, slipped sideways in the sky, then came slowly round. The coast disappeared from the cockpit windows and was replaced by a broad and craggy expanse of sierra, its foothills studded with olive and vine, and beyond that a vast, tawny plain which came to a misty stop about sixty miles away. The only feature that relieved that distant expanse was the lake of Fuente de Piedra, where flamingos waded. From here the lake was just a dull, oval mirror laid on a lion-skin rug. Away from the coast there was cloud: it lay above them like a smooth grey ceiling. The plane swam up to it, was quickly engulfed, then floated free, and the nose cone gleamed again in the sun, beneath an infinity of blue. Meanwhile Captain Amanda Symons took radio leave of Málaga Tower, changed frequency and reported their position to Spanish Air Traffic Control. A minute later they were climbing through ten thousand feet and Borja let the autopilot have control.

'What are you doing tonight?'Amanda asked. She meant in Manchester. Neither of them lived there; the airline operated mostly out of Gatwick and Luton. She had guessed that he would be stopping over like herself.

'Shooting straight off, actually.'Borja had learned his English idioms from his partner. They sounded at odds sometimes with his Hispanic appearance and residual Spanish accent. 'I've got a first night to get to.'

Amanda looked about as surprised as an airline captain is permitted to look when on duty. 'You're appearing in a play?'

'It's not my first night. It's my boyfriend's.'There. He'd done it. And because neither he nor Amanda but the autopilot was now flying the plane, this announcement had no impact on its steady progress through the air and accordingly went unregistered by the hundred or so passengers behind them.

'Oh,'said Amanda in a bright tone that very nearly succeeded in disguising her instinctive disappointment: a disappointment that Borja nevertheless recognised – and was all too familiar with. 'Is he an actor?'

'James? Only in his private life,'said Borja with the ghost of a smile. 'He manages a theatre. He doesn't have to do much on first nights except worry. And he likes me to be there to hold his hand.'

'It must be nice. I mean, having a partner in the theatre.'

'Well,'said Borja, 'I don't want to exaggerate it too much. He's only the manager there, not the director. It's like being first officer rather than captain.'

'All the same,'said Amanda.

They reached the top of their climb as they crossed Hinojosa beacon and the autopilot adjusted their heading onto a bearing for Madrid. Amanda returned to the subject of Borja's boyfriend a few minutes later. 'Isn't it difficult having a permanent relationship with someone in the theatre? I mean, it does have a certain reputation... Or am I prying? Sorry.'

'It's OK. But is the theatre so different from our profession in that way?'

'I'm not sure. A female airline captain doesn't get chatted up all that often by junior stewards, you know.'

'You can join my club,'said Borja. 'Not that it's something I miss that much,'he added rather carefully. He glanced sideways at her: a petite woman with neat dark hair and a pleasing profile. 'Are you ... single?'It was a safe question now, disarmed by his earlier announcement.

'At present, yes.'

'Well, there's more to life than stewards, no? People with the same rank as you. Other captains?'

'You might have decided that I'm totally undiscriminating. But it isn't true. There's only two pilots in this outfit I might have been remotely interested in. One of those is gay.'

'Really?'said Borja, genuinely astonished. 'Who?'

Amanda giggled. 'You, you fool.'

'Oh I see.'Borja was silent for a moment while he took this on board. He had guessed his captain fancied him, not that she would actually say so. Then, 'And the other?'

'I'm not sure I should tell you. You might...'

He turned slightly towards her. 'Have I told any of your secrets before?'he asked, mock-serious.

'You've never had the opportunity.'

'OK then. I promise to be an oyster of discretion. Do we say that? Crossing my heart.'

'Well then, what about Captain Holmes? Andy to his friends. Don't you think he's rather nice?'

'Andy Holmes? I'm not sure that I do. He's very unsmiling. I've heard he's a stickler for procedure. No joking on the flight deck. Very Scottish Calvinist he strikes me. You don't think so?'

'I know what you mean. But maybe the coldness is part of the attraction. Part of the challenge. He's got wonderful ice-blue eyes. Don't tell me you never noticed.'

'Hmm,'said Borja, non-committal. 'Of course I've never actually flown with him.'

On the panel in front of them the VOR needles smartly about-turned, indicating that they had passed overhead the beacon at Madrid. You wouldn't have known it otherwise, though. The clouds lay thick beneath them.

TWO

James collected Borja's ticket from the box office and made a point of paying for it in cash. Even though Borja wouldn't be occupying the seat until some time after the interval and the house would not be a sell-out, he didn't want to pull rank by simply instructing the box office to leave the seat next to his unsold.

As he walked away from the window he was waylaid by a slim young man dressed in off-black jeans and T-shirt. It was Nick, one of the assistant stage managers and a very new addition to the company. He looked somehow surprised to find himself in the place where he stood, and surprised to find James there too. 'Oh James,'he said. 'We were looking for you. I mean Mike is.'Mike was Nick's boss, the production manager. 'There's a bit of an emergency.'

'OK, tell me.'

'The Fire Department just rang. They're coming to do an un-something inspection in about ten minutes.'

James grimaced. 'They must have known it was an opening night, for God's sake. They do it on purpose. And the Public Health?'

'Just Fire as far as I know,'said Nick.

'Well that's something. Where's Mike?'

'Upstairs in the ... in your office. Not panicking.'

They found Mike sitting at James's desk, his back to the big window on whose frame James had pinned a King Cong postcard which was captioned: Don't panic. Count to ten. Then panic.

'It's all OK, surely,'James said. 'We get this over during the break at the end of the dress-run and let the public in on time as usual.'

Mike made an it's-not-that-simple kind of face. 'It's all OK. Yeah. Bar one thing. Emergency lighting.'

'It's up and running, isn't it?'James was just checking, confidently expecting yes.

'It was. Till three bulbs blew at the weekend for some reason. That took all our spares. LX reordered and they're coming tomorrow. But another bulb went this morning. We're one down.'

'Jesus,'said James. 'They'll close us. Does Guy know?'

'No.'

'Let's keep it like that. He's got enough to think about.'

There was a moment's silence and then Nick, sitting quiet and forgotten at the other end of the big room, said, 'I think I've got an idea.'

The fire chiefs arrived in full uniform a few minutes later and began their torch-lit procession round the building – the mains switch having been thrown, to simulate emergency conditions. Miraculously the dress rehearsal had ended on time and the stage and auditorium were clear. As James and Mike led the way out of the foyer Nick waited behind and, as soon as they had turned the corner into the darkened dress circle, unscrewed the emergency bulb nearest to the front entrance, shot out of the front door, legged it up Pembridge Street, round two street corners, and then turned in at the stage door where he placed the bulb in the nearest socket – which was now vacant following a hectic rearrangement two minutes earlier. It was a version of that old familiar school trick in which one face makes two appearances in the end of year photograph. Nick had disappeared by the time James, Mike and the fire officers completed their progress, but there was the evidence of his recent, inspired visit, shining out most satisfactorily like the grin of the vanished Cheshire cat.

It was well after the interval by the time Borja arrived quietly in the dress circle, whispering his sorrys in the darkness as he knocked knees with the people already sitting, attentive, in James's row. He sat, still in uniform, and gave off that unique combination of odours – to which James alone was receptive – that was partly aircraft, partly Spanish cologne, and partly simply Borja himself. For half an hour they sat side by side, the tall, still vaguely blond Englishman, and his smaller, trim, dark-haired Spanish mate. For over a dozen years now their friends had told them they made a handsome pair. Borja picked up the threads of the plot reasonably quickly – it wasn't that difficult – and by the end of the piece he was laughing at the jokes along with everyone else. Then it was house lights up and a shuffling transfer upstairs to what by day had been James's and everybody else's office but was renamed the Regent Room when refurnished with buffet tables for occasions such as this.

Neville, the author of the play, had got there first. 'Watched the whole thing,'he said, 'from the safety zone of the circle bar. Doesn't do to get too close in on a first night.'Neville was their senior by some fifteen years, bulky tonight in a moth-friendly suit, and ruddy of face. 'Champagne?'He flourished a bottle a little unsteadily and, thanks to the skilful deployment of glasses by Borja and James, managed to execute the manoeuvre of filling them up without spilling a drop. 'Like mid-air refuelling,' Borja said to James. James reflected for a moment that the champagne wasn't actually Neville's to offer but then took a good swig to banish the thought.

'Hóla, pilot!' This was Guy, the artistic director; he was Neville's age, but tall, slender, nervy: a questing pine marten.

'It went well, didn't it?' Borja said. 'I only caught the last forty minutes but the bus seems good.'

'The buzz,' James clarified.

'We came through,' said Guy, nodding. 'Now who's got the champagne?' He wandered off before James could direct his attention to the nearest bottle. But of course it wasn't exactly champagne that he wanted.

'We had a panic earlier,' James confided. He told Borja the story about the fire inspection, and Nick's brainwave about swapping the emergency bulbs around.

'Jesus,' said Borja, hoisting dark eyebrows above lustrous eyes. 'You people take some liberties. Can you imagine what would happen if we did that?'

'The same as would have happened here if we'd got caught. The theatre would close and I'd be out of a job for ever and a day. But we didn't get caught. That's the trick of it.'

'Who is this Nick character?' James's mention of the younger man had caught Borja's attention. 'Have I met him?'

'He's a very new ASM. Nice, but new. I'll introduce you.'

Nick had arrived without James having very much to do with it. He had been interviewed by Guy and Mike when James and Borja were on holiday, so James had only met him after he'd started. James remembered Guy introducing them on the pavement outside the theatre. Nick had been smiling a vague kind of a smile and was wearing the weirdest pair of desert boots that James could remember seeing. He had kept looking down at them as if they were the source of some surprise to him too. Then he had dipped them, one after the other, over the edge of the kerb as if testing the depth of an invisible puddle. He was not much more than average height, but looked taller because of his slim build, with deep brown eyes that shone shyly through spectacles and displaying a gap between his top front teeth.

'He's quite attractive in his own quiet way, I think you'll agree,' said James to Borja. Ten seconds later

Nick came up to them with a confident manner that he had not demonstrated during his previous contacts with James but which was undoubtedly born out of his successful resolution of the afternoon's little problem. James introduced him.

Borja decided Nick looked nice. Nice enough to start a conversation with. 'What brought you into the theatre?' he asked.

'God, you don't half begin with difficult questions,' said Nick, sounding alarmed.

Borja hadn't thought the question difficult. 'I thought it was easy enough,' he said.

'I didn't know quite what I was,' Nick began, confessionally. 'I did a music degree at university.'

James's eyebrows rose slightly. He'd forgotten that bit of the CV. Nick didn't look to him like someone who had done a music degree.

'But what do you do with that?' Nick went on, addressing the question to himself. 'I don't play an instrument well enough to be in an orchestra – let alone be a soloist – and I don't compose. And who wants to be a teacher?'

'We-ell,' James said, in a beg-to-differ tone. He had spent three years of his life being exactly that.

'You just care a lot about music,' Borja offered helpfully. Nick flashed him a smile that struck him as almost pathetically grateful.

'Like Alexa,' Borja said in an aside to James, which caused Nick to consider asking, who's Alexa? before deciding not to. He had found that musical comparisons rarely flattered him. Instead he heard himself saying, 'We're all going to the Queen's afterwards. Just for a laugh. I mean, for fun. Are you two coming?' Then he stopped, surprised by his own boldness, pleased but at the same time alarmed by it.

James looked at Borja. 'You've never been to the Queen's, have you?'

'Meaning that you have, I suppose.' Then he smiled and shrugged and said, 'Yeah, why not?' over James's mumble of, 'Well-yes-once-or-twice-but-only-in-a-crowd-of-us-sort-of-thing.'

'I suppose we all have to go in that case,' said Guy resignedly. 'I hope it's not going to be full of people all off their faces on E.'

'Don't worry,' said Mike, who had just materialised beside them. 'It's only Tuesday.'

It was just a couple of blocks from the theatre to the club, which was fortunate, because it meant everyone could walk. Getting a company of actors plus stage management and crew into a fleet of cars was always difficult. 'Ah … I don't think I'll tag along, if you don't mind,' Neville said to James as they all began to drift up the road, a loose swarm of buzzing insects.

'And getting home?' James was concerned.

'Well actually,' Neville confided, 'I don't think that's going to be a problem tonight. There's a certain little lady … you haven't met her but you will … who lives near the cinema and… A very nice little filly, I think you'll agree when you do… Ah, I go this way.' Neville branched away where two streets forked, leaving James to wonder how he managed it. Neville was fifty-something, stout, and given to wearing ancient tweed jackets and plus-fours. There was no accounting for taste in the end, he decided.

The club was a let-down. There was hardly anybody else there, and the few who were did not recognise them, which rather defeated the object of being a theatre company hitting the local night spot en masse. People had a desultory couple of drinks and then began to drift off in ones and twos, the glittering bubble that had been the earlier part of the evening suddenly, sadly deflated.

At a suitable moment James and Borja took their leave; they had a four-mile drive to get home. Only Guy seemed impervious to the change in mood, and they left him at the bar counter with the younger of the two stage electricians, who was called Throat.

THREE

It seemed they had been asleep for only a moment before the phone was ringing, brusquely spilling James and Borja into the rush and scurry of the new day, though it was still dark this end-of-winter morning. James reached the phone first although Borja was close behind him. After listening for a second, James handed the receiver to his friend. 'It's your mother,' he said.

James's Spanish was not so rusty that he needed Borja to tell him, once he'd put the phone down, what the news was but Borja told him anyway. 'My father's dead.'

James embraced him quickly. 'I'm sorry darling. Come back into bed and talk.' The morning was cold and neither of them had on a stitch of clothing.

'Mama wants me to go.' Borja had never referred to his mother as Mama when speaking to James before.

'Then of course you must go.'

'It was a heart attack. Sudden and quick. She sounds awfully upset.' Borja was taking it quite calmly, James thought. Although Borja had never exactly fallen out with his family they had not been very close since Borja had first left Salamanca in search of a living and a life fifteen years before.

Borja would have to ring the airline as soon as the main office opened, they decided rationally once they were back under the warm duvet, and ask for a few days' leave.

'I don't know what it'll be like at home,' Borja said. 'Because it's not just a home; a farm's a business. It'll all be totally different. Will Javier and Simón let my mother hold on to the reins? I somehow doubt it. I guess they'll want to take charge. One or other. Or both.' His tone of voice made all the possible outcomes sound gloomy.

A further possibility occurred to James, or rather it seized him like a loop of wire pulled tight around the diaphragm. It was a crazy, panicky thought, unworthy of someone who had lived so long with a person like Borja, but he couldn't help it. He clutched at Borja's forearm. 'You will come back, won't you?'

Borja gave a little laugh of surprise: a small laugh like a child's, one that James had rarely heard. 'Of course I'll come back. What a question! And even if you took yourself out of the equation, my job's here, and my salary.' He paused a second. 'To say nothing of the uniform.'

Somehow, James discovered, it was that weak little joke that most reassured him.

At nine o'clock they left their home together, with barely a glance at the Palladian splendours that encircled it, and drove back through the forest, which they called the time-warp, into the workaday world. By this time Borja's programme was settled: the result of three or four phone-calls. He would fly out that afternoon from Luton to Madrid in the jump-seat, and then take the train to Salamanca where, late tonight, one of his brothers would meet him with a car. Now he drove in convoy with James as far as the motorway junction: James dawdled for a few seconds, watching Borja's car disappear down the slip road before accelerating away towards the town.

Later in the morning, opening the office fridge in search of milk for a coffee, he was a little startled to find it half filled by a large slab of ox liver. His admin assistant, Linda, rushed to explain that it had been left there temporarily by Neville while he did one or two errands in the town. As well as being the author of the current play in production and one of the heroes of the previous night, Neville was Borja and James's landlord.

James left the liver to rest in peace and caught up with Neville during his lunch break, in the Seven Stars.

'What's with the liver?' he asked him.

'Do you mean mine?' Neville's visits to the Seven Stars were frequent and time-consuming. He laughed. 'You mean in your fridge, of course. Sorry about that, but it's turning milder. No, dear boy, it's animals. I've been given a cat. In itself a small misfortune. Can happen to anyone. But this particular cat refuses to partake of anything out of a tin, even one not opened in his presence. And nor will it eat steak or anything like that; its front teeth are missing. So it's liver twice a day I'm afraid. Nothing else will do. It has to be cut up very small, first thing in the morning.' Neville shut his eyes and grimaced. James found it hard not to feel sorry for him. Having seen Neville many times late at night he had some idea of what it might feel like to be him at breakfast time.

James bought Neville a drink. Although Neville had inherited Sevenscore, the extraordinary property of which James and Borja rented one part, he had not inherited an income to go with it and the proceeds from the play that would be entertaining the county for the next four weeks would, James knew, simply disappear into the black hole that was his overdraft.

Later in the afternoon Neville arrived in the theatre office and discreetly removed the liver.

Since Guy would be watching the second-night performance and there were no evening meetings to attend, James found himself suddenly at a loose end at half-past five. Beginning the drive home alone and thinking about the prospect of a long evening without Borja, he decided he could spend at least the early part of the evening in the Rose and Castle. Neville would be there and James would have a couple of pints with him before going the last mile up the hill. Neville, who would be well into his whiskies by the time James got to the pub, would always appreciate the lift.

The thought of a pint became increasingly attractive and James decided to break his journey at the last pub on the town's outskirts for a preliminary half. It was not the first time he had ever been here; Borja and he came in sometimes to drink a quick beer and rekindle their astonishment at the décor. The place had been done up to look like a Wild West town, complete with sheriff's office and railroad station, and you pushed through little waist-high swing-doors to get to the loos. On Saturday nights it was quite a fashionable hangout, but at six o'clock this Wednesday evening the place echoed only to James's own footsteps.

Except that, at one table, a lone young man sat nursing a pint of bitter and that young man was, astonishingly, Nick. James took himself over and said, 'Mind if I join you?' And Nick, whose immediate boss, Sally, reported to Mike who reported to James, was hardly going to send him away.

'Shouldn't you be getting ready for the show or something?' James asked without irony. He didn't have everyone's work schedules at his fingertips.

'I'm not working this one,' Nick said. 'I'm on the book for the next show. Early starts and early evenings for the next couple of weeks – for a change. Last night I was just helping out. All hands on first nights.'

'And your help was pretty bloody welcome. I won't forget your saving the fire inspection from disaster in a hurry.'

'Where's Borja?' Nick asked, looking into James's eyes suddenly out of his own bespectacled brown pair almost as if he suspected foul play, and at the same moment James was surprised to see a resemblance in those brown eyes to Borja's.

'I'm surprised you haven't heard. I told everyone I've spoken to today. Obviously the bush telegraph doesn't work as well as I thought.' James told him the news.

'Oh, wow. I'm sorry.' Then Nick disengaged his eyes from James's and swallowed a mouthful of beer, having said all that could reasonably be expected of him.

James asked, 'Why are you spending your evening off in this dire pub on the edge of nowhere?' Though Nick might as reasonably have asked him the same question.

'It's just round the corner from my flat.'

'Really?' The theatre company was a tight-knit group of people – though that was not exactly the same as saying they all liked each other – and James did think he knew roughly where everybody lived. 'I thought you had a room with Sandra and Will.'

'I did have. Then Sandra's sister split up with her husband and they needed the room for her. I moved out at the weekend.'

'Oh no,' said James, feeling sympathy but not surprise. How messy other people's lives were, he thought, and then remembered uncomfortably that it had been the same for him when he had split up temporarily with Borja all those years ago in Seville and they had ended up sleeping on sofas belonging to different friends. That was worlds away now, like a past that belonged to somebody else. He hauled himself back to the present. 'Anyway, your new place. What's it like?'

'It's a shit-hole.'Coming from this rather thoughtful young man who was a graduate in music the phrase startled James a little.

'Oh?'

'It's basically someone's back room with all their junk in it. I've got my own key and a gas ring but…'

James could visualise it all too easily. 'So you plan to stay here till you're pissed enough to go back and face it, is that right?'

'More or less.'

'Well,'James said, looking around him, then at Nick's nearly empty pint glass and at his own nearly finished half. Somebody would have to make a suggestion soon and it would be easier for him. 'We could go on and have a pint or two somewhere a bit nicer than this…'

He let the suggestion float, tentatively. Nick looked up, a little surprised perhaps but not at all displeased.

'I'd run you back afterwards of course. Which means we wouldn't be making too much of a night of it.'

'Where?'asked Nick simply.

'The Rose and Castle, by the canal.'

'It's your local, isn't it?'Nick half guessed, half knew. He too had a rough idea where everyone at the theatre lived. 'I went out there for Sunday lunch once. It was a bit crowded.'

'That's Sunday lunchtimes. On a weekday evening it's really laid-back. You'll like it. How did you get out there anyway?'

Like most junior members of the company, Nick had no car. 'On the back of Sandra's bike,' he said matter-of-factly. Sandra and Will were great bikers. When you went round to their flat you were always having to move pistons or spark-plugs before you could sit down on the sofa.

'I hope it won't be too anti-climactic to ride in the passenger seat of an ancient Escort,' said James.

Neville was already installed in his corner in the top bar when they arrived at the thatched village pub. The bar was intimate, with benches around the walls that could accommodate ten and a half people if everyone was matey, plus there were four small square stools. When it got busy later of an evening everyone simply stood on the stone-flagged floor.

The bottom bar offered even less in the way of seating, but there was a fruit machine, a coal fire in winter, a low beamed ceiling to bump your head on, and scenes of canal boats and bridges that had been painted directly onto the walls by a local artist. There was even a skittle alley, for the local variety of the game which required mercifully little space.

'Neville, this is Nick.' James got the formality out of the way.

'Delighted to meet you, dear boy.' You never knew when Neville was sending you up, sending himself up, or just being himself. 'But here's Borja's father not yet cold and there's someone new invited up to the manor.'

Both James and Nick laughed. But Nick still thought it wise to spell the situation out carefully. 'Borja doesn't have to worry about me. I don't dance at that end of the ballroom.'

Neville smiled. 'What can I get you both?' Then he leaned across the bar. 'Lily,' he said. 'You couldn't possibly lend me a tenner out of the till so I can get these good people a drink?' And to Nick's amazement, though not to James's, Lily, a bright, no-nonsense-looking woman with pepper and salt curls, did just that.

They talked about theatre, mostly about Neville's play. When the glasses were empty, Nick, a little red-faced, put his hands in his pockets and insisted on buying the next round himself. James knew how little Nick got paid: he was also conscious that time was moving on and that somebody would have to eat something sometime, so he suggested that Nick and he had steak and chips from the bar menu, firmly adding, 'On me', to counter any indecision on Nick's part. For form's sake he asked Neville if he'd like to join them, but he said no. He'd had a steak a month or so ago and it hadn't agreed with him. Meanwhile there was a pork pie and some potato salad waiting for him when he got back.

Nick ate the steak and chips like a child on exeat from boarding school or a newly released prisoner. James noticed this and tried not to let his smile catch Nick's attention. He stood another round of Pedigree. After that the landlord bought them another, and a local farmer treated them to yet one more.

'Look,' said James to Nick as they left the Rose and Castle a little after closing time, 'I'm not in a fit state to drive you back to town. You can have a comfy room at my place and I'll run you into work when I go in in the morning.' There had been a light fall of snow while they had been in the pub and the car park was just covered: a white carpet patterned with black tyre-tracks. The snow clouds were retreating, their backs silvered by an emerging full moon.

They took Neville in the back of the car. It was only a few hundred yards up the hill on the public road; then came the half mile through the dense wood they called the time-warp where, though you might still have a crash among the trees, the police couldn't touch you since it was private land.

They stopped at the kitchen door of the Court House. 'Come over to my place. Have a drink,' said Neville.

'Maybe later,' said James, feeling suddenly proprietorial towards Nick. Nick was his guest, not Neville's, and he didn't want a pre-emptive visit to Neville's place to upstage Nick's first impression of his own.

Nick was momentarily bewildered, getting out of the car to find himself in a patch of moonlight among the silhouettes and deep shadows of old stable-blocks and trees, with Neville lumbering off through huge double gates to cross what looked like a vast whited-out garden to get home, while James called to his disappearing back, 'Can we come in about twenty minutes, say?'

Then James led Nick into the Court House, the high-roofed, Dutch-gabled house that was their part of Sevenscore, via the brick-floored kitchen. It wasn't until you had walked into the living room and clicked on the light that you realised you had come to somewhere a little bit out of the ordinary … as your eyes focused on inlaid walnut writing-desks, French marble-topped commodes, Chinese silk wall hangings, a solid mahogany dining table and an Afghan floor carpet – these items picked out at random as your surprised stare went ricocheting round the room.

James led Nick through the other rooms of the house while his guest's eyes grew wider and wider, as James hoped they would. 'It's like Aladdin's cave!' Nick said with the hyperbole of the half drunk. They toured the seven opulently furnished bedrooms on the ground floor – upstairs was nothing but a barn-like loft – and the three bathrooms that could also just about be described as opulent provided you made allowance for the nineteen-fifties plumbing.

'Choose a bedroom,' said James. 'They've all got beds made up; they're all equally damp. But we'll put a heater on.' Nick chose the Chinese bedroom because it looked south. 'How do you know it looks south?' asked James in genuine wonder.

'I can see the moon through the window.' Nick spelled this out patiently, as if to a rather dim child. Then he looked more searchingly through the window, cupping his hands against the pane to screen out the indoor light. 'Hey,' he said. 'What am I seeing? Have you brought us to Italy, or what?'

What he was looking at among the moonlit cypress trees was a pair of identical renaissance buildings, each the size of a largish detached house, whose roofs sparkled with new snow; there were two symmetrical colonnades that reached out like arms between the two blocks but failed to meet and, in the central gap between them, an ornamental rectangular lake with a statuary fountain in the middle.

'There was a mansion once between the colonnades where the lawn now is,' James began to explain. 'It was burnt down. All that's left are the wings: the two pavilions, they're called; they're believed to be designed by Inigo Jones. Neville lives in the left-hand one: the East Pavilion … but you'll have worked that out yourself of course, since you've already discovered the south. If you want to satisfy your curiosity further we can stroll across the lawn and join him for a drink. If not…'

But Nick's curiosity was whetted by the idea of an Inigo Jones pavilion and his amazement seemed to have sobered him up. They unbolted the front door and set off across the wide, white lawn where the centre building of the ensemble had once stood. Their feet made a slight chumfing sound in the snow and their footprints soon joined the track that Neville's had made a few minutes before. They turned left along the colonnade, a snow-dusted corridor between bare-twigged shrubs, that led to Neville's front door. A welcoming light above it gleamed out in competition with the full moon above. Just for a few seconds James put an arm lightly around Nick's shoulder, slightly drunk and thinking, I'm his boss, I shouldn't be doing this; but doing it anyway and being dispassionately curious as to Nick's reaction. But Nick didn't react at all. He was chatting away fluently about the classical buildings of Venice and broke neither his stride nor his syntax.

Neville was finishing his pork pie in his thirty-foot double cube drawing room when they arrived. The whisky bottle was open, inviting, at his side.

Nick had never before found himself sitting down to drink whisky at midnight in such a grand setting but had he ever imagined doing so he would not have envisaged the room in quite the state this one was, the floor heaped with piles of manuscripts, cast-off gumboots, a bale of hay – half-breached and spilling onto the carpet – and logs strewn everywhere for unwary feet to trip over. The fire in the glorious Adam chimney-piece was out. 'Can't get this thing to go at all tonight,' said Neville. It didn't look as though he had really tried.

'Come on, let me,' said Nick and, in a businesslike, stage-managerial way he got paper and sticks together, put a match to them and then carefully placed the scattered logs, smallest first, onto the blaze he had created. Within a few minutes a large black cat with an inscrutable expression on its face had appeared from nowhere and extended itself in front of the hearth as if to bestow a seal of approval on Nick's efforts.

They sat and enjoyed their nightcaps around the flames. Then Neville, who had appreciated Nick's interest in the buildings and given him a fairly expansive history of them, said, 'Come and see the other pavilion.' He took a massive key from a hook, led them out, around the colonnade and in, through the door that was identical to his own, to the twin building. The West Pavilion had never been converted into a dwelling and retained the lofty proportions of the ballroom it had once been. A grand piano – a very old one – sat at the far end, beneath a vast mirror. Nick went over to it and lifted the fall-board. It folded back, unexpectedly, in two sections. 'It's a Broadwood,' he said. 'About eighteen seventy.'

Neville and James exchanged glances. 'Your little friend knows his stuff,' said Neville.

'Play something,' James said.

'No way.' Nick giggled. 'I'm far too pissed.' But he fingered the chord of C major and said with a suggestion of surprise as well as pleasure, 'It is in tune though.'

But there was a bone-chilling dampness in the air of this building and they left it quickly, shivers running down their backs. They said good-nights at the parting of the ways; Neville continued round the curve of the colonnade towards the beckoning light above his front door, while James and Nick struck out across the lawn towards the Court House. And as they drew near to the door, perhaps affected by the snowy moonlit strangeness of everything, Nick put an arm round James's shoulder in imitation of James's own gesture when they had first crossed the lawn an hour ago. But James, sobered up a little by the chill of the ballroom, made no response, thinking, very deliberately, that though he was gay, and might be more attracted to Nick than he had at first realised, he was thirty-six and not a fool. And Nick slid his arm away again as, with the full moon shining brightly on their backs, they stopped to open and then go through the front door.

In the morning the snow had gone and Nick had to be shaken awake. James gave him an Alka-Seltzer for his breakfast.

On the way into work, in the car, both their minds were focused on the same thing, namely that there were six spare bedrooms in the house where James lived, while Nick made do with another family's cramped box room. 'I'm quite a good cook, you know,' said Nick out of the blue, which gave James an enormous jolt since it echoed, almost word for word, what William, the only man who had ever caused him to stray from Borja's bed, had said to him when they had moved in together all those years ago in Spain.

'I'd have to ask Borja,' he said. It was not a non-sequitur.

As they neared the outskirts of the town they both became preoccupied with another thought. Their arrival together at work, in James's car, when Borja was well known to have left for Spain the previous day would have a galvanic effect on the engine of theatre gossip. Even if James were to drop Nick a hundred yards short of the building and let him walk from there, someone would be sure to spot that and the picture would look even worse, guilt and deception stamped all over it like smudgy postmarks. 'Is there anything you need from your flat?' James asked. 'We can call in on the way if you like.'

'Just to clean my teeth would be nice. But you needn't wait. I can walk in from there.'

'What time's your call?'

'Ten o'clock.'

'It's quarter to already,' James said, checking the dashboard clock. 'I really don't want you to be late because of me.'

'Yes, but won't it look… I mean, for you?'

'I'll wait for you.' James was touched by Nick's sensitivity to his situation. 'And don't worry about me – or yourself – and what people might or might not think. I reckon we should just tell truth and shame the devil. Don't you?'

Later that day James phoned Borja at his parents'– or rather, his mother's – farm outside Salamanca. From the office phone. The city treasurer wouldn't query a solitary, one-off, call to Spain. Would he?

FOUR

Borja filled James in with the situation where he was as best he could: he didn't have much privacy in a house packed with family, something which James, hearing a soundtrack of sparrow-like chatter in the background, fully appreciated. Borja was surprised though, especially in the middle of his own domestic and funerary preoccupations, to be asked to consider the possibility of Nick's moving in with them as a paying guest, even if only until he could find a more comfortable place for himself in the town.

'But he might lose the incentive to move out once he got used to the place,' Borja objected. 'He's not going to find a place like ours – with a garden, views across the fields and a grand piano thrown in – in the town centre. Not that he can afford. How come he knows about the place?'

James explained how they had met by accident the previous evening and then it had got too late – which Borja correctly interpreted as too drunk – to drive him home.

'You always were quick off the mark,' Borja said, not sounding totally pleased. 'Anyway, technically speaking we've got six spare bedrooms, not just one. Why not have all the assistant stage managers come to live with us? Won't it get a bit difficult if the others start asking?'

James said he thought Borja would agree that Nick was a special case. He'd met him and liked him, hadn't he? As for the rest of the staff, living in the depths of the country with a piano and the boss for company might not have a universal appeal.

'Look, let me think it over,' said Borja finally. They agreed to talk again the following day and then hung up.

Borja already had plenty to think about.

His eldest brother, Simón, had met him at Salamanca station late the previous evening. They had embraced warmly – perhaps because it was over two years since they had last met. 'You'll find Mama in a bit of a state, I warn you,' Simón said. 'You know how tough she's always been? Well, not this time. She's still in shock.'

Which was true. When they had driven the ten miles out of town towards the hills, Borja's mother met him at the door, and hugged him, in floods of tears. This was something new in his experience of her, as far as he could remember. So was the way she was dressed. Black jogging pants and toe-capped leather farm boots – though nothing unusual there – were topped with a brocade waistcoat, black, red and gold, that must have been her dead husband's, yet that Borja had never seen before. The ensemble gave her an unhinged look. Another new thing that night was that the farmhouse was full of brothers and sisters, two of each. Even in his earliest childhood when he had been the 'baby'and his elder sisters nearly grown up, they had rarely all spent a night under the same roof. His old, chestnut-beamed bedroom had been commandeered by his two sisters – just for the one night, they said – so he made himself up a bed on the living room furniture. At least he would have the room to himself. Or so he thought. He was not to know that one of the cats had recently had kittens in that room – until he discovered in the middle of the night that he had parked his legs in exactly the place on the sofa that mother and babies regarded as their home.

In the morning Borja's mother sought him out while he was briefly alone and took him outside into her garden, a humble oasis where a few oleanders sprouted from the dust to give shoulder-high privacy to the table and outdoor chairs that huddled together under an awning. Again she was wearing that extraordinary waistcoat. This morning it occurred to Borja that it looked like part of a matador's suit of lights. She drew him down into a seat beside her. 'About all this,' she said, and gestured around her, at the sheep pens and the barn, at the small fields tumbling away beyond the low stone wall. 'You know of course how things are now.' She turned large dark eyes, like searchlights, on him. 'Two thirds of the estate becomes mine automatically, and the other third is divided in five…'

'Mama, please don't…' He didn't want to hear it all spelled out like this. It had all been gone through painfully with both his parents years before.

'Of which you had your share, as you know, when you decided to become a pilot and needed that money then and there. So that the other four fifths of that third…'

'Yes, I remember. As for you, Mama,' he said this with a smile, 'your talents are wasted. You could have become a maths teacher.' He found a moment to wonder how, when his own hair was beginning to display a tiny number of silver threads – although the number was still a single-digit one, he liked to think – his mother's, like the mothers of most of his Spanish friends, had remained an astonishing, uncompromised raven black.

'Don't tease me, I'm serious. That portion belongs to your brothers and sisters. You know that already. You also know that, when I die, two thirds of my share gets divided between your brothers and sisters: Simón, Javier, Conchita and Purificación. The other third is mine to dispose of as I want. And I want to give it to you.' Despite her businesslike tone up to now, her eyes were again brimming with the tears that, over the past two days, had been only too ready to come.

'Mama, please.' Borja took his mother's hand. 'I knew what I was doing when I took my share and got out. I don't want to get my share back again when you die – as if it was some kind of a fix. And what would the others say? You can imagine how they'd feel about it.'

'Borja, don't you think that that's your problem – all of you – when the time comes? I only wanted you to know what I wanted. What I wanted for you. How I felt about…' She had to stop for a moment. When she had composed herself she carried on, clenching her face in order to get the words out while she was still able to. 'I want you to know that you were … wanted. Not, as you thought, that your father and I didn't… Oh my darling, how I wish it could be you!'

'Mama? Wish what could be me?' Borja asked, now moved near to tears himself but not quite following his mother's train of thought.

'I wish it could be you, here, managing the farm for me.'

Borja remembered what James had said to him in bed the previous morning. You will come back, won't you? It no longer seemed quite such a ludicrous anxiety to have had.

'I'm the youngest, not the eldest, Mama, so it wouldn't be a very practical thing to wish for. Non?'

'I know all that, of course, but…'

'I wouldn't be the right one, whatever the case. Me a farmer? I don't think so. And you've always known that in your heart. You thought of me as a future priest, remember, when I was younger; never a future farmer or a businessman.'

'But now you're a pilot, not a priest. And you've done so many practical things in between. You ran a tourist office, managed concerts…'

'I never actually ran the tourist office. Kept it going when the boss was away, maybe…'

'Simón and Javier have so little experience of anything beyond the farm. What do they know of business?'

'What do I?'

'What if the two of them fall out?'

'And what if I was here and all three of us fell out?'

His mother was silent for a second, then gave him a sideways look. 'You always were my favourite, you know.'

This gave Borja a jolt. 'You shouldn't say such a thing. Though I know youngest sons often are.' He was flattered and disconcerted in equal measure to find himself cast in the role of Joseph – the visionary, rainbow-coated one: Rebecca's son.

'If only you'd stayed in Salamanca and not been...' She shaded her eyes with a hand, and the tears she had had been so determinedly withholding began to fall.

'If only I hadn't been made the way I am.' Borja said this gently but quite firmly. This scene had been played out between them several times over the years. It grew only marginally less painful with each repetition. 'Mama, darling, you know it's better the way things are.' He realised, as he spoke, how unsatisfactory this sounded, and thought bitterly how puny was the power of comforting words against the raw pain of human suffering. 'I'll come and see you more often, if you like.' This wasn't much better. His mother's tears now became an unstoppable outpouring, and Borja took this as the most eloquent of rebukes for being the person he was.

At the same moment he realised, with as hefty a shock as if a sea wave had hit him, that his mother's waistcoat really was part of a suit of lights. At once he thought of Rafael, though Rafael had never worn, let alone owned one. As a torero he'd never made it quite that far. Where had this one come from, then? He bit hard on the fact that in every family, even your own, there were questions it was impossible to ask.

The funeral would not be for another three days. By the end of his first twenty-four hours at his family home, what with the overcrowding, and the pressure on him of his mother's wishful thinking, Borja decided to move out of the claustrophobic environment, at least for the evenings and nights of the remainder of his stay. With four siblings and their spouses to share the work of arranging the funeral and comforting the widow, he did not feel unduly guilty about the prospect of not being at his mother's side twenty-four hours out of every twenty-four. He telephoned his oldest friend in Salamanca.

'Of course stay the nights with us,' said Marisa. 'We were so sorry to hear about your father. We'll be coming to the funeral naturally. But it'll be nice to see you, quite apart from that. Alberto and the youngsters will be delighted to hear you're coming. Especially Borja. He's talking about becoming a pilot and he's got so many questions he's been waiting for the chance to ask you. I hope he won't be too much of a nuisance.'

The Borja in question was Marisa's son, now sixteen. 'I'm sure he won't be a nuisance,' said Borja the elder. Later that day he borrowed the smaller of the two farm trucks and drove the ten miles back to Salamanca.

Alberto and Marisa lived in the heart of the old town on the Calle el Rosario, sandwiched between crumbling convents and just a stone's throw, in different directions, from the university, the two cathedrals and the Plaza Mayor. They paid for the upkeep of their sizeable old house by renting out its honeycomb of rooms to students. It was a lively place to stay in during term-time, Borja remembered, though it was a good few years now since Borja had been there. And he had never arrived in a truck before; finding a parking place in the narrow streets was no easy matter. But he accomplished it at last and presented himself finally to his hostess at the heavy wooden door.

Borja couldn't help noticing that Marisa's handsome face no longer shone quite so brilliantly with youth's first light, and it occurred to him now that perhaps his didn't either. The beginnings of lines showed around his old friend's mouth while her swept-back mane of hair, black with a just perceptible sheen of chestnut, was threaded with fine silver capillaries. Perhaps, he now thought, the faces of your contemporaries were the truest mirrors to the stealthy changes wrought upon your own features by the advancing years.

Alberto's manner, gruff but friendly, had not changed at all in the nearly twenty years that Borja had known him. And as he had never looked particularly young, even as a student, so the approach of middle age had altered his appearance very little. Meeting the children, on the other hand, was like coming upon new people. Carmen, whom Borja remembered as the twelve-year-old of their most recent encounter, was now a dark haired and oval-faced young woman of eighteen who, facially at least, took after neither of her parents. As the afternoon passed, Borja discovered this new person to be charming, solicitous and moody by turn. Physically she sat on the borderline between sensual beauty and heaviness, like a rose in a too hot hothouse or a ripe dark plum. Whereas her younger brother, Borja's namesake, looked as fresh-faced and uncomplicated a sixteen-year-old as any you might meet.

Having two people in the house with exactly the same name for several days looked as if it might pose problems of communication and so it was quickly agreed that Borja junior – Borja López Carballo, to give him his full name – would be known by his in-family nickname, Rizo, for the duration, while Borja senior was allowed to retain his own forename unchanged. Rizo did not immediately leap upon the pilot with questions about speed-brakes and automatic direction finders, but when dinner-time began to approach in its leisurely Spanish way and Borja made noises about heading out to the supermarket to get some wine, it was no surprise to anyone that the youngster should decide to tag along with him. Borja had no objection. Actually he found this readiness to accompany him on such a banal expedition slightly flattering.

They had only gone a little way along the street before Rizo sprang his first question. Only it wasn't quite the sort of question that Borja had been expecting. 'You and James are maricones, non?' he queried brightly, just as they passed a nun, laden with bags of shopping, letting herself in at the door of one of the convents. Borja felt his heart sink. He stopped, leaned against the convent wall and turned to Rizo. 'Yes,' he said wearily. 'What of it?'

'Because I think I am too.'

It was dusk, and the street and Rizo's face were alike lit by a mixture of end-of-day light and the stuttering flashes of street-lamps that were just coming on. The face was turned slightly upwards to Borja's own. Borja was still the taller of the two, though only by an inch. 'Oh,' was all he found to say. Then he thought that, God in heaven, things had changed since he was in his mid-teens. Then, such intimations had been the source of private doubts and secret, hidden, anguish: not something, in Spain at any rate, to blurt out matter-of-factly to a family friend in the hearing of whoever chanced to be in the street. Certainly he himself could never have done so. But now he felt he ought to turn his initial, surprised 'Oh,' into the preamble to something more constructive. 'That's very honest of you,' he said, and smiled to show that he wasn't put out by the announcement. 'But you need to know that not everyone who jumps to that conclusion at the age of sixteen really is maricón. There's a lot of living to do before anyone's really sure about it.' He told himself, I will not pry into Rizo's private thoughts, or into his sex life if he already has one. He would not say, What makes you think that?

But Rizo told him anyway. 'I have a friend. We… well, you know.'

'Well, no, I don't know. At least, not exactly. And do you really think you ought to be wanting to tell me? I mean...'

The look of disappointment that crossed the boy's face made Borja waver. 'Look, if you really want to talk, well, we're standing in the doorway of a convent right now. Suppose we go on and get the wine and than we call into a café on the way back. OK?'

A few minutes later they were seated at a pavement table – for though it was dark now the evening was unseasonably mild. Rizo had an orange juice in front of him, Borja a beer. 'You're going to tell me it's a phase, aren't you?' Rizo said. 'Did people tell you that? And when did you know it wasn't?'

Borja shook his head in wonder. 'Nobody knew about phases in Salamanca in the seventies. Nobody ever gave me advice as a teenager. And I never thought to ask. As for your second question, it was when ... no, not when I first had sex, but when I met and fell in love with James when I was twenty-one and a quarter.'

'That sounds incredibly romantic. Except for the exactness of the maths.' Rizo attended a bit noisily to his orange juice.

'Oddly enough, people do remember things like that. As you will discover, if you haven't already.'

'So how long was there between meeting James and falling in love?' Rizo's eyes were shining with curiosity and wonder.

'About six weeks.'

'So either you were twenty-one and three eighths when you fell in love, or else only twenty-one and one eighth when you first met.'

Borja laughed. 'I see. Well, I'm pretty impressed by your maths too.'

'I think maybe we're not really in love,' said Rizo, 'Me and Manuel Peñafiel. He's cool. He thinks we should go to Madrid and disappear among the drop-outs. See life and get into drugs and so on. Cool but crazy. But I still don't think it's love. It may be that we're simply friends who … do things.'

'I think that's very normal,' said Borja evenly, trying not to feel curious about the precise nature of the things that Rizo and his friend did. 'Being a teenager is supposed to be all about experimenting, after all. My teenage experiments weren't very adventurous or very successful. I hope yours will fare better. Only – you'll have to put up with me talking like an adult now – don't hurt yourself in your experiments, physically or otherwise; and don't hurt other people or let others hurt you.' He paused, took a sip of beer. 'Sorry to preach, but you brought the subject up, not me. Oh, just one more thing. Do you know about Aids?' Rizo nodded. 'And how to make sure you avoid it?' The boy nodded again.

'Then I think I've probably given you all the information I can.' I sound like a pompous prick, he thought glumly.

Rizo looked steadily at Borja. 'When you were a teenager, what came first: sex or falling in love?'

Borja managed something like a laugh. He sounded uncomfortable. 'In my case it was falling in love. I'd have liked the sex to come along too, but the other person didn't and that was that. But everybody's experience is different. Don't rush yourself into falling in love; be cool about it. It'll happen when it happens, in its own time.' He stopped, looked down at the last half inch of liquid in both their glasses. 'Perhaps we'd better get back home and ready for dinner.'

Dinner was a convivial meal, when it eventually happened. At table, in addition to Marisa's family were two of the student population of the house, one of each sex, and Borja enjoyed quizzing them about life as it was lived today in the university that had been his own second home for three years… It seemed like only the other day. Conversation continued long after dinner, with Alberto bringing out a bottle of coñac, while Carmen and Rizo, who had both had wine at dinner, went out to meet younger friends in the streets. The frank exchanges Borja had shared with Rizo earlier in the evening began to fade from the forefront of his mind, as he became caught up in tales of lectures and student pranks, sometimes involving the very same teachers and staff that he had known fifteen years ago. It was two o'clock before he got to bed.

The room Marisa had given him brought back a very particular memory. In fact he had almost jumped when Marisa had showed him to it in the afternoon, and he hoped she hadn't noticed. For this room had once been Rafael's room. The first time they had shared a room together it had been here, twelve years ago. Rafael had invited him to share his bed and he, rather primly, had chosen to sleep on the floor – an arrangement that was not maintained when Rafael, a few weeks later, came to visit him in Seville. But then, just days later, Rafael was killed. Borja had not been in here since. He stood, looking round it for a minute, then stripped, put out the light by the door and got into bed.

As is the nature of things, Borja only realised that he'd got off to sleep when he was woken up. A crack of light fanned open across his face and then swept shut again. Wide awake suddenly, he knew that someone he couldn't see had come into the room. One of the students drunkenly mistaking his room for their own? 'Hóla,' he said, and then, 'Qué tal?' somehow sure by now, though he still couldn't see or hear him, that the uninvited visitor was none other than the boy whose name he shared.

Borja switched the bedside light on. Rizo stood there in a white night-gown that must have belonged to his grandfather. He walked towards Borja, who now sat bolt upright in the bed. With a sudden shock – Borja felt as though iced water were pumping through his veins – the reason for Rizo's visit became alarmingly clear.

'I wanted...' Rizo began.

'You didn't,' Borja said. 'You don't.' The words came out in a hoarse whisper. 'We don't.' He climbed – almost jumped – out of bed, wrapping the top sheet around him in one movement as he did so, so that it shrouded him as he pushed Rizo back towards the door. 'You must go,' he whispered. He felt the hair on his neck bristle. He opened the door and, over Rizo's shoulder, peered out. Mercifully the landing was unpeopled, dimly lit and quiet.

'I just thought...' Rizo started again, but now sounding close to tears.

'Just go,' Borja said. 'Quietly. Now.' Trying to do it gently, but with nervousness rendering the action a brusque one, he propelled Rizo out through the door, then pushed it shut between them. He remained for several seconds pressed flat against his side of it. But he felt no pressure from the other side, nor was Rizo's voice raised in protest, and after a few more seconds he heard quiet footfalls retreating down the passageway. He returned to bed, shivering, and rearranged the sheet around himself. But he didn't feel able to turn out the light.

FIVE

There was no avoiding the younger Borja the next morning. It was Saturday and there was no school. Borja decided on a proactive approach. It was already his plan to spend the daytimes out at the farm, returning to Salamanca in the evenings. He decided now that he would take Rizo with him today, then he could have a straight talk with him in the privacy of the truck on the way. It was possible that Rizo would say no, that he would want to avoid just such a private chat and find that he had better things to do. But he didn't. He wasn't yet too old to find the idea of a ten-mile trip in a farm truck quite exciting – only too old actually to admit it. So after a late, informal breakfast at which Borja could eat nothing and Rizo did not manage much better, they set off.

Borja was feeling sick and, almost physically, heavy inside – like a carelessly grazing swan, he thought, that has swallowed a fishing weight. Rizo was silent and subdued. Borja glanced sideways at his face as they crossed the Rio Tormes, leaving the town centre for the suburbs. If that profile was giving anything away at all it was that Rizo felt frightened. It was only when the last of Salamanca's outskirts were behind them and they were out in the open, undulating countryside that Borja felt relaxed enough to find some words to say. 'Look,' he finally began. 'What happened last night shouldn't have.' The boy continued to stare straight ahead of him, impassively, through the windscreen. He rubbed his lips together but made no sound. Borja went on. 'If I have anyone to blame, it's myself. For talking too freely to you yesterday. People of my age and people of your age shouldn't share those intimate things, I think. I also think we have to clear the conversation from our minds as if it never took place.' He didn't just mean the conversation.

The truck breasted a series of low hills each one of which showed the road ahead descending and then climbing towards the next summit as if they were on a huge-scale, but quite gentle, roller coaster.

At last Rizo spoke. 'I suppose you're right. I mean that I got stupid and would have behaved like an idiot if you hadn't stopped me. On the other hand I can't see myself actually forgetting what happened. That doesn't seem possible. I mean, not for me.'

It struck Borja forcefully that he was no more likely to be able to forget the previous night than Rizo could but he made no attempt to say so.

'After all,' the boy resumed, 'it's the experiences we've had that make us the people we are. If we started writing some of them out of the story, well … we'd never really grow up, would we?'

'My God,' said Borja, wondering for a moment which one of them was supposed to be the older of the two. 'I suppose,' he said slowly, 'I don't have the right to tell you what do with the inside of your own head.'

They turned off the main road towards the high Sierra but then, long before foothills had grown into mountains, turned again onto the familiar cart track. Borja's mother welcomed the young visitor as warmly as if he had been another of her own grandchildren – there were three of those here this morning – and Borja began to feel pleased with himself for bringing him to the farm. His presence was providing his mother with a refreshing distraction from funerary activities and thoughts. It became the excuse for a quite decent lunch, with paella, cold sausage and cheese – more like a Sunday than a Saturday really, and so much so that a few members of the family required a short siesta afterwards. Not Borja, though. Having brought Rizo out here he felt obliged to keep him entertained, since the grandchildren, Borja's nieces and nephew, were far too young to count as company, and so the two of them set off on an exploration of the farm, with its steep-pitched fields, stands of holm oak and stream-chiselled valleys. Rizo had been there some years before and had much the same tour on that occasion. But it seemed a much more fraught and complicated thing to be doing this time round. Now the ground beneath their feet had altered; today they were exploring a new farm.

They had not gone any distance when Rizo said, 'There's another thing I wanted to ask you.'

Borja felt his heart sink. 'What is it?'

'You know when you're flying, and the autopilot's on, how does it know which side to approach the arrival airport from, because you might have a change in the wind direction, no?'

A wave of relief swept over Borja. He actually laughed.

'Sorry,' said Rizo. 'Was it a very stupid question?'

'No,' said Borja, 'it wasn't. It was a good question, and it has a very beautiful answer. It's all about STARs.'

'Stars? Estrelas?'

'More like spiders'webs, actually – it stands for Standard Terminal Arrival Routes.' And he explained how the bearings of the criss-crossing pathways were keyed into the autopilot in sequence so that the plane could track unerringly from way-point to way-point, threading its way without mishap through the maze of airways that surrounded busy airports.

After that the boy wanted to know about spoilers and speed-brakes, and following that he needed to know what you actually did if an engine caught fire in mid-flight, and how you navigated the Atlantic Ocean where there weren't any VOR beacons…

Back in Salamanca the evening passed easily enough. But, pleading a slight headache – which by now he really did have – he excused himself from the family's after-dinner conversations and went out for a walk in the fresh air of the dark streets. His feet took him almost instinctively towards the Plaza Mayor. It had been the hub of his social life, as well as everybody else's, in his student days and seemed the most natural place to gravitate towards even now. On the way he passed the massive Baroque church of La Clericía which, unusually for a Saturday evening, was open and brightly lit. A small crowd of people was issuing from its main door. Clearly there had been some special service, or maybe a concert or other event. Borja lingered a minute or two, watching the people until the human stream had diminished to a trickle. He moved to resume his progress towards the Plaza Mayor but just then his attention was caught by one of the last stragglers to leave the church: a woman, in conversation with one or two other people, carrying a guitar case as well as a bag of some sort, slung over her shoulder. She stood out from the others because of her fine head of hair which, even under the colour-subduing influence of the street lighting, was a striking copper red.

Borja found himself crossing the street, waving to catch her attention and calling out, a little uncertainly because he still wasn't a hundred percent sure, 'Alexa! Alexa?'

The woman turned towards his voice and studied him silently for a second or two. Then she called out, 'Borja!' in her turn and moved towards him, and they embraced in the unsatisfactory way that people must do when one of them is encumbered with a guitar and a case full of music.

Then they both talked at once, since they had communicated nothing more than Christmas cards for the last ten years, while the little knot of people that had gathered round Alexa in the hope of discussing technicalities of the classical guitar faded away into the background.

They were soon on the way to the Plaza Mayor together, Borja carrying the precious instrument like the gentleman he was. Alexa had just given a concert in La Clericía. She was on her own in Salamanca, would be spending the night in a hotel just off the Plaza Mayor and would be returning to Seville and Mark in the morning. Mark was the man she lived with, half American, half Spanish. Borja had known him in his Seville days too, but Mark hadn't lived with Alexa then.

The Plaza Mayor seethed with young people, as it always had. Borja and Alexa squeezed among chairs and columns of cigarette smoke at one pavement café and miraculously found two seats free. One or two people sitting nearby had been in the audience at Alexa's recital and greeted her without any show of bashful hesitation but then, understandingly, left her to talk to her companion in peace. Alexa wanted to know what brought Borja all alone to Salamanca. She had forgotten, till he reminded her, that this was where he had grown up. He explained the present circumstances: his father's death, the impending funeral, the overcrowded family home and his mother's rather overwhelming attentions to her favourite son. He told Alexa about his friend Marisa and her husband and about their hospitality, which explained his presence in the centre of Salamanca this evening, but made no mention of their son.

'Is your father's death upsetting you?' Alexa asked.

'We weren't close,' Borja said. 'We had a difficult relationship. Obviously.' He looked down at the table.

'The gay thing, you mean?'

'It's water under the bridge now, anyway. My mother's more or less all right about it, provided she doesn't have to meet James or have the thing thrust under her nose. But Papa?' Borja looked thoughtfully at

Alexa for a second. His conversations with Alexa had been rare, but they had all been serious ones. 'I'll miss him, of course. People always do.'

'I asked because you looked troubled,' said Alexa a minute or two later. 'Something's worrying you.' She had ordered a glass of moscatel, Borja a beer; the waiter brought them at that moment.

Borja was momentarily taken aback. 'I see you for the first time in ten years – we've both grown through ten more years of life – and you tell me I look troubled.'

'But I've seen the look before, remember,' Alexa pursued. 'When I talked to you properly for the first time, and you asked me to play Bach for you on the piano. When Rafael had just died. You had the same look then.'

'I see,' said Borja and took a swallow of beer.

'I don't want to be nosey, but if there's anything you want to talk about, well, I'm here – just this one evening – as I was there then, that day in Seville.'

Borja smiled. 'I see. But no. Something and nothing, as they say. I found that one of my friends'teenage children had a bit of a crush on me.' He took a measured swallow of beer. 'It was a bit disturbing for a moment, but in the end, no harm done.' Then he remembered something. 'Oh my God,' he interrupted his own thoughts. 'I was supposed to phone James today. I'd completely forgotten. Now it's past midnight.'

'Not in England, it isn't. It's only just gone eleven over there. You can still get him, can't you? Without getting him out of bed, I mean.'

'Yes, I probably can. You don't have a mobile, do you?' Alexa shook her head: they were far from universal then. 'Look, do you mind if I leave you a minute? Then we can finish our drink peacefully and I'll see you back to your hotel.'

'You hardly need to do that,' Alexa said. She pointed across the brightly lit square. 'It's that one over there.'

Borja threaded his way among the tables to find a phone inside the café. In the thronged interior of the bar it was not easy to locate the pay-phone, and when he did there was a young woman using it, but Borja – uncharacteristically – scowled at her so aggressively, and jingled the coins in his pocket so impatiently, that she gave in to his bullying tactics and wound her conversation up as quickly as she could.

He dialled the UK code and then the familiar number. James answered. Borja said, 'Hallo darling,' and then to his great surprise he found that he was saying, 'I've thought about what you said. You know, about having Nick to stay with us as a lodger. And yes, that's fine by me.'

SIX

Nick moved his belongings out to Sevenscore the following day, using the theatre's Transit van to carry them. That was a quite accepted practice; it wasn't even a question of James having to turn a blind eye to it. On the money they were paid it was hardly possible for ASMs to go hiring vans at the weekends. Not that Nick's moveable goods filled the van; his bags and cases could have gone into James's car, but Nick was wise enough not to push his luck by asking.

Late in the evening, when they'd both returned from the theatre, James cooked sausages and eggs for Nick and himself. The first night of a new domestic set-up.

They ate at the big mahogany table in the living room and, after Nick had done the washing up – how quickly new routines became established – settled themselves, with a glass of wine each, before the hearth where a fire burned between brass fire dogs, 'So tell me about Borja,' Nick said. 'How did you come by him?'

James smiled. He was feeling very comfortable in Nick's company: he found Nick's new over-familiarity surprisingly endearing. He started to tell him the story: of how they had first met on a Spanish train when they were both quite recently out of university, how they had shared a hostal room in Madrid, then how James had courted Borja by letter until, months later, Borja had come to Seville where James was working, to start a new job himself. Except for a traumatic couple of months a few years into their relationship – which James wasn't going to go into tonight with Nick – they had been together ever since.

'What, from the very day he arrived in Seville?'

'That very day. Well, we'd been writing, as I said. Me doing the wooing, if you like, he being pleasantly shocked by me – he was a good Catholic boy back then

– but unable to stop answering my letters. He was as attracted as I was… Well, more than attracted, and he found he couldn't just tell me to get lost. I mattered to him more than anything else, even on the strength of one meeting. It was the same for me, of course. And still is,' he added with plonking carefulness. 'For both of us.'

'I know that,' said Nick. 'It shows. Anyway, so he showed up in Seville. And?'

'He had a job interview at the tourist office. I waited in the street outside and took him for a drink when he came out. He was in a very neat suit and tie but he had his overnight things in what looked like his old school sports bag.' James grinned at the memory. 'We went to a bar I knew but which he didn't, in the old part of Seville. It was called the Gitanilla, the Gypsy Bar. Then, because I was staying with this American guy – called Mark – who taught at the same school as me…'

'I didn't know you'd been a teacher.'

'Everybody has a past. You'll have your own, one day. Anyway, I took him back there. I only had a single bed in Mark's back room, but Borja and I shared it and that, as they say, was that. Next day we started looking for a flat together, and were able to leave poor Mark in peace a week later. He lived in a street whose name you could never forget: Virgen de la Luz.'

'Virgin of the Light,' translated Nick. 'How beautiful. And was it …?'

'Apt, do you mean? Well, no, not literally,' James attempted to clarify. 'Neither of us was exactly…'

'No,' allowed Nick, 'but all the same.' And this time it was he who got up to refill the wine glasses.

For the first few days after Nick's arrival at Sevenscore his work schedule corresponded to James's and they travelled together into town and back each day in James's car. But this harmony of timetables was a mere coincidence and would not last beyond the next weekend. Nick did not expect to be granted the use of the theatre's Transit van in perpetuity – not and remain on speaking terms with the rest of the stage management at any rate – and so he negotiated the purchase of a small, semi-reliable motorbike, complete with L-plates, from Mike, the production manager. But Nick was not a total paragon of guileless consideration. He guessed that the new-old machine would be prone to breakdowns and calculated that, in an emergency, it could easily be lashed to the open boot lid of either James's or Borja's car. He borrowed a length of rope from the stage management store to keep in his saddlebag just in case.

Borja had been told about the motorbike over the phone. So he was not surprised, when he returned at last from his visit to Spain, to see the shabby, L-plated contraption standing next to James's car in the car park of the Rose and Castle as he drove up. He parked his own car alongside and made his way into the cosy – and deeply un-Hispanic – top bar to find James and Nick ensconced there, enjoying an early evening drink with Neville. It was not at all unpleasant to find them all here together like this; it made him feel that he was returning, not just to a lover, but to a family. And especially on this particular occasion.

Borja had also often had the same feeling of returning to a family when he went to James's theatre. At those times he was very conscious of its warmth, both physical and atmospheric, in contrast to the colder, lonely element in which he worked. There were undercurrents, he knew, of rivalries and petty animosities in this theatre family, but he perceived them only dimly and knew that, as an outsider, he was not subject to their power. But this was even better, somehow: coming back to James and Nick. Perhaps because he needed warmth and comfort more than he usually. Perhaps it had something to do with the personality of Nick. He had been expecting to recognise in himself some small signs of jealousy – his partner was, after all, however innocently, sharing their house with a younger man. But to his surprise he felt no twinges at all. He shook Nick's hand and looked into his intelligent, attractive face. He thought, quite simply, what a sweet young man.

Once the most basic courtesies had been exchanged Borja, now with a drink in front of him, gave James an account of his time in Spain, of his mother's grief and her response to her youngest son's arrival. That his own feelings about his father's death were complex James already knew. Meanwhile Neville and Nick politely found topics of their own. But after a little while Borja, glad of something more positive and concrete to talk about, brought up the subject of his meeting with Alexa in Salamanca.

Borja had told James about his unexpected encounter with Alexa over the phone. He'd told him that he had mentioned to Alexa the Sunday night concerts that were given at the theatre from time to time, and suggested she might be in the frame to do one next time she was England. Subject to James's approval, that was.

'Well, not only mine,' James said now. 'Though I'd be as happy as anything to see her again. But there's Guy to be asked, plus the board – which in practice means having a word with the chairman. Though that might not pose too big a problem. She still has red hair, I take it?'

Borja nodded his answer. 'There's another thing, though. She brought something else up right out of the blue. She wants one of us, either you or me, to sit on some sort of committee, spending money on a memorial to her old teacher, Eulogio.' Borja added, turning almost apologetically to the others, 'People we knew in Seville.'

James took it upon himself to explain how, years ago in Seville, Borja had organised a concert in the Alcázar at which Eulogio, Alexa's piano teacher, had played.

Borja reclaimed the story. 'And now Eulogio has died, and there's money in the will for a foundation – scholarships and things – which Alexa seems to be responsible for organising.'

'Good old Alexa,' James said. And he treated Nick and Neville to the story of how she had transported her Bechstein piano from Reigate to Seville on the back of a lorry and then got involved with a German guitarist, later abandoning the piano and taking up the guitar. She had pursued it so single-mindedly that it had become her full time career.

'A woman guitarist in Spain,' wondered Neville out loud. 'Do they tolerate that?'

'Why not?' answered Borja. 'There are women bullfighters these days. Women airline pilots too – I fly with one quite often. And Alexa manages to make a living at the guitar. Which answers the question, I think.'

'All right,' said Neville, 'I was only asking.' Borja's occasional moments of forthrightness sometimes struck a jarring note with Neville's whimsical musings.

Neville thought that Borja should accept the invitation to sit on Alexa's committee or trust or whatever it was going to be. Borja did not. There was a brief, polite debate at the end of which James accepted the task. It would involve the odd expenses-paid trip to Seville, after all.

'I meant to tell you all,' he said, as he returned to their table with refilled glasses, stooping under the low beams, 'Guy wants to come out at the weekend to thrash out the new season.'

'Fine by me,' said Borja. 'I won't be here.' He was off to work again the following day, on a 'W'flight that would take him from Birmingham to Pisa, from there to Gatwick, off again to Fuerteventura and then back to Birmingham. He would be at home on Friday night but then off again the following morning, home on Monday night. James was always acutely conscious of where his lover was, hour by hour, during his tours of duty, and thought of him ploughing his lonely furrow through the troposphere and then touching down in the various places on his itinerary moment by moment – even when delays and other incidents rendered his calculations void.

'I've got a young lady coming to stay at the weekend,' Neville said a little tentatively. 'The one you asked about the other night. Lives in town near the cinema. I said I'd introduce you. Maybe Nick,' he waved a hand in Nick's general direction, 'could keep her entertained while we do the author director manager stuff.' He looked at Nick and gave him such a guileless smile that Nick could do nothing except grin his assent.

After they had taken Neville up the hill and seen him amble off across the lawn to his own comfortable dwelling, the three younger men had their first meal together at the Court House. It was Nick's turn to cook. He did pork chops with an accompaniment of leeks and a sort of fried rice which managed to use up most of the leftovers in the fridge. With a hefty application of soy sauce it managed to taste much better than it might sound. Then, feeling emboldened rather than incapacitated by the two or three drinks he had had, he offered to play something to his two hosts on the ballroom piano. He picked up the heavy iron key from the hall table and led the way across the dark lawn to the West Pavilion. At one point he placed an arm expansively around both James's and Borja's shoulders, but only for a moment. Conscious of his junior status, he quickly dropped his hands to his side again, before either of his hosts could shrug him off.

Tuesday afternoon was the cheque round. The accountant filled them in, clipped them to their supporting documents, invoices or whatever else might be needed, then either James or Guy signed them at lunchtime and James took them across town to have them countersigned by the chairman of the theatre board. It was a weekly ritual that suited both James and his overall boss. James could have deputed the task to someone else; it simply involved a walk and then a wait while the chairman brandished his fountain pen at the paperwork. But the weekly visit provided a useful opportunity, seized sometimes by James, sometimes by the chairman, for an off-the-record chat about theatre business. From time to time over the years understandings had been arrived at in the course of these informal chats that had saved time and unpleasant wrangling at subsequent board meetings.

The chairman, who occupied the position in a strictly honorary capacity, was also the leader of the Conservative bloc on the county council and the owner of the town's principal commercial hotel, the Three Feathers. It was to this establishment, halfway along the road to the station, that James now made his way. You went in, nodded to whoever was on reception duty, and walked through the gilded, pilastered lounge bar, then knocked at an unobtrusive door at the far end of it. A different kind of chairman would have proposed to hold these regular Tuesday meetings in the bar itself over a civilised drink. It would have been quite private: nobody ever went in there in the middle of the afternoon. It was a source of mild regret to James, as he passed the rows of gleaming optics and polished hand pumps Tuesday after Tuesday, that in seven years this had never happened. His chairman was not of that kind.

The chairman's call of 'Enter' brought James into as small and spartan an office as he had ever seen. The single window was minute and six feet off the ground: a ventilator, nothing more. The chairman sat behind a plain mahogany desk on which stood a single telephone. No papers littered it. Instead, a large and pristine leather blotter with attached pen holder occupied its exact centre. No pictures adorned the walls, no filing cabinets or other office furnishings cluttered the small space. There was no computer. It was clear that the business operation of the Three Feathers Hotel was carried out elsewhere and by somebody else. Certainly James's chairman played very little part in it. It was difficult to imagine what he did in here, day after day, with so little in the way of tangible office accoutrements to keep him busy. James had long ago come to the conclusion that this room, together with the telephone that furnished it, was dedicated almost exclusively to the enjoyable pastime of hatching council-chamber plots.

'Sit down, Mr Miller. I hope you are well.' Nobody else called James Mr Miller. From the most part-time of part-time usherettes to the vice-chairman herself, everyone knew him as James. He sat.

The chairman leafed through the cheques and invoices, reading carefully, sometimes questioning, while his fountain pen performed aerobatic displays a few inches above the sheaf of papers. 'Three new pump-action screwdrivers?' he queried.

'Some new casuals on the pantomime strike. Not very clued-up, I'm afraid, and heavy-handed into the bargain.'

The chairman looked up at James with an expressionless stare. 'Perhaps they were a bit too casual.' He was not the kind of man who made jokes. If he had been, that would have been one of them.

'And the autumn season? Will Mr Levington be telling us what he has up his sleeve soon?'

'Guy's thinking hard about it, I know that. There's going to be a big planning meeting in about a week. We'll have something to put forward at next month's board meeting, you can be sure of that.'

'It might be an idea,' the chairman said this every time, 'if you and Mr Levington could come and have a little chat with me about it first. Just so that the three of us know exactly where we're going when the moment comes. Eh?'

James indicated that the point was noted. 'I also wanted to bring up another thing,' he ventured. 'About Sunday concerts. We have one or two slots free later in the spring.'

'Ah yes, Sunday concerts. Have we ever done one that made money?' The chairman's stare brought owls momentarily to James's mind.

'Several, actually. You see, I've been approached … or rather, I've been talking to a rather splendid guitarist, who does classical recitals all around Spain. She…'

'A woman?' The chairman opened his eyes even wider. 'And unknown in this country?'

James admitted that, yes, that was so. 'I've talked to Guy – Mr Levington – about her and he's all in favour. But I thought I'd…'

'Tell me, Mr Miller.' The chairman paused for some seconds to indicate a major change of subject. 'Have you found out any more about the carpet?'

The chairman had been wielding the carpet question like a baseball bat at these meetings for as long as James had known him. It never failed to floor him. 'The carpet? Er, no. It remains…'

'A mystery.' The chairman concluded James's sentence with a triumphant gleam in his eye. In truth there was no mystery. Both of them knew it but the game being played between them required them both to pretend they didn't. A very substantial and expensive carpet had been purchased for a production of The Seagull some years ago and then disposed of afterwards. It was the manner of its disposal that had caused the problem. The city treasurer, who sat on the board, had decided that the carpet was an item of such major worth that it should feature in the theatre's accounts as a current asset and – in that case, where was it now? Either the carpet itself or the money resulting from its resale. But the treasurer's interest had come too late. Already the famous carpet had been cut into seven pieces of different sizes and could be found all over the town, if you knew where to look, furnishing the hallways and living rooms of various members of the theatre staff. That was four years ago now, and still the chairman brought it up every time he wanted to stop James in his tracks, or give himself time to think about something else during a meeting.

'I've looked into it time and again, as you know,' said James. 'Drawn a blank each time. I'm really sorry, but I don't know what more I can…'

'Well maybe if you could just ask around one more time, perhaps? You never know. You might suddenly stumble over something. Don't you think?'

'I'll see what I can do. I promise.' James saw himself stumbling only too literally over corners of deep-pile in the flats of several of his employees. He made an effort of will and wrested the conversation back to where he wanted it. 'Alexa…'

'Ah yes. The guitar lady.'

'I should declare an interest, I suppose. I've known her for about twelve years. We belonged in the same circle of friends in Spain. On the other hand, that's given me the opportunity to know her work very well. She's very special indeed, believe me.'

'We had Paco Peña last year.'

'Who showed a tidy profit, remember.'

'Yes, but how much Flamenco do we actually…?'

'Alexa doesn't do Flamenco. She's classical. Bach, Handel, Scarlatti, that kind of stuff.'

The chairman had not been aware, up to now, of Scarlatti. ‘Well, maybe, maybe. Perhaps, Mr Miller, you could bring a proposal to the next board meeting – with a budget. And maybe some literature about the young lady in question? With publicity photos if she has some. Then the board could get some kind of feeling about her. If you see what I mean.’ The chairman looked up at James in a very direct fashion.

James saw exactly what he meant. ‘I’ll see what I can do,’ he said.

SEVEN

Saturday morning. The Friends of the Regent were holding their regular coffee morning in the foyer. People milled about with cups of instant and biscuits, exchanging gossip and feeling good because the coffee and biscuit money would go to help the theatre's ever-precarious finances. In fact, the worse the quality of the coffee the better they felt, for by so much more would the theatre benefit from their generosity. James was being politely present, having just finished dealing with his post in the office above. Through the big, windowed front doors came Neville, looking – James thought – faintly sheepish.

'Glad I've caught you,' Neville said. 'Looked for you at the manor but you'd already left. The thing is, old chap, I'm in a bit of a pickle. You know I said I'd invited Rita to stay the weekend.' James looked blank. 'Rita. The filly who lives near the cinema.' James remembered. 'Well, it turns out that I'd already invited another woman as well. My ex-fiancée, Maya. I'd been thinking it was for next month, but apparently it wasn't. She rang late last night to confirm she was coming.'

'So you said…?'

'Well naturally I said she was to come.' Neville looked surprised, almost hurt, that James might have imagined any other possibility. 'She's motoring over all the way from High Wycombe. I couldn't possibly have put her off. We were engaged, after all. Look, the thing is, I was wondering if you could possibly find a bedroom for one of them on Sunday night. It's going to be damned awkward having the two of them around the place together without all three of us sleeping under the same roof.'

'Don't forget, our house will be pretty full too, with Nick in residence and Guy staying over the weekend.

But I don't see why not. Provided she doesn't mind staying in a house with three male strangers.'

'Well,' said Neville, 'it's not as if any of you…'

'Don't bracket Nick along with the rest of us,' warned James. 'He doesn't appreciate it.'

'Well all right, but he's only a kid. Maya's a stately galleon of forty-six, and Rita's almost on the same scale. I don't think either of them would show up on Nick's radar, or he on theirs.'

'Who gets to choose which one of them we have?' James asked. 'And by the way, do you want a cup of awful coffee?'

'No, thank you, but maybe a Bourbon biscuit…?' He helped himself from a nearby dish. 'I think, on balance, it might be better if you were to put up Rita, the one near the cinema. She'll keep for another night. Whereas Maya…'

'Who comes all the way from High Wycombe…'

'To tell you the truth, I still hold out a sort of hope that she and I might be able to … after all these years … sort of get something more lasting together again.' He stopped. His expression did not look excessively hopeful.

'And your game plan starts with inviting her over on the same weekend as you've invited this creature from behind the cinema?'

'As I said, that wasn't the original intention. And she doesn't live behind the cinema, I only said near it. But we'll have to wait and see what happens. There's nothing else to be done.' Neville shook his head.

James could think of quite a few other things that could have been done quite easily – putting one of the women off till another time struck him as one of the more obvious ones – but he knew from experience that there was little point in sharing this insight with Neville.

'Anyway,' said Neville, suddenly all bright again, 'if that's all OK you're all invited to Sunday lunch at the East Pavilion to make up for any inconvenience. Including the boy of course.'

'What boy is this?' Chris, the honorary secretary of the Friends of the Regent was doing her circuit of the little crowd of supporters, selling raffle tickets. She had just arrived at James's elbow. Her eyes twinkled. 'Which boy?'

'Nick Parker,' said James and found to his surprise that there was pleasure to be tasted in the act of pronouncing his name out loud. 'One of the newer ASMs. Have you met him yet? He's staying with Borja and me out at Sevenscore.'

Chris raised an eyebrow. 'Indeed?' she said.

It was Neville's idea to go down to the Rose and Castle for a drink before lunch on Sunday. The weather was fine and they went on foot. Rather than go the long way round through the time-warp wood and down the public road, they took the slightly shorter route across the fields, going by way of the old carriage drive. It wasn't a drive now, being completely overgrown with grass, grazed by sheep and indistinguishable from the fields it passed through, except for its double line of graceful Lombardy poplars, still asleep in this early springtime but with buds already swelling and red. Neville walked in front, twirling a stick and with Maya at his side. She had arrived the previous night. Next in the procession walked Nick with Rita alongside. Rita had arrived in a taxi about an hour ago and was more than a little put out to find Neville already à deux with another female. James brought up the rear with Guy, whom he had driven out to Sevenscore at the end of the show the previous night – Guy didn't drive – and who was now talking about everything under the sun except the forthcoming season of plays.

Arriving at the Rose and Castle they found one or two groups of customers sitting along the canal side, at wooden tables under the pub's thatched eaves. But the ladies felt it wasn't quite spring-like enough to join them and so they trooped inside, Guy ducking his head under the beams, where they stood jostling with the Sunday morning regulars at the top bar. From time to time one or both of the women managed to squeeze into a vacant seat for a few minutes – but only for a few minutes because sitting down rather sidelined them from the principal centre of animation, which consisted of Neville and Guy, standing with their backs against the counter and, spurred on by each other's presence, entertaining the whole room with theatre stories. Between them they had a repertoire that stretched back through half of two lifetimes – and also stretched, just occasionally, the credulity of their audience. They were a strikingly contrasted pair: Guy, lean and ascetic looking with cropped grey hair, only the light in his brown eyes giving an indication of his mischievous, restless temperament; Neville a round-faced fifty-year-old cherub – in tweeds and a woollen tie, despite the informality of the occasion.

'I was approached by Leonard about a part in the pantomime before Christmas,' said Guy. 'Dick Whittington. He met me by chance in Pembridge Street.' Leonard was an elderly and distinguished actor who lived nearby. Many years ago he had held the post that Guy now had, as artistic director. He was now over eighty. 'Oh dear, I said. I'm afraid it's all cast. If only I'd know you might be interested… If you'd come along a bit earlier. But there's nothing left at all. Well, only the Cat…'Well, we walked along in silence for a bit and then Leonard said, in that very measured way…' Guy imitated Leonard's resonant, senior actor's tones. ''The Cat. Ah Yes. And … How Do You See This Cat?''

James knew many of these stories already. He had a more limited repertoire of his own from which he produced one or two gems. But he knew better than to try to compete with the two older hands when they were in harness together and on top form. Besides, he was enjoying watching the innocent delight stealing across Nick's face as he listened, entranced, to all the old tales for the first time.

It was already two o'clock when Neville, their host for lunch, began to let his thoughts turn in that direction. They left the pub and canal side, setting off again up the old carriage drive, this time in a kind of V-formation, like a skein of flying geese, with Guy setting the pace and still in full anecdotal flow at the front.

'Do you suppose Neville's actually done anything about lunch?' Nick asked James at one point.

'On past experience I'd say not,' James answered.

Experience had informed him correctly. When they all trooped through the front door of Neville's Inigo Jones pavilion residence, and then turned into his kitchen, Neville produced with a kind of vague pride a rolled joint of pork with neatly slashed skin for crackling … once it would be cooked. 'How long do you think it'll take?' he asked, optimistically directing the question at the ladies, who were expected to know that kind of thing.

'An hour and a half,' suggested Rita helpfully.

'Two and a quarter, maybe?' Maya hazarded.

'How much does it weigh?' asked James.

'Seven and a half pounds,' said Neville. He sounded quite positive about that.

'Then it's simple,' said Nick. 'Twenty minutes per pound and twenty over. That's … er … two hours fifty minutes – plus a little time to rest.'

'Perhaps we ought to put the oven on now,' suggested Guy.

Neville thought that, in the light of Nick's astute and helpful new calculation of the cooking time there would be time for a small whisky while they waited. What did everybody else think?

The outside temperature had risen a little since they had decided against sitting out of doors at the pub a couple of hours before. Or perhaps it was they, Neville and his guests, who were no longer quite so sensitive to the cold. They took their whiskies, which were not as small as all that, out into the garden with them.

The early promises of spring were very much in evidence in that sheltered place. From between the pale flagstones of the pathways and in amongst the gravel of the drive, the flowers of Siberian squill sparkled up at them, blue and bright as children's eyes. Clematis shoots were already climbing, lithe and green, among the still bare apple trees in the walled orchard. In the herb garden fennel and dill were sprouting green and purple plumes.

'Well, Nick,' said Guy suddenly. 'What do you think we should do: kick off with a costume drama, or a musical?'

Nick knew perfectly well that Guy was not seriously consulting him; he could as easily have launched the discussion by addressing the question to Neville's cat. Nevertheless, he was startled enough by the question to become suddenly tongue-tied, even though he felt vaguely flattered that the crucial meeting had been opened in his presence. The ladies looked as though they felt the same. Perhaps that was how Guy liked to play things: the cameras had been let in on the cabinet meeting, and thereby he was flattered too.

James saw Nick's embarrassment and spared him any more by answering the question himself. 'Costume drama,' he said at once. 'If only for the sake of change. Last autumn began with a musical. So…'

Guy, who loved nothing better than to make snap decisions that startled everybody to bits said, right then, let it be The Mystery of Edwin Drood. Neville would write a stage adaptation: cast of no more than eleven, the smaller parts to be doubled. Could Neville have a list of scenes by mid-May and the finished script by – say – the end of July? Had he read Edwin Drood, by the way?

Neville had. Had Guy remembered that Charles Dickens never actually finished the book? The lack of an ending might make any stage adaptation a little unsatisfying in dramatic terms. Unless Guy wanted Neville to write an ending? Neville said he felt under-qualified to finish a literary task whose completion had eluded Dickens.

'Not Edwin Drood,' said Guy. 'I didn't mean Edwin Drood. I meant the other one. The chap with peacock feathers in his hat.'

'Barnaby Rudge,' said Neville. 'It's extremely long. With riots, the burning down of Newgate jail, gin flowing flaming along the gutters of Chancery Lane…'

'Just the job,' said Guy. 'Good. That's settled.' It was probably the flaming gin that clinched it. He liked to set pyrotechnic problems for the design department to get their teeth into. 'Now there's this new play called Bouncers. I'd like to see if we can get hold of the rights to that one.'

Nick remembered that his lunch invitation was, at least notionally, contingent on his keeping the two women entertained while the other three held their planning meeting. That meeting now seemed to have started, its progress fuelled by Neville's generous dispensations of whisky, while its participants ambled to and fro in the rose garden. But the goal of splitting the party into two groups, towards which James and Nick were separately working, proved elusive. James was trying to keep Neville and Guy together and focused on the business at hand; Guy, who had decided that Nick was really quite a lovely boy – and why had he not noticed before? – was trying to keep him engaged in conversation; Nick was trying to draw the two women away from the others by various conversational strategies, while Neville was determined to show off the shy March beauties of his garden to Rita and Maya. So they travelled together in an ever-changing grouping and their winter-garden-party conversation bounced around, remarks ricocheting off people for whom they were not intended, in a Babel of semi-communication.

‘He’s always proposing marriage to people. Then he wakes up in the morning and changes his mind. It isn’t fair on the women.’

‘A stage version of Moby Dick? Are you out of your mind?’

‘Just look at those lovely golden aconites.’

‘They did it at Leicester a few years ago.’

‘That vacant plinth for a statue. It’s like The Draughtsman’s Contract.’

‘A female whale? No way.’

‘And the bassin. Are there fish in it?’

‘In that case he’d have called it Moby Fanny.’

All the time Neville kept topping up people’s glasses from the whisky bottle he was carrying in the hand that didn’t have a glass in it. ‘We have to see the snowdrops.’ Neville opened a door in a lichen-covered brick wall. It opened upon a small wood, still with winter’s sleep upon it but whose floor was a foaming sea of white. Snowdrops had multiplied there unchecked for more than a century. A stage-set for the Sleeping Beauty. They saw a starry-flowered magnolia growing against a wall. Through its branches peered a blue mop of aubretia growing from a crack between the bricks. The colours of the Virgin Mary. Rita gave Nick a kiss on his left cheek.

'You're a very sensitive young man.' Guy wondered why he hadn't thought of the idea first.

'Play something for us, Nick,' urged Neville. Nick weighed this up while Neville lumbered off, with Rita in tow, to get the ballroom key from the hall table in the Court House. Nick decided that his eye-brain-finger coordination, despite a fairly major intake of beer and whisky, might just be up to one particular Chopin Nocturne which he had learnt as a boy and which was relatively simple and reassuringly slow. Neville ambled back across the lawn with the key, Rita now fastened on his neck like a limpet-mine that would explode in only a matter of time, and everyone drifted into the great, chilly, West Pavilion. Nick's gamble paid off. He acquitted himself beautifully, aided and abetted by the ballroom's flattering acoustic, into whose well of resonance his one or two shooting-star wrong notes disappeared without trace.

It was James who suggested that perhaps the joint in the oven might need basting, or at least looking at. Guy observed that it was getting dark outside and Neville thought that everyone's glass looked a touch empty, though that might just be a trick of the fading light.

They returned around the colonnade to Neville's pavilion and Nick heroically suggested that the two ladies join him in the kitchen and help to prepare the potatoes for roasting and get the veg sorted. James thanked him in an aside. 'You played very beautifully just now, by the way.'

'It's all very well my getting them into the kitchen,' said Nick. 'But how am I going to keep them there?'

'I think I've got the solution.' James took the two women's glasses from them, topped them up from a fresh bottle and then bore the glasses, and the bottle tucked under his arm, with great ceremony into the kitchen; it was like laying a trail of corn to decoy pheasants, he thought. No longer able to decide whether this was a wise, or even a kind, thing to do, he topped up Nick's glass at the same time.

Lunch was as substantial, and as generously accompanied by wine, as it was late.

By the time the meal was over, the programme for the autumn season had been mostly settled and it was nearly bedtime. There was the small difficulty of persuading Rita that she was staying the night in the care of James: a fellow guest along with Nick and Guy, and not rooming with Neville who by now looked as though he would have his hands quite full with Maya. It was Guy who tackled the problem. 'Right,' he barked, as if it had been ten o'clock on the first morning of rehearsals. 'Time to go.' He stood up and offered his arm to Rita to take. Once she had hesitantly inserted her hand into the gap formed between his elbow and his waist, he clamped his arm to his side as smartly as if he'd been a human mousetrap and marched out into the night with his captive. James and Nick followed him across the lawn to where their own porch light beckoned.

Once indoors, Rita was very ready for bed indeed and had to be unwound from everyone's shoulders in turn before she could be persuaded to cross the kitchen to the Blue Bedroom. Back in the sitting room Nick slumped on the sofa. 'I've got hiccups,' he said, demonstrating the fact in the middle of the announcement.

'Make your thumb and forefinger into a ring,' instructed James. 'Both hands. Interlock them but don't let them touch. Hold them steady like that for exactly one…'

Nick hiccupped.

'Try again. Keep them apart for one minute and you won't…'

It wasn't going to work.

'This always works,' said Guy. 'Lie on your back on the floor.'

Nick did as he was told. Guy leaned down and seized his ankles, then, to James's surprise as well as to Nick's, lifted his legs in the air. After that – and this took some doing – he stepped backwards up onto the sofa behind him and, once he had got his balance, lifted the whole of Nick's body off the ground so that only his hands and forearms still trailed along it.

'Guy, please,' said James from a nearby armchair. 'Put him down, for God's sake. He doesn't like all that.'

A moment later Nick arrived back on the floor with a harmless but audible bump. 'The hiccups seem to have gone,' he said.

Nick was in bed and already asleep when light shone across his face. The door to his bathroom had opened and Rita stood framed in it in naked, ample, splendour. 'What time is it?' Nick asked.

'Oh darling, I don't have a watch,' Rita said. 'You look so lovely lying there. And my bed's so cold and damp. Would you mind very much if I…'

'Actually,' said Nick, 'I don't want to be unfriendly or anything but I'd rather you didn't.' He snuggled down into the bed and pulled the clothes up over his head. A moment later he felt the weight of his visitor sitting down on the bottom corner of his bed. 'Oh darling,' he heard. 'You'd find me ever so…' Through the blankets he felt a hand run down his arm. But he lay there rigid and after a minute his discouraging response and the nocturnal chill of the bedroom had their effect on his naked visitor; soon he was aware of the darkness returning as the door clicked shut, and then of a second click as Rita exited their shared bathroom by its other door to return to her own Blue Room.

In the morning James was as solicitous of Nick and as concerned for his well-being as a mother hen: making breakfast and black coffee, finding orange juice and aspirins. Guy was already up and taking an energetic turn around the grounds. He didn't believe in hangovers. James drove them both into town, Guy brightly talking, Nick somewhat subdued in the back. Rita had been left to sleep herself out; Neville could take responsibility for her when she rose. James considered his own responsibilities towards her to have been amply discharged – as did Nick.

While Guy sprang up the stairs to the theatre office James hung back and caught at Nick's elbow as he prepared to make his way backstage via the auditorium. 'Look. I feel a bit responsible. I have to thank you for all your help yesterday – cooking, understanding, tact and all that. And for playing the piano so nicely. Only I'm sorry if one or two people got a bit…'

'You don't know the half of it.' Nick managed half a grin, and told James the story of Rita's mixing up the two bathroom doors. 'If it was a mistake, of course.'

James looked at him. 'Oh dear,' he said. Then, 'You haven't combed your hair this morning. Here, let me.' He took his own comb from his jacket pocket and gently combed and parted Nick's black hair, as he had used to years ago for Borja. But whereas Borja had always laughingly protested or, dog-like, shaken himself away, Nick stood still, a study in docility, in front of him and let himself be groomed. 'The trouble is,' James said when he couldn't reasonably prolong the coiffure any further, 'you're such a lovely, lovable guy. Damn it, you've nearly got me doing it now.'

'Well, that's really flattering but I'd respect you more if you didn't.' The moment of passivity was past.

'Well, thank you!' James was badly stung and let it show. 'What's that meant to mean?'

'I meant, even more than the considerable amount I respect you already.' He laughed, which made his teeth and eyes suddenly sparkle.

'Go to work,' said James. 'I'll buy you dinner sometime soon. I owe you that at least.'

Nick turned and disappeared through the red-curtained doorway into the hidden gilded splendour of the dress circle. James stood and watched the door he'd gone through, his eyes focused on its bright brass handle for several more seconds.

Neville spent most of that morning, as he told James later, explaining to Maya and Rita that when he had proposed marriage to both of them, at separate times during the course of the previous day, it had sort of just slipped out and he hadn't really meant it.

EIGHT

Flying is freedom, Rafael had once told Borja. Borja's heart still agreed with that proposition, despite the fact that he had been flying jets as a job for nine years now. It was still exciting. Despite the absence of novelty these days, he retained the sense of being at peace with himself that he had experienced the first time he had ever taken to the air as a passenger, years ago, in an old Caravelle that was plying between Seville and Valencia.

Did he really find flying such a peaceful experience? people asked him. Was it a job totally unencumbered with the stresses and strains that other people experienced in the course of their working lives? Was there never the slightest frisson of … danger? Well yes, he would admit, there was always that. Rafael, his lover for so short a time, had been killed in an air crash. That had made him want to be a pilot in the first place.

How bizarre, people thought. They didn't say it to his face, but he could see the thought etched momentarily on theirs.

Yes, but the premature end to that adventure with Rafael had brought him back to James, had brought James back to him… It was complicated, all that, and very long ago…

Yes, there was always danger, there was always risk, as in everything you undertook. And over the years there had been moments, of course there had, when Borja had felt, in the words of the old flying school adage, that it would have been 'better to be down here, wishing you could be up there, than up there and wishing you were down here'.

There had been the time when they had made landfall over the wrong bit of Brittany after crossing the Bay of Biscay, bound for Luton, and it had taken a few anxious minutes and some fraught exchanges with ATC in Nantes to sort out a new route home.

There had been landings in bad weather. Once, arriving at the mountainous island of Madeira where the short runway jutted into the sea at both ends and looked, on approach, as small as the deck of an aircraft-carrier, they had hit a sudden squall of wind and rain seconds before touchdown. As they aquaplaned along a suddenly invisible surface he had seen himself careering off the end and plunging over the edge, taking all his passengers with him. When, as actually happened, the wheels got a grip on the tarmac at the last moment and enabled him to brake to turning speed – and a hair-raisingly fast turn that had been, just feet from the precipice – he felt the applause that erupted from the passenger cabin, a spontaneous gesture that was quite usual at that alarming little airfield, might have been replaced by a more solemn recognition of their deliverance had the passengers realised just how close to disaster they had come.

There was the occasional worry over danger from the passengers themselves: hijackers, mad people or drunks. So far, in Borja's experience, no-one had ever intruded into the cockpit and the few incidents with drunken passengers had been contained quite easily by the cabin staff. He could only recall one occasion when a captain had been obliged to wade down the aisle to wag a forefinger.

If anything did give him more cause for anxiety it was what they called at flying school the making breakfast factor. That meant the possibility that in performing an oft-repeated routine action you might one day screw it up. Switch on the oven instead of the grill to make the morning toast. Switch on the electric kettle when it was empty. Spoon sugar into the milk jug instead of into the cup. Raise the wing-flaps instead of lowering them on finals. Easily done, but there was one small difference. The sugar in the milk was just a nuisance. Stall on your final approach, though, and you'd bought it.

This was why so much care had to be taken with every move and every action. Pilot and co-pilot checked and verbally reconfirmed everything with each other as they went along: pre-flight checks, taxi drills, top-of-climb checks, pre-descent checks, pre-landing checks. It was like a series of litanies. On a short flight, say Luton to Amsterdam, when descent began almost as soon as the climb was complete, the litanies followed each other almost without a break, except for the constant, necessary interruptions created by radio conversations with air traffic controllers on the ground. On those flights there was hardly a spare minute for casual chat with the person sitting next to you. But this morning, since today's was a somewhat longer flight – all the way to Athens and back – there was.

Borja hadn't flown with Amanda Symons for some time: not since the day before his father had died. He told her about that once they had started to relax into the cruise, safely above the clouds that blanketed the English Channel. Amanda made appropriate polite noises. She was flying the plane this morning, Borja dealing with the radio and other secondary operations; in the afternoon, on the inbound sector, their roles would be reversed. This role reversal procedure was essential for the career of first officers like Borja in order for them to accumulate enough flying hours and a sufficient number of landings to qualify for the rank of captain. Borja was very conscious that in just a few more weeks he would himself have notched up the requisite number of hours and landings – the next requirement was a vacancy arising for a captain. But, one thing at a time, he told himself. They passed over Koksy beacon on the Belgian coast and Borja reported their position to

Maastricht Control. 'This is Silverwing four one three overhead Koksy on Upper Golf One, eastbound. Level three three zero, at zero nine two three. Sprimont next.'

'You were going to a theatrical event last time I saw you,' said Amanda once Maastricht had acknowledged. 'How did that go?'

'Oh, I'd rather forgotten about it. That was the evening of the night my father died. Now I remember, it was a big success. Oh – but it nearly didn't happen.' The memory came back to him. He told the story of how Nick had saved the day with his emergency light bulb trick at the unscheduled fire inspection. 'And the ending to that story,' he concluded, 'which you'll find bizarre, is that the chap has come to live with us.'

'With you and your boyfriend?'

'Yes.'

'I do find that bizarre.' Amanda let it go at that so there was silence for a moment – which was then broken by Borja.

'How are you getting on with Andy?'

'Andy?'

'Should I say Captain Holmes?' Borja prompted.

'Oh that Andy. All in the past, I'm afraid. My interest in him is completely at an end. Since at least ... since last Friday. And it's funny you telling a story about dud light bulbs. Because I think I can cap it. You know what a reputation he has... Captain Holmes I mean. As a stickler for rules and details. I heard that at Gatwick a couple of weeks ago he threw a whole morning's departure schedule into chaos. He'd arrived at the threshold with a queue of planes behind him all waiting to take off. Then he announces to the co-pilot that he's used the wrong wording in calling off the taxi drills and all the checks have to be gone through again before he can move off onto the runway. He's positioned right in the middle of the taxiway so the queuing planes can't get past him and they just have to sit waiting there till he's finished.

'Well, by now there's about five inbounds doing scenic tours of Sussex and demanding to be let down, so the tower clears them all to land one after the other. So all the take-off slots were missed and everyone had to be re-allocated. It was a Saturday morning and all. You can imagine the chaos.'

'Yes,' said Borja. 'I can. But if the cause of the problem was his sticking to the rulebook, then we shouldn't really be complaining. Better to be too careful than too lax, surely?'

'All right. But to make a fuss about a first officer's phraseology? I mean! It wasn't that the checks weren't done, they'd just been incorrectly called off.' She affected a blimpish voice. 'Non-standard communication.'

'Or so you heard. You weren't actually there,' Borja said gently. 'Stories go round. They get exaggerated.'

'No, I wasn't there. And like you, I'd have put it down to the rumour mill and thought no more about it. But then there was last Friday. And I was there. And he did it again. But not Gatwick this time. It was on Gran Canaria. He had the first of our two flights out, I had the second. When I got there I saw his plane still sitting on the tarmac. He wouldn't take off. He said the plane had gone sick, was unfit. All it was was, was this.' She pointed to the nose-wheel lock indicator light front of her and then, with an emphatic sigh, to its identical twin on Borja's side. 'The other one was working perfectly. It was quite safe enough to get home with. Just one deployment. But he insisted on getting the engineer out, which couldn't happen till the next morning. A four thousand mile round trip to change a light bulb, can you imagine?'

'So he and his passengers had to stay the night.' Borja made the obvious assumption.

'You'd think so, wouldn't you? Far from it! He insisted on flying his passengers back on my aircraft, leaving me with the night stop.'

'Why on earth did he…?'

'Oh, it was a little trick he did with the hours. Creative timekeeping. He said that if he went first he would be out of hours but he had the discretion to waive that. Whereas, if he stayed, we'd both be out of hours and both sets of passengers would have to stay in hotels, costing the company money. I argued with him. First that his calculations made no sense. And if he could waive his hours' limitation, then so could I. Also that if he wasn't being such a big girl's blouse about the indicator light the company wouldn't have any extra costs at all. But it was no use. In the end he was the senior officer – just – and his decision overruled me. The simple fact was, he just wanted to get home that night.'

'With the result that you couldn't.'

'Which wasn't hugely convenient. I didn't have a change of clothes or anything for the bathroom. Added to which it was the start of…' she wasn't quite sure how to say it to a gay first officer, 'that time of the month. I hadn't brought too many… Fortunately one of the cabin crew…'

'Poor you.' Borja thought for a second then smiled. 'I suppose some people might say you were a bit improvident. But all the same.'

'Improvident? We're going to Athens and back today. We're still in March. I bet you haven't brought an umbrella with you.'

'No,' admitted Borja, 'you're right.'

'Change of shirt? Pyjamas?'

'OK, you win.' His smile became a sly grin. 'But I always carry a toothbrush in my bag.'

'You would.' Amanda said it with a laugh. She might not have done if Borja had confessed to having the other stuff as well.

Borja was able to join James – and Nick – for supper late that evening. He retold the story that Amanda had told him, about the captain whose punctiliousness had led to her being stranded in the Canaries without a tampon.

'I'd have thought getting to stay an extra night in the Canaries was one of the perks of the job,' said Nick, 'especially at this time of year. Still, the other captain does sound a bit of a wanker. All that fuss over a light bulb.'

'Well, I was told all that in connection with another story about a light bulb.' Borja shot Nick a mischievous smile, then was serious. 'Planes are different. Theatres may catch fire, but people have a reasonable chance of getting out alive. They never fall out of the sky.' He stopped. He never could make a remark like that, however inadvertently, without thinking of Rafael. James knew that too and looked at him thoughtfully for a moment. Borja went on. 'There are good reasons why pilots are over-cautious sometimes. I agree it sounds pretty selfish of him to disappear with someone else's plane and leave her behind with the sick one, but I can understand his feeling he didn't want to fly home with a broken light.'

'What would you have done?' James asked, the ghost of a challenge in his voice.

Borja thought before replying. 'I honestly don't know. I mean, I hope I wouldn't have left a lady stranded and taken her plane. And he was hardly expected to know about her monthly … thing. But about the light… Well, without having been there I couldn't say. I might have decided one way or the other. It's a feeling you have, being on the spot.'

James nodded sympathetically, knowing the feeling all too well.

'His decision will have cost the company a lot of money,' Borja concluded. 'They can't criticise him for it … and yet, privately they'll remember.'

'Managers do,' said James. He leaned across the table towards them with the wine bottle.

NINE

At the board meeting, which was held in an echoingly large committee chamber in City Hall a week or two later, Guy Levington announced his plans for the autumn season. They would kick off with the new dramatisation of Barnaby Rudge that Neville had promised to deliver…

Did Mr Levington mean Neville Sanders? Councillor Matthews wanted to know. And could Mr Levington guarantee that Mr Sanders would deliver the scripts on time on this occasion? Councillor Matthews recalled an occasion when…

The chairman fixed the councillor with a death-mask stare and said he had no doubt that Mr Levington and Mr Miller between them would ensure that Mr Sanders respected the timetable he had been given. He turned, expressionless, to where Guy and James sat side by side. They nodded, almost imperceptibly, in return.

Following the costume drama would come a new play called Straight and Narrow, which had just completed a successful run in the West End – Guy skated rather quickly over its subject matter; next a revival of a popular favourite, Noel Coward's Hay Fever; then another, quite gritty, new play which was called…

Guy went on with his presentation, supported by James, whose job it was to take the board through the budgets and box-office targets for each show. Later in the meeting he would have the tougher job of presenting the show reports – the actual financial outcomes – of all the productions since Christmas. For the moment he took a back seat as the board questioned Guy further about his choice of plays. He knew that the matter had already been sewn up in the chairman's back office at the Three Feathers Hotel and that the board's vote on the season would be just a formality. As it proved when the chairman, still gravely nodding his approval of Guy's programme, called for a show of hands.

'Unanimous, I believe,' said the chairman, peering in both directions along the strangely banana-shaped table. 'No abstentions?' There were none. He banged his gavel lightly against its wooden anvil. 'Now I would like to draw the board's attention to a proposal of Mr Miller's to add one more Sunday evening event to the spring programme. Perhaps Mr Miller would like to speak to it himself?' He peered along the table at James. The chairman occupied the centre of the convex side of the board table, James and Guy sat a little way down on his right, the company secretary a little way away on the left. The chairman's closest supporters on the city council sat directly opposite him on the concave side, while his opponents always found themselves seated, by some strange accident, on the two extremities of the table: those on the concave side facing almost away from each other and finding it difficult to maintain eye-contact let alone any sort of concerted opposition to anything the chairman, sitting midway between them, wanted to push through.

James stood up and told the meeting about Alexa: about her talent, her growing success in Spain; he mentioned the box-office success that had attended Paco Peña's concert a year or two before…

'That's all very well, James,' said Councillor Stackpole from the other end of the table in a voice that would have carried along a station platform – though given the length and shape of the table one could see his point – 'but Paco Peña was already a household name when he came here. Whereas this lady-friend of yours…' A ripple of unease ran round the room: was Councillor Stackpole not perhaps slightly out of order? The chairman delicately fingered the handle of his gavel.

'This … musician. Has anybody in the city heard of her? Let alone heard her play? And let us not forget that the Sunday events, unlike our mainstream productions, do not attract subsidy; they must pay for themselves.'

'For God's sake,' Guy muttered to James privately. 'It's one woman and a wooden chair. You'd think it was going to break the bank.'

'I'm very happy to declare an interest,' James said resolutely, looking at Mr Stackpole and trying hard not to turn it into a glare: he left that to the chairman. 'Alexa and I have been personal friends for over twelve years. I've followed her career closely during that time. I wouldn't be putting her forward if I didn't think she was well worth it.' He fished among the papers on the table in front of him. 'I have some of her promotional literature here.' He passed it along the table towards the chairman.

'Hmm.' The chairman examined it carefully, stopping when he came to a portrait-size photograph of Alexa, admittedly taken some four or five years previously, in which her long mane of copper hair flowed forward onto one shoulder, partly shading one of her eyes. The other eye shone a brilliant blue-green. 'Tell me,' he asked in a quiet, clear voice, directing his question at James, 'is her hair that colour naturally?' He held the photograph aloft then allowed it to be passed around the table from hand to hand.

'Yes, absolutely natural,' said James. 'And for all I know, it may be the same colour everywhere.' Another ripple ran round the room.

'Then perhaps,' said the chairman slowly, 'we owe it to the good people of the city to let them see her for themselves.'

The vote, when it came, was unanimous.

When the meeting was over, James and Guy returned to the theatre to enjoy a quiet drink in the circle bar along with the one or two board members with whom they were on first-name terms. There were a few wounds to lick – the question of the disappearing carpet had been raised yet again by the city treasurer – but all in all it was an occasion for a little, understated, mutual congratulation. Surprisingly soon the sound of clapping came from the other side of the wall and then a small influx of playgoers wandered into the bar, and the original small gathering was diluted, mingling with the new arrivals; in a few minutes they would be joined by members of the cast, back in their day clothes now but with their cheeks aglow with make-up remover and their eyes still shining with that special, post-performance light.

Nick came rushing through the swing-doors, still in his blacks, which made him look even slimmer than he was. 'Thank God you're still here,' he said, arriving at James's elbow. Then, 'Sorry,' to the person James was talking to and who had been cut off. But the playgoer faded away. Keen to engage the manager in conversation, he was less interested by the boys in black. 'It's my bike,' Nick said. 'It's packed up and I didn't want to walk all that way if I could help it. Would you mind terribly if…'

'What time are you in tomorrow?' James asked him.

'Nine thirty.'

'Me too. Leave the bike here. Someone can sort it in the morning…'

'Throat said he'd look at it for me.' Both the theatre electricians were called Mike. Since that name was already spoken for by the production manager, they were known respectively as Throat and Hand.

'I'll take you home and bring you in again in the morning. No worries.'

The relief that flooded Nick's face touched James. They had not seen much of each other for a week or two:

their timetables had been different; Nick had gone home to his parents one weekend, and when Borja had been at home Nick had tended to cook for himself and, sensibly, not join his two hosts too often unless asked. James still hadn't had the opportunity to buy Nick the dinner he'd offered him as a reward for his gallantry that complicated Sunday. Though he had certainly not forgotten.

'Tell you what. Why don't we have that meal out I've been promising you? Seems like this might be a good opportunity.'

Nick tried not to look too eager, but without much success. James could almost imagine he saw a tail wagging behind him. 'Yeah. I mean, that'd be great. Mind if I run and get out of my blacks?'

'There'll be a beer waiting here for you when you get back. After that, Chinese OK? There's a rather up-market new one just opened on Cutler Street.'

There was bound to be someone in the restaurant who knew them, of course. That always happened in life, causing things that were simple and needed no explaining to appear complex and in need of justification. This time the someone was two people: Chris, the honorary secretary of the Friends of the Regent, and Sammy – actually Samantha – who was the president. Nobody knew for certain if Sammy and Chris were a couple. They never referred to themselves as if they were, and nobody from the theatre had been so ill bred as to ask them to their faces. On the other hand nobody was so well bred as to leave the question unasked in the tail-chasing round of theatre gossip.

'Oh hallo,' Sammy greeted them brightly. 'Celebrating a successful board meeting?' Chris nodded and grinned.

James noticed with relief that they were seated at a table for two so that they would all be spared the awkwardness of the do join us, no thank you we're talking business charade. 'Board meeting was fine. Season's been accepted without a fight. Show reports … well … I'm still here, complete with hair and finger-nails.'

'And where's Borja today?' Chris asked. This was not said pointedly. It was a standard question, almost a game really, because James always knew and the people who knew him knew that.

'Bedding down in an airport hotel at Gatwick if all's gone to plan. He'll have flown back from Tenerife this evening and he's got an early morning trip to Tangier tomorrow. Then tomorrow evening he's coming home for a few days.' James extended a hand towards his companion. 'I don't know if you've met Nick yet.' The two women gave vague yes-sort-of nods and smiles. 'He's the one I told you about, Chris: he's our new lodger out at Sevenscore. This is his reward for listening to my life story.'

Why on earth did I say that? James asked himself immediately. Not only was this a public announcement that he was treating a very junior employee to a meal, but what he had said was actually untrue: the reason he had given for the treat was actually more eyebrow-raising than the simple reality. Still, it was said now and could not conceivably be changed or amended. He smiled, gave a small finger-wave – which Nick copied – and then they moved off to find another table for two at a distance wide enough to be discreet, but not so far away as to constitute a snub.

'But you haven't told me your life story,' Nick said, once they were sitting down. 'Only bits of it.'

'Well maybe that's about the right amount. Perhaps I should keep the rest in reserve – as a kind of penance in store.'

'There's no penance about it. I'm interested.'

'Well then, I only know little bits about you. So maybe you could fill in some of the gaps for me too.'

'Then I might find I had to buy dinner for you,' said Nick.

They both knew better than to embark on a thoroughgoing exchange of life histories in chronological order. Nevertheless, James's flustered fib to Chris had set the tone for the next part of the evening. A certain amount of mutual autobiography was clearly on the agenda. It was some time since James had been so indulged. Very young people would swap life stories at the drop of a hat; but as people got older they were less likely to do so: the stories were too long, too complicated – eventually too sad.

It struck James with some force that, after fourteen years of sharing a life with Borja, he had very little to tell that wasn't about his partner rather than about himself. Nick already knew the story of how they had met. Now James found himself explaining how, on first visiting England for a holiday, Borja had fallen so much in love with the place that he'd wanted them both to leave Spain and settle there for good – to James's initial horror and stunned disbelief. But a year later they had done just that.

They had needed jobs. They had worked together in the box office at one of the London concert halls. It had seemed like a good idea while Borja got acclimatised. He had already managed a concert in Spain and was good at maths. But he had other ambitions for the long term. He had dreamed for some time of becoming a pilot. James saw this as a dream only. His lover was a linguist and a Shakespearean scholar; James had chosen not to see his practical side, had not remembered being told how he had excelled in physics and mechanics as well at school. Being a clerk in the oficina de turismo in Seville hadn't given him the opportunity to display such skills. So it came as quite a shock to James when Borja first negotiated with his parents for the money and was then accepted as a full-time student at flying school. Forced to live apart now for a time, except at weekends, James found himself at a bit of a loss. Not wanting to return to teaching, he had embarked on a training course in arts management, was then able to secure a post as front of house manager in the nearest theatre to where Borja was training, moved here to the Regent when Borja joined the airline … and that more or less brought the story up to date.

It was still mainly Borja's story. James found himself half wishing he had been able to present something of himself that was all his own to the likeable, interested young man who sat opposite him. For Nick was very likeable, he'd discovered that early on. He'd realised not long after that that he was also very attractive, even if not in the most flamboyant of ways.

Nick was telling a story which must have cost a bit to tell, since it was against himself. It showed a willingness, James thought, to trust him, to expose his vulnerability. And James was flattered.

The story was about Nick's breaking up with his last girlfriend. He was quite candid about it. They had been very attracted to each other and had 'gone out'together for about six months. Sex had been part of the deal but it hadn't really fired either of them up all that much. In the end she had found someone else who was, 'hunkier, more exciting and with better earning prospects,' as Nick self-deprecatingly put it.

'He might have been all of those things,' James heard himself unguardedly saying, 'but I doubt he was better looking.' He stopped abruptly, flushed, and looked at Nick – who, equally pink, looked back at him.

'Ready to order, sirs?' The waiter had materialised.

'Not quite,' said James and they both buried their heads more deeply than was strictly necessary in the mock-leather-bound menus.

Of course he shouldn't have said that, James realised. All the same, he did think Nick nice looking; there was no point denying it to himself. He had a full-lipped mouth, not too big, which showed a nice set of teeth, when he smiled, with a fetching gap between the top front two. His nose was non-eventful but smallish and straight. His hair was quite long and thick, shiny black. He had unfashionably long sideburns… His eyes were large and, for a British boy, unexpectedly dark and lustrous behind their not very thick glasses. For the second time James was reminded – by the eyes in particular – of Borja. Nick was tallish and lanky, Borja trim and compact, a little shorter than James – who considered himself to be of exactly average height. But there were other Borja-like things about Nick. The way he looked at you sometimes, the way he smiled to himself as he planned in his mind what he was going to say to you, the infinitesimal twitch of the lips as he listened to your answer... Borja when he was Nick's age, twelve or so years ago.

By the time their meal was finished Sammy and Chris had long gone, so they were able to take their departure more anonymously than they had arrived. Nick was quite garrulous in the car going home, while James had to concentrate quite hard on the driving. Safely back at Sevenscore, while Nick got the living room fire going and James uncorked a bottle of something red – he gave the label no more than a cursory glance – Nick was talking and asking questions about Alexa. She had caught his interest when James and Borja had first mentioned her. Now, with her concert at the Regent scheduled for just two months from now, he looked forward to the opportunity of meeting her. 'Her teacher,

Eulogio,' he changed tack slightly, 'I heard him play once.'

James was surprised. 'You heard Eulogio play? How could you have done?' James did a mental calculation. Eulogio had retired from concert giving in London over fifteen years ago. He had come out of retirement a year or so later to do the concert in the Alcázar that Borja organised. 'You were still a child.'

'When I heard you talking about Eulogio, just his first name, it didn't ring any bells. But just the other day it clicked. Eulogio Pérez Cabrera, wasn't he? And I did hear him. He came out of retirement one more time. He came to London when I was a first-year student. I suppose he did the other European capitals at the same time. He played the last three Beethoven sonatas. Very much the grand old man. I went to hear him at the Wigmore Hall. He played very … what do people say … magisterically? magisterially? But he made a mistake at the beginning of the last sonata. It was very dramatic. It begins, with a big handful of notes, da-daaah, pa-pom.' Nick mimed the hand movements as he sang out the four-note motif. 'Only he missed the second jump: da-splatt. There was a sort of gasp in the audience. Then, without looking round at us, he held both hands in the air – just as if he was stopping traffic – for what seemed ages, though I suppose it was only a couple of seconds. Then slowly he brought his hands down. The silence was incredible, electric. And he started again. And of course he played the whole thing without dropping a stitch.'

Nick stopped and looked at James, his eyes shining with the memory, reflecting the firelight. James said nothing. He had lived the moment too, in Nick's telling of it. Then Nick remembered something. 'I think I've got a tape of him playing, somewhere among my stuff. Would you like to hear it?' He wouldn't have made the suggestion sober.

James would not normally have wanted to hear it all that specially much. He was not a great aficionado of solo piano music, even played by someone he had known personally. But just at that moment, if Nick had suggested listening to the complete Ring Cycle or all of Bach's forty-eight preludes and fugues, he would probably have said yes. 'That'd be great.'

'It's only an old tape, taken from the radio.' Nick became faintly apologetic in advance, then went off to the Chinese bedroom to rummage for it. In his absence James put another log on the fire and topped up their wine glasses as a precautionary measure. He felt his whole body shivering suddenly. He must get that under control before Nick came back. With an effort of will he did.

The recording was almost unlistenable. There was nothing wrong with the music, Schubert's glorious second set of Impromptus, nor with Eulogio's playing, masterly and mischievous by turns. But the tape had been recorded years ago from an imperfectly tuned radio, had been bounced around in a student's, then an ASM's luggage, and had stretched from frequent playing. Both Nick and James grew increasingly uncomfortable as they listened, but neither could face the further embarrassment of being the one to suggest cutting their losses and turning it off.

James found himself idly taking in the fact that Nick's jeans were coming unstitched at one point on the leg seam. He had another pair of trousers, James remembered, which had been turned up on the inside and which hung down on his ankle where the stitching had given way. He would have liked more than anything right now to be able to say, 'Give me that, I'll mend it for you,'the way he did with Borja. But he knew that Nick would be mortified if he were to suggest it.

At last, after twenty-five minutes, the tape spooled its groggy way into the brilliant coda of the last Impromptu … and cut off six seconds before the end. The tape recorder's play button jumped up with a loud click that made them both start.

'Shit,' said Nick. 'I'd forgotten it did that.' The tape had cut off just before the final resolution into the tonic, with the pitch and the tension rising through a succession of dominant harmonies and suspensions like a towering, glistening wave that seemed must break any second. 'We can't just leave it like that,' he said. 'Not without the final cadence. Come with me.' Nick got up.

James obeyed, half guessing what he was going to do. Sure enough Nick led the way out into the hallway where he picked up the torch and the heavy ballroom key from the small table, unbolted the garden door and led the way across the pitch dark lawn, round the chill colonnade, and opened up the West Pavilion. The sudden switching on of the light gave a surprised appearance to the interior as if, like an elderly dowager, it was not used to being woken up so late at night, its ballroom days having ended centuries ago. Nick marched towards the piano and lifted the fall-board. Then he sat down, found the shimmering C-minor dominant tremolo on which the tape had gone silent, and broke into the thunderous downward scale in the tonic – the mountainous wave breaking at last in a torrent of foam – five full octaves – in Schubert's day the full compass of the instrument – from top to bottom in six seconds in an echoing crash. Nick took his hands from the keys and stood up. The lofty space went on ringing for several more seconds in a fading, ghostly, F-minor… We only hear the half-life of an echo – which means it is ringing still.

James never discovered how he found himself at Nick's side so immediately. He caught him by the waist with one arm and round the shoulders with the other. He had turned the unprotesting Nick towards him and they were kissing, comfortably, easily, but intensely, as if it had been the thing they always did. They took their time over this moment, both savouring it to the maximum because both knowing that it would soon have to come to a stop. Then – not that then has much meaning in relation to events that take place outside time and are not subject to measure by the artificial convention of seconds – they were standing apart, neither of them aware that either he or the other had broken free. They stood for a moment, looking at each other, half bemused, half wondering, like punch-drunk boxers, or like bull and matador, what – and whose – move would be next. Then Nick said, almost but not quite managing to make his voice sound normal, 'We'd better go back inside.'

They retraced their steps towards the door, switched off the light and locked the pavilion, walked round the colonnade and back across the lawn, James deliberately not putting an arm round Nick but walking at his side, and neither of them able to think of a single thing to say.

'I think it's time I went to bed,' Nick said flatly as they went indoors.

'Sure,' said James. 'See you in the morning.' And Nick turned sharp right into the Chinese bedroom and shut the door behind him. His bathroom was on the far side of his room, James's was en-suite with his and Borja's own bedroom. They had no awkward, toothbrush-carrying confrontations in corridors to face; there was no need for their paths to cross again before the morning.

James returned to his armchair beside the log fire. He poured out another glass of wine and sat staring, eyes unfocused, into the flames. The country silence was so intense that he was conscious of a whooshing in his ears:

the faint, ever so faint, hiss of the fire mixed in with the singing of his blood.

How could he have been so stupid as to kiss the boy? It was like striking a match in a firework factory. And that was before considering the impact it might have on Nick, the repercussions on their relationship as employer and employee, landlord and lodger – and Nick shared not just his home but Borja's too. He remembered the misery that had sprung from the last time... It had started with a simple kiss between him and William, back in Spain twelve years ago. But what it had led to! At least he'd had the excuse of being young then. Now he was thirty-six. Nick was twenty-four, as he and William had been back then.

Involuntarily he inhaled deeply. He topped up his half empty glass. He thought ahead, with a sick feeling, to the morning: to the awkward silence of the breakfast table, the uncomfortable proximity necessitated by the car journey they would make to get to work, the sensitivity of the antennae of the gossip machine to any subtle change in their behaviour when their paths must cross at work. Nick would never say anything, of course. Of that James was profoundly certain, but the smallest sign of a change in temperature between them would arouse suspicious talk as surely as winter flowers will bloom at the slightest hint of a milder day.

He could not allow any of that to happen. Could not let a night go by in this way. What had gone wrong must not be allowed to fester until morning but must be righted before they both slept. He drained his glass, got up and walked towards Nick's door. He knocked but without waiting for an answer went in.

It wasn't easy to see if Nick was surprised, or pleased to see him. His facial reaction was not the first thing to strike James. The bedside light was still on and Nick, who seemed to be indulging in a similar process of introspection to the one that James had just snapped out of, was sitting on the side of the bed. Presumably he had been just about to get into it, since he was naked from head to toe. Although he sat facing James his hands were resting between his thighs and so, fortuitously, they already hid from view what his natural reflexes might otherwise have been startled into covering up.

Of the two of them, James, it appeared, was now the more surprised. 'I…' he began, but his train of thought was derailed by the unexpected vision of male nakedness. He was more than taken aback by the quality of Nick unclothed. For, while his arms and chest were the slender, not unattractive, youthful picture that meeting him in his clothes had led him to expect, his legs – of which James had had no great expectations, seeing him always in shapeless jeans – would not have disgraced an athlete or a dancer. Lightly striated with black hairs, they were muscular and shapely. 'I just wanted to say…'

He sat down on the bed, draped an arm around his shoulder. He had no idea now what he wanted to say, could not imagine what words would burst forth next. The wine suddenly caught up with him, and threw over his head a cloak of dizziness.

Nick spoke. 'Look, we shouldn't be here together like this. I may have been stupid just now to let you… No, that's not fair, because I did too. What I mean is, that's not the way I am. I mean, you can enjoy something for a moment or two in a way that surprises you, if you like, but that doesn't mean it's the way you want to go.' His body was not totally at one with his sentiment though, and his hands, unless Nick had deployed them very carefully indeed, and thereby defeated his intention, could not have concealed from James the fact that he was substantially excited.

By now, so was James. He rolled round onto Nick, half flattening him back on the bed. But Nick was not prepared to be compliant again, would not submit to being kissed, still less to being touched anywhere else, and, with some force, pushed James off him to the side. 'Look, don't,' he said, in a small voice, 'Please don't. I've made one mistake tonight. I'm not going to make it again. And please don't let's fight.'

James got the message at once and backed off, stood up. 'I only came to say I was sorry. Now I'll have to do it again. So, sorry, and I'm sorry. You took me by surprise, that's all.' He went out and closed Nick's door behind him. 'Fuck it, fuck it, fuck it,' he said to himself. He didn't exactly feel shamefaced. Not yet at any rate. Just wretchedly stupid.

Breakfast was exactly the silent meal of dust and ashes that James and Nick had each, separately, imagined it would be. Neither of them said much at all until they were in James's car, going to work. Even then, the only exchange that touched on the previous night was a model of terse brevity.

James went first. 'I already said sorry about last night. I won't go on about it. Only … I'd like it if, some day, you managed to forgive me.'

'I will do – one day,' said Nick, quite affectionately but striking a chill in James's heart at the same time. 'But it may take a little while. Sorry. And I have to say sorry to you too, remember. You weren't the only one who…' He tailed away. James had heard that somewhere before, he remembered. Then it had been at the end of a passionate, eventful, eight-month affair. Now, in some weird process of ellipsis, this stage had been reached after just one kiss. Was that what growing up meant?

Nick went on, almost to himself: ‘Why do people who’ve already got someone – someone lovely, I mean – always want someone else as well?’

James swung into the roundabout that crossed the motorway. ‘I’ve no answer to that,’ he said.

TEN

Borja had an early flight that day: Gatwick, Tangier, Gatwick. He had spent the night at a hotel near the airport. There was to be one novelty about today's otherwise routine trip: he would be under the command, for the first time, of Captain Holmes, the Andy Holmes whom Amanda had first admitted to fancying and then, following the Gran Canaria experience, gone off in a big way. Up to now Borja had never exchanged more than a gruff hallo with him, and, though he guessed they were of similar age, had not yet had to choose between addressing him as Captain, or by his first name. Now, signing on for duty together in the operations room, meeting as team mates for the first time the moment had come.

'Good morning … Captain.' The man could take it how he wanted.

He took it straight. 'Good morning Borja. Call me Andy.' This in a brisk, lightly Scottish, accent. No hint of a smile, though, as he added, 'Must be my lucky day. I've drawn the gay Spaniard.' On the other hand, it wasn't said sarcastically or maliciously either.

Non-committally, Borja said, 'I hope I come up to scratch on the luck question at least,' and was quietly pleased with himself for thinking his reply up in time. All too often he only found the right quip much later.

Andy would fly the outward leg to Tangier; Borja would pilot their return in the afternoon. They got down to work, examining the flight and fuel plans that lay spread on the desk in front of them, checking the weather reports for the way-points along the route. There was some pre-dawn fog in the Strait of Gibraltar – which was exactly where they were going – but they both knew from experience that it would evaporate within an hour or two of sunrise. There was one annoying piece of news, though. The plane itself was not ready for them. The pilot who had flown it in to Gatwick late the previous night had reported something wrong with one of the engine gauges. The engineers had almost finished with it, but they would miss their intended take-off slot by a few minutes. The next one would not be available till forty minutes later. 'Bugger it,' said the captain, speaking for them both.

He was quite attractive, Borja had to admit. A little less than average height and lightly built, but trimly muscular, he had the same build as Borja in fact – and Borja was not unattracted by it in others. Facially he was quite different though, having blondish hair, a remarkably fair skin for someone of his age, and very blue eyes – ice-blue, Amanda had said. He didn't seem to be much of a conversationalist though, and they sipped the scalding cups of coffee that their enforced wait seemed somehow to oblige them to have in near silence.

It was still dark when they were driven out to the aircraft a little later, though a pale blur was just beginning to lighten the sky in the east. Once on board, with the log checked, the two pilots separated, the captain walking round the outside of the plane, checking with his eyes and hands that everything that was visible looked right and was firmly attached, while Borja stayed in the cockpit, checked emergency systems, started the auxiliary power unit and began his scan-check of all the flight instruments. The captain returned presently, spoke to the purser and agreed to board the passengers without further delay; they could be told about the forty-minute wait once they were on board. There was always a chance that an earlier slot would appear suddenly, but that was not something you could take advantage of if half the passengers were still roaming around the Duty Free.

Checks and calculations continued, with Borja in intermittent radio conversation with the tower for updates of wind speed – north-easterly, five knots – which explained the coldness of the morning, as also the clear sky, now visibly lightening by the minute. Now came the formality of the captain's briefing, when, in a kind of antiphonal recitation, the take-off procedure and emergency drills were spelled out by the captain and agreed by the co-pilot sitting on his right. Andy did this meticulously, poker-faced.

'Take-off runway is zero eight right, using flap five. Transition altitude six thousand feet. We're expecting clearance for a standard instrument departure via Midhurst, turning left after take-off to intercept Midhurst VOR radial zero six eight. After Midhurst VOR, route via Airway R eight. On take-off, you announce any malfunctions and I'll say stop or continue. If either of us calls stop I'll close the thrust levers and apply maximum braking. And you?'

'I'll note the rejection speed,' recited Borja, 'select reverse thrust, check the speed-brakes have deployed, and call the speeds on deceleration.'

And so it went on. It reminded Borja of serving at Mass when he was a child, in the old Latin days, when the whole great ceremony began with the quiet exchange between priest and server: 'Introibo ad altare Dei.' ' Ad Deum qui laetificat juventutem meam.' There wasn't a lot of humour apparent in those exchanges either.

The dispatch officer arrived in the cockpit with the load sheet for the captain to check, and simultaneously the tower called up to say there was a slot free unexpectedly. Could they be ready for engine start in two minutes? Borja turned and looked at the captain. Andy thought hard for a split second, then nodded.

'We'll go for it.' Dispatch took his cue and, with a curt nod, got out of the way. It would be a rush now to get the final check-lists finished in time. Borja knew that Andy's decision had put them both under extra pressure and he guessed from the tension visible in his face that Andy was privately stressed even more. Rumour had it that he had been hauled over the coals by senior management for holding up the traffic for half a morning at Gatwick a few weeks before – the Saturday morning Amanda had told Borja about – as well as for calling an engineer out to Gran Canaria to check a nose-wheel indicator light.

Nevertheless, a somewhat breathless five minutes later they were trundling down the two-mile taxiway to the western extremity of the airport, Borja selecting the wing-flap angle of five degrees and rapidly calling off the control-surface checks as he went through them. At last, and no more than twenty minutes late, they were turning towards the holding point at the runway's end, the taxi drill completed just in time. Borja dialled their allocated 'squawk'code on the transponder – this was the code that would identify them to ground radar as they proceeded on their morning's journey – and then, before the captain had even applied the toe-brakes for the anticipated hold, the tower was calling, 'Silverwing five one, you're cleared for take-off. Wind seven three at six.'

They continued to turn onto the runway, Andy's right hand inching the throttle levers forward. His co-pilot studied the gauges and called, 'Engines stabilised.' Suddenly, as the aircraft completed its turn to line up on the centre-line, a beam of light, more powerful than a searchlight, swept into the cockpit. The sun had risen behind their backs as they taxied and now it struck them with full force, blazing over distant trees. 'Wow,' said Borja, involuntarily screwing his eyes up for a second and rummaging in a pocket for his sunglasses. 'That's powerful.' Andy had his sunglasses on already. He seemed in no mood for exchanging pleasantries – too wound-up perhaps – and merely grunted a grudging agreement as he advanced the throttles to take-off power. Borja glanced again at the gauges. 'Power set.' At once they were pushed back in their seats by the rapid acceleration of the take-off run. As speed increased Andy stopped steering the aircraft by the nose-wheel tiller, and switched to the rudder pedals to hold the centre-line.

Borja called, 'Eighty knots.' Then, 'A hundred.' In a second or so he would call 'V-one,'the last moment at which it would be possible to do an emergency stop on the remaining runway. After that they were committed to take off whatever might happen, and when the pre-calculated take-off speed was reached, Borja would call, 'rotate', the captain would pull smoothly back on his control column, the elevator flaps would rise and up would go the nose wheel into the air where, after a few more seconds, the rest of the plane would follow it.

But today it didn't happen quite that way. Borja called V-one at a hundred and thirty-eight knots, then, 'Rotate,' at a hundred and forty-seven. But instead of seeing, out of the corner of his eye, the captain's right hand smoothly leave the throttle levers to join his left hand on the control column, there was a flurry of movement and a shout. 'What...? Ow...!' Andy's hand was beating at his head, thrashing his right ear. A tiny object spun through the air between them and landed, weightlessly, on Borja's lap. The control column remained unmoved, the nose wheel stayed on the ground, the speed indicators were climbing inexorably while the whole plane began to shake with the gathering power of the engines, and through the window ahead Borja was conscious of the onrush of the end of the runway, lights and gantries, trees and fences, the London to Brighton railway line clattering with commuter trains… He heard himself shout, 'I have control,' and yanked sharply back on his own control column. The plane practically leaped into the air, a racehorse taking a particularly formidable fence. Below them the railway line ceased to threaten them with death and destruction and became an irrelevance of straight lines on a flat surface while the Sussex landscape unfolded like a flower under the risen sun. Borja remained gripped by terror and incomprehension. Beside him Andy was scarlet-faced and gasping. 'We go around?' Borja asked.

'No.' Andy's voice was thin as a thread. 'I have control.' His hands were already back on the yoke. 'Select undercarriage up.'

'You OK?'

'Yes. Fucking insect.'

Borja glanced down. The thing that had fallen onto his lap was trying to crawl across his thigh; it was a large wasp, damaged beyond recovery and dragging its entrails after it. He brushed it onto the floor with disgust.

Gatwick tower called them up. 'Silverwing five one, do you have a problem?'

'No,' Borja said, almost shouted.

'Because your take off looked…'

'Yes. Gust of wind. No problem.'

Andy glanced at him, nodded faintly. There was a degree of relief on his face but he was still too shocked for it to register much else. He turned the yoke to bank the plane, initiating the two hundred degree turn onto the Midhurst radial. The sunrise swept away out of sight like a lighthouse beam, returning one minute later to light up the cockpit from the other side. The runway they had taken off from in such a heart-stopping fashion now appeared below them to the left. Borja called, 'One thousand feet;' Andy said, 'Flap up;' Borja carried out the command; Andy straightened the plane out as they intercepted the Midhurst radial, and Borja reported their position to Air Traffic Control. The English Channel appeared, a trough of liquid gold beyond the Downs. Except for the racing of the two pilots'pulses which still seemed to fill the cockpit with vibration, things were beginning to return to normal.

Andy spoke. 'I'm sorry.' The words were coughed up like fish bones. 'I'm really…'

'Look, don't…'

'No, I have to say it. I've never reacted so unprofessionally to any … ever. Never thought I even could. I nearly killed us. Killed you. All those poor sods behind us…'

'Look, don't think about it. It was just incredibly unlucky timing. It would have been the same if it happened to me…' He interrupted himself. 'Passing Midhurst, four thousand feet.'

Andy nudged the plane gently right, following the flight director bar, to track to Southampton. 'Thank God for your reaction speed, that's all I can say. Oh, except thank you.'

'A wasp. Where did it come from?'

'My shirt pocket? I haven't worn this one for months. It might have…'

'That's right.' Now Borja saw it clearly. 'Queen wasps get sleepy in autumn. They crawl into holes to hibernate. When the temperature warms up in spring, or there's bright sunlight…'

'It could happen so easily. Incredibly dangerous. To a driver, a train driver passing red signals… It buzzed in my ear, stung me, gave me a scare. I didn't have time to think…' He stopped, shook his head, painfully conscious at that moment of the awesome fragility of human existence. 'Um… I suppose we ought to log it as an incident?'

'I don't see that we need to,' said Borja complicitly. 'It involved nobody except the two of us. You heard me tell Tower it was a gust. I'd have to explain that.'

'So, not just a good pilot but a friend.' With the waterways of Portsmouth and Southampton glistening beneath them they turned leftward out to sea across the Solent and the Isle of Wight. The sky remained a cloudless blue as, one by one, the Channel Islands came in sight, passed slumbrously beneath them and then, just twenty-five minutes after take-off, they crossed the Brittany coast and simultaneously reached the top of their climb. That always signalled the beginning of the most relaxed phase of the flight. Andy spoke to the passengers, about the route, their height and speed, about the weather – which was still behaving impeccably all along their way. But he made no mention of their startlingly violent take-off: he had a healthy respect for sleeping dogs.

The purser came onto the flight deck with coffee. He was a young man whom Borja had worked with once or twice before, named Martin; he was still in his twenties. Clearly he knew Andy too, because he wasn't too much in awe of him to say, 'That was one hell of a take-off back there. Passengers had their eyes popping out.'

'The wind,' said Andy casually, but it didn't sound good enough. 'Windshear,' he added a little recklessly.

'Windshear?' Martin's tone indicated that, given the weather conditions that morning, he could only believe this with a bit of an effort, but he wasn't on quite such familiar terms with his captain as actually to say so. He stayed and chatted amiably for a minute or so, then left them to drink their coffee as they monitored the indicators – just to make sure that the autopilot was doing as it had been told.

'Isn't it time they made you a captain?' Andy asked. 'You must be the same age as I am.' He half smiled. 'And you're not too bad a pilot.'

'Actually I haven't quite got there in terms of hours and landings. I was a bit of a late starter. Funny thing, though. I just need exactly one more landing under my belt to qualify.'

'The one you're going to do on the way back this afternoon? That's great. We'll have to celebrate afterwards. Well, touch wood, anyway. I'd better take special care to get us safely to Tangier first.' The frostiness that had existed between them at the beginning of the morning was quite gone, thawed by the heat of their shared experience of fright and danger. Andy asked, 'What made you become a pilot?'

'I suppose I fell in love with flying. Because…' Borja saw no point holding this back. 'Because I fell in love with someone who flew. Not a pilot. A steward.'

Andy smiled. 'How romantic. What happened to the steward?'

'I don't know if you'd call this romantic or not. He died.'

'Aids?' Andy queried gently.

'No. This was a year or two before all that started. He was killed in an air crash. At Valencia.'

'That one,' said Andy nodding. 'When the plane broke in two? Microburst, wasn't it? Not that they called it that back then. Well I'm very sorry. Sorry for you, I mean.'

'He was very brave. A survivor told me. He should have been seated but he moved to sit with someone who was panicking. Moved to the wrong spot as it happened and it cost him his life. But things work in strange ways. We had this affair – which was brief – because I'd split up with my partner. And that was because he'd gone off with somebody else. Strangely, Rafael's being killed enabled me and James to get back together again. We still are together. Eleven years on.' Borja looked at Andy. 'Are you married?'

'I was. For – don't laugh – seven years.'

'And then?' Andy had received very frank answers to his questions. Borja didn't expect him to be less open in return.

'We broke up because of me. I'm not just being a gentleman saying that. It was entirely me. I wasn't good at devoting myself to just one person. I don't suppose I would be now. I'd always played the field and I couldn't just switch that side of me off once I got hitched. Much as I loved her. My wife. Lizzie. The other thing was – and maybe I have something in common with you here – I'd just qualified as a pilot.'

Borja nodded. 'It's clear. Flying equals freedom. That's what Rafael used to say. All that opportunity. Women … away from home.' He smiled. 'It's a fairly common story.'

'Yes, all of that. But it wasn't only women.' Andy looked sideways at Borja for a second and Borja briefly met his look, his eyebrows slightly raised in surprise. 'I don't know which was the chicken and which was the egg. Whether I found I was not exclusively interested in women because of the 'opportunities'– your word – young men, away from home – or whether I took up flying because at some subconscious level I already knew there was another new thing I wanted to try. But either way, you're not the only one on this flight deck who's responded to the charms of male flight attendants.'

There was light cloud over the Bay of Biscay but the coast of Spain came up over the horizon as clear as Borja could remember ever having seen it. There was no need to switch on the weather radar to verify their landfall point. The city and docks of Bilbao unfolded beneath them as unambiguously as a map. They got a weather update from Spanish Air Traffic Control. Clear all the way, they were told. Only, the morning fog had not yet cleared from Gibraltar Strait. The two pilots looked at each other. 'That should have gone by now,' said Borja. Fog in the strait could sometimes close Tangier.

'Let's not spoil their holidays quite so soon,' Andy said. There was another whole hour before a decision would have to be made. 'There's still time for it to clear before we get there.'

There was no fog where they were just then, crossing the Cantabrian Mountains and then the tawny plains, cut with lakes and rivers, of northern Castile. 'Don't you miss it?' Andy asked. 'I mean Spain.'

'I told you that I fell in love with flying when I met Rafael. Well, I fell in love with England when I met James – in much the same way. I had already studied the literature at university…' Andy looked surprised. Borja went on. 'I did tell you I was a late starter as a pilot. That's partly why. I had to brush up my maths and physics later in my twenties. Well, loving the language and loving an English boy and never having been there, of course I wanted to go there and see it. I wasn't disappointed, which may surprise you, because it's true that it's often cold and rainy and all the people in the back today are flying to the southern sun to get away from it. My life in England has been happier than it ever was in Spain – up to now at any rate – so, if I do miss Spain from time to time, it isn't very often. And I fly there pretty regularly in this job. Here we are, for example, just abeam Madrid right now.' The city was coming into view away to their left, under a bit of a haze. A jet leaped into sight, a gleaming speck, rising from an unseen runway beyond the city's edge.

'We're hardly in close contact with the country, viewing it from thirty thousand feet,' objected Andy. 'You can't smell the cigarette smoke for one thing.'

'You can't ring the bell and walk in the procession,' said Borja. 'You don't see the whole of the country like this from a café table in the Plaza Mayor. From up here we've got mountains and the lot.'

'Only on a clear day like today. Half the time you only know you're here because the instruments say so.'

They drifted uneventfully on, across the Sierra Morena, and then Borja said, 'I have to show you this.' It was Seville, laid out like the orb of a spider's web below them, its shining waterway, the Guadalquivir, gliding through its southern corner. 'Can you see the plaza de toros by the river? That's where I used to live.'

'What? In the bull ring?'

'No, you pillock, in a flat nearby, but I can hardly point that out from up here.'

'Hey, that's great.' Andy picked up the hand mike and spoke to the passengers. 'Passengers on the right hand side of the plane will have a grand view of Seville where, you might like to know, our co-pilot was born in the bull ring.'

'Oh my God,' said Borja, torn between mortification at what Andy had said and a sort of quiet delight at the idea that he cared enough to say it. It was only a moment later that he remembered that he had called his senior officer a pillock while on duty.

A few minutes later their course took them out to sea again, crossing the coast near Cádiz, impregnable on its ten-mile-long peninsula, and then it was time to get back to work. Presently they would turn east and begin their descent into Tangier. Borja took his leave of Spanish ATC and changed frequencies to speak to Maghreb.

Who told them quite categorically that Tangier was closed.

'Tell them we'd like to do one or two circuits at the holding point if we can,' said Andy. 'That'll still give it thirty minutes to clear between now and landing.'

Borja put in the request but ATC was un-persuaded. Permission to hold was refused. They must head south to their designated alternate, their diversion airfield, Rabat. ATC cleared them to a lower flight level, which Borja dialled in the altitude capture window, then gave them their new heading to fly down the coast. This too was fed into the autopilot. 'Visibility excellent all the way after Tangier,' they were told. 'Left turn at the holding point and you can request a visual landing.' Andy passed the bad news on to the passengers adding brightly that Rabat was just twenty minutes down the coast, though without drawing their attention to the fact that twenty minutes in a Boeing 737 covered a lot of ground. Should he be unable to fly the passengers back to Tangier – if, for example, their flying hours ran out before the fog lifted – the passengers would have a long and gruelling trip to make by coach.

By this time the two pilots could see the fog ahead of them. It was very local indeed, confined to the strait and extending just a mile or two inland on both sides. It looked like a wodge of tissue paper that someone had packed between the rough corners of Africa and Europe to stop them knocking together. Near one edge of it the Rock of Gibraltar rode clear like the humped back of a whale. Further south the long crescent of the African coast could clearly be seen, just as Air Traffic Control had promised, and mountains floated, blue and misty, in the furthest distance.

Borja had landed at Rabat once before on a diversion from Casablanca. Andy had never been there. 'It's very easy,' Borja told him. 'The city's right on the coast, easy to spot, with a big harbour, and the airfield's just behind it, a few miles inland. But they didn't give us much guidance the time I landed there. We more or less did our own thing.' He pulled the arrival charts for Rabat from the clipboard at his side and placed them at the front; those for Tangier now went to the back of the bundle – which was referred to as the library. They would not be wanted just at present.

They followed the coast southward, their straight-line track gradually converging with it. Except for one patch of wispy cloud in the middle distance it was clear all the way. They passed the mouths of great rivers which, while appearing strangely motionless, ceaselessly poured semicircular fans of red silt into the green Atlantic. The two colours had a distinct dividing line between them as if they had been meticulously painted on the water.

'Top of descent?' Andy queried.

Borja peered at the DME. 'Ninety-five miles to run.'

'I'd have thought we were nearer than that. Never mind.'

Borja glanced at the Rabat let-down chart. It all looked quite straightforward. Less than three minutes later the autopilot closed the throttles and lowered the elevator planes. The two control columns automatically moved forward. Andy made some adjustments to the aircraft's trim. Descent had begun.

They were passing abeam the small cloud bank that obscured a few miles of coastline, but ahead all was still clear. Borja spoke to Maghreb ATC, announcing that descent had started, then changed frequencies to talk to approach control at Rabat tower. Despite several attempts, though, Rabat tower proved elusive. Andy wasn't worried about that. 'We'll get them soon enough. Anyway, it's all going to be visual once we pass the holding point.'

He was right. Five minutes later, with twenty minutes still to go – that meant they had about seventy miles to cover – and now down to fifteen thousand feet, Borja got through. 'Good morning Rabat. This is Silverwing five one. Fifty miles north of the holding point. Flight level one five zero. Request a visual approach and landing.'

Permission was granted. Which was just as well, because Rabat tower disappeared from the airwaves again almost immediately afterwards. Andy was still less concerned about that, though, than he was about the time they were taking to get there. 'I thought they told us twenty minutes from Tangier to the holding point. We've been going twenty-five already.'

Borja checked the DME and speed indicator. 'We'll be at the hold in three minutes. Is that OK for you? Or would you like me to re-check everything?' They descended through ten thousand feet. Borja switched on the landing-lights.

'Re-check the STAR chart. Look at those distances. No, hang on, it's OK. We're there. I can see it.' The city on the coast had come into focus some way ahead. From his left-hand seat Andy had the better view and presently he spotted the airfield lying some way inland, behind the town just as Borja had described it. The coast came to meet them and they crossed it at a gentle angle just before the instruments told them they had reached the holding point. Andy disengaged the autopilot and initiated their turn left towards the airport. Below them the land was a patchwork of dark gloss-green orchards and bare red earth as bright as broken brick. Borja tried again to get Rabat tower. This time he was successful, but their responses very faint. 'You're not on our radar,' they told him. 'Push ident.' Borja pressed the identify button on the transponder. 'You're still not there. You sure you have the right squawk code?'

'What the hell's going on?' Andy wanted to know. They were rapidly approaching an airfield that had cleared them to land but now wanted to argue about who they were. He took the hand mike and spoke to Rabat tower himself. 'Forget your radar. Look out of the window and you'll see us. We're west-north-west twelve miles. We have visibility fifty miles. We're cleared for a visual approach. Request you confirm clearance to land, please.' All this was taking time and they were heading directly towards the airport without any particular approach in mind. 'Is the area clear of traffic?'

Rabat tower reluctantly agreed that there was no traffic in the area. They had a twelve-minute window in which to land. There was virtually no wind. They could land from either end of the runway. Andy said they would land from the north and promptly turned the aircraft sharp right in order to fly onto their final approach in an S-shaped course that would be long enough for them to lose height in a comfortable, rather than precipitate fashion. Abeam the runway threshold, though still some miles to the west, Andy told Borja to start the stopwatch, in order to help him hand-fly the approach more accurately. Predictably enough, the tower was no longer accessible by radio; at least they had been in contact long enough to confirm their precious clearance to land. 'Like being a real pilot again,' Andy said, when Borja had called, 'Sixty seconds gone,' the signal for Andy to turn the plane back to the north. Borja had the feeling that Andy was quite enjoying himself.

It was during that hundred and eighty degree turn that Borja got his first full view of the city of Rabat on the ground beneath them. He thought the place had grown considerably since his only previous visit some five or six years ago. There was much more high-rise building than he remembered, and the harbour looked somehow different. Maybe he had simply remembered wrong. He called the altitude, another sixty seconds gone, and Andy straightened the aircraft out, so that they were now flying northward, away from the airfield. In two minutes he would turn right one last time and fly straight down the final approach onto the runway. He called for Borja to deploy the speed-brakes.

A minute later: 'Gear down, flap twenty. Landing check.' This was Borja. Another litany was gone through as the two pilots agreed their final check-list before landing. Borja read off the stopwatch count again and Andy initiated the final turn. 'Cabin crew, seats for landing,' he announced. 'And now,' he said, privately to Borja, 'we'll see if I've got it right.' He meant that, if he had flown all his turns accurately, when they straightened up out of this last one, they should find themselves lined up perfectly with the runway centre-line and at exactly the right height, given the three-mile distance that their calculations with the stopwatch and speed indicators told them they had left to run.

The moment of truth arrived. Andy straightened out. The runway lay dead ahead of them, the glide-slope indicator bars alongside it appearing in just the right configuration to confirm their height as ideal. Andy adjusted their speed. 'Not bad,' said Borja. Stronger words of praise were frowned on.

Once more they were facing directly into the sun, by now an African, mid-morning one. It filled the whole of the southern sky with glare, a vast circle of platinum radiance that extended almost to the ground. Only a narrow band of heat haze came between it and the horizon. It was uncomfortable to look at. Not that you wanted to, or really should. Andy's eyes were glued to the runway ahead and Borja's were mainly fixed on the instruments, the altimeters and speed indicators in particular. So why, once he had called 'one thousand feet'did his eyes stray upwards, beyond the runway, to where that blinding platinum disc and the low heat haze met? And why, having done so, did he keep his eyes focused there a full two seconds? He never knew. But his gaze lingered there just long enough for his eyes to pick out a pinprick of light – something glinting in a sky against which you could scarcely have seen a munitions factory on fire – and then to interrogate the pinpoint further, until what he saw chilled the blood in his veins, and made the skin around his temples tighten to his forehead like a clammy hand.

Years before, when he was in his teens and early twenties, when travelling as a passenger in a car, he'd been able to see – or thought he had been able to see – cars approaching round blind bends, just a second before they appeared in his physical field of vision. 'Car coming,' he would shout, and many a driver, James not least, had blessed him for this strange gift, if gift it was, on the treacherous mountain roads of Spain.

He said it now, to Andy, though this time using the jargon of his trade: 'Traffic, twelve o'clock.'

Andy looked up, exhaled fast, audibly. They both now saw, lined up in the sky ahead of them and approaching their own runway from the other end, the silhouette of another plane, a jumbo-jet, with landing lights ablaze and undercarriage down.

'Eight miles,' said Andy. 'He's got five and I've got two.' The runway itself accounted for the other one. The planes would be closing the gap between them by one mile roughly every twelve seconds. 'I'm going on in. Agree?'

'Agree.'

'He must have seen us first. He's on a longer approach. Sun's behind him.'

Borja was already trying to make contact with the other aircraft on the VHF. A scramble of squeals was all he could make out. 'Five hundred feet. No contact with traffic or tower.'

'We keep our nerve. We land.' Andy's voice was silvered with a sheen of fear. He was talking to reassure himself as much as Borja. 'Climb, you bastard, climb,' he said – a whispered prayer that Borja simultaneously uttered in Spanish: 'Sube, coño.'

Still the radios only squealed, and still the oncoming jumbo bore down on them, huge now in their terrified visions, darkening the platinum sky. 'We tell the passengers – Brace?' Borja could only croak the words. 'Two hundred.'

'No point. It's either.... Fuck you, climb! ...He's going...'

'He's going up,' Borja almost yelled. 'He's going up.' They hardly dared to believe it. Only when they saw the wheels start to retract into the jumbo's wings did they know for certain that Armageddon wasn't going to be just then – that they'd see at least a little more of life before it came. 'One hundred.'

Andy made an impeccable landing, a third of the way along the runway, the way it told you in the textbooks. If it hadn't been for the thunderous roar of the 747 passing over their heads at three hundred feet, throttles open at full go-around power, the passengers behind them would never have noticed that anything was amiss.

Until, that is, they turned off the runway towards the terminal building and the full truth of their situation at last struck the two pilots squarely in the face. For there at the terminal was no rooftop announcement of the airport's name: Rabat. On the contrary, as they trailed along the taxiway towards the apron, they saw themselves and their passengers welcomed, in letters three metres high, to ... Casablanca. They had come to the wrong place.

ELEVEN

James usually had the office to himself immediately after lunch. Guy would return to the rehearsal room leaving a small pile of illegible memos about things that urgently needed doing. Linda, his admin assistant, usually took this time out to do whatever errands had to be run in the town, and the front of house manager, Jack, who worked mornings and evenings, had afternoons free as a matter of course. James was glad of this today. He was still struggling to pull himself together. He was finding it hard to make sense of what had happened. He hadn't intended to have sex with Nick. Well, he hadn't had sex with Nick, though in the end that had been because Nick hadn't wanted it. If he were to tell Nick now that his intentions in taking him out to dinner the previous night had been totally innocent Nick would never believe him. People did have some choice in the matter of what they did and didn't do. In principle there was such a thing as freewill; James didn't doubt it. But in practice, sometimes, it didn't seem to work. The mechanics of one's cock seemed to have a built-in override of everything else, and that was not restricted to one's teenage years either. They never told you that in R.E. or Philosophy.

James's ruminations were brutally cut short when he climbed the stairs to his office. It was not empty. Guy and Linda were standing in the centre of the room, talking, trying to arrange something. '…Ah, good,' said Guy, turning at James's entrance. 'Here you are. Linda can't come to London tomorrow.'

'Sorry, James,' said Linda. 'It's Debbie. She's been sent home from school with the 'flu. I can come in to work, OK, but I'll need to get home at lunchtime, so…'

Guy was going to London with James the next day in order to audition some young actors and actresses for the final production of the spring season, and also to interview candidates for the stage manager's job: Sally, the present incumbent, would be leaving in a few weeks'time. It was quite a routine thing and usually Linda would travel down with them and manage the reception desk in the lobby of the small hall they hired for these occasions, checking candidates and auditionees off on lists, letting them go through in the correct order and so on.

'We'll have to get one of the ASMs to come instead,' said Guy. 'Why not have Nick?'

James's heart sank. He tried to think of some reason not to have Nick. 'Um, doesn't he have a heavy load of propping to do for Kiss Me Kate?'

'They've all got propping to do,' said Guy brusquely. He looked at his watch. He was late for rehearsal and he hated that. 'I suggested Nick because he's so sensible. He wouldn't have to be told what to do; he can be left to get on with it without leaving us with cock-ups to sort out. Look, I leave it to you. Do what you think best, but get someone. OK? I really must go.' He looked at his watch again and strode out of the room.

'I'm really sorry,' said Linda again. James waved her apology aside, while she put on her coat, collected bundles of cash and a paying-in book from the safe, and exited the office en route for the bank.

James sat down at the long table in the centre of the room and let out a long breath that sounded like a sigh. There were three ASMs to choose from. He would simply ask one of the others.

There was a knock at the door. James said, 'Come in', and Nick entered, glancing around the room cautiously as if suspecting that other members of the management might be hiding behind the furniture. Though James guessed that Nick had made pretty sure James was alone in the office before coming to see him.

'Oh, hi,' Nick greeted him a little nervously. 'I wondered if I could have a word.' He had regressed to junior employee mode since the morning.

'I guessed you might,' said James without enthusiasm.

Something in James's demeanour or look alerted Nick. 'James, are you OK?'

Nick had never addressed him with his name at the beginning of the sentence before. Involuntarily James shook his head slightly and winced. He hastily rearranged his features into a hangdog smile and said, 'So-so.'

Nick sat down at the table opposite him without being asked. 'Am I part of the problem?' he asked directly, trying to look hard into James's eyes but finding, unexpectedly, that he could not.

'No,' said James quietly. 'Not really.'

'You see,' said Nick. 'What I came to say was, maybe it would be better for everybody if I moved out – out of Sevenscore, I mean.'

It was what James had expected to hear. That didn't prevent his heart from sinking yet further. 'Where would you go?' he asked flatly.

'I don't know exactly, yet. I'd have to ask around. Maybe when Sally moves out…'

He sounds so sad, James thought. He doesn't really want to go, but he thinks he ought to and it's all my stupid fucking fault. He wanted to walk round the table and put his arms around him, comfort him, the poor kid. But there was a spark of hope in what he'd just heard in Nick's voice. He doesn't want to leave.

Nick looked at James strangely, peered at something in his eyes that he hadn't seen there before. Then he got up and walked round the table to where James sat, put his arms round his shoulders from behind, his chin on James's shoulder, and pressed his cheek against the side of his head. How hot his skin feels, each of them separately thought, and Nick pretended to take no notice of the faint trail of wet that escaped the corner of James's eyelid.

'I don't want you to have to go,' James said, his voice much fainter than a whisper. He found Nick's hand with one of his own and grasped it tightly.

The phone rang on James's desk at the other end of the room. James stood up awkwardly, half pushing Nick down into the chair he had just vacated. 'Don't go. Wait here. But I must get this. I'm sorry.' He adjusted his face with a swipe of his hand and took the few steps towards the desk, eye-balling the King Kong postcard that was pinned to the window frame behind it. Don't panic. Count to ten. Then panic. He picked up the phone.

Nick heard him say hallo and then watched him listen in what appeared to be an astonished silence while the person on the other end seemed to be having quite a lot to say. Then James said, 'I thought you were going to Tangier,' and Nick realised it had to be Borja on the phone. He got up to go, but James motioned to him to stay. There was more lengthy explanation from the unseen Borja, punctuated only by whistles of surprise and grunts of sympathy from James. Finally he said, 'Right, ring me later, then,' added more quietly, 'I love you too,' and put the phone down.

'Bad news?' Nick queried diffidently.

'You could say that. Don't worry, no-one's hurt.' James had seen that look on Nick's face. 'Only Borja won't be coming home tonight. He's been suspended from all duties. It seems they landed at the wrong airport in Morocco and caused another landing plane to have an abortion or whatever it's called.'

Nick surprised himself by a giggle which, though it was quickly stifled, pleased James. 'So where is he?'

'Casablanca.'

'Casablanca,' Nick echoed. Then, 'Look, whether I move out of the Court House or whether I stay, I wasn't going to move right away today in any case ... unless now you'd prefer...'

'No, Nick. I said I wanted you to stay. Well, even more now, perhaps. Especially tonight. I'd be grateful for your company this evening.'

'I'd like that too,' Nick said and for a worrying moment James thought he was going to follow his own example and crumple into tears, but he did not. 'Only we're not going to...'

'No,' said James seriously. 'We're not. Oh, one more thing before I forget. D'you fancy a trip to London tomorrow?' James explained about the auditions and interviews and about Linda's Debbie having 'flu.

Nick was only too happy to have a day out as a change from prop shopping. Before he left the room he gave James his hand to shake, rather formally. James took it and said, 'Oh, by the way, could you nip into the off licence and get us a bottle of wine for tonight? I won't have time.'

He took a note from his wallet and handed it to Nick, who turned and headed towards the door. 'Casablanca,' he said to himself one more time, then looked back at James as he reached the door, chuckled and said, 'Play it again, Sam.' The door closed behind him.

If you needed to lick your wounds after an ego-bruising and potentially fatal experience, then the palm-bedecked poolside, open to the blue African sky, of a hotel on the outskirts of Casablanca was not the worst of all possible places to do it. Borja was regretting that he had nothing less casual to wear than his pilot's uniform. He had had no reason to suppose that he would not be returning to Gatwick that day – where his overnight bag was stowed safely in his locker in the pilots'room. He remembered teasing Amanda about her improvidence in arriving on Gran Canaria without a change of clothes or tampons. He should have taken the lesson to heart instead, he now thought.

Then he told himself that any too obvious signs of frivolity, such as lounging around in shorts or swimming trunks, might raise eyebrows in the present circumstances. Not that there were any of that morning's passengers on hand to see him. They had been given lunch at the airport and left to wait there until someone in Tangier, over two hundred miles away, could arrange for a fleet of coaches to come and pick them up. Only the cabin crew were there to share the poolside with him. They seemed a friendly and supportive bunch and were not too miffed at the prospect of an unscheduled night stop in Casablanca. Still, you had to be a bit careful. The cabin crew might be interviewed themselves at some stage in connection with the morning's events and you didn't want to give them the chance to say anything, even by accident, that might show you in an unprofessional light. As for Andy, after an initial frantic session peering at charts in the cockpit with Borja, he had been spending most of the afternoon on the phone to company headquarters. Borja's heart went out to him. They had got into this mess together, but it was Andy who had been flying the sector – and he was the captain. If there was a can to be carried, he would have to carry it the furthest.

Just as he was thinking this, out came Andy to join him. It was funny to think that, until earlier this morning, Borja had always thought of him – unlike the more easy-going captains with whom he had always been on first-name terms – as Captain Holmes. Now, as he stepped, cap-less and blond headed, into the sunshine, he was impossible to think of as anything other than Andy, as if he were a friend he had known for years. He looked much younger than he had ever seemed before, fresh faced and with a small, snub nose that gave him an almost teenage look. He seemed very vulnerable right now, a boy in trouble, and Borja felt suddenly very protective towards him. Nobody would be allowed to hurt Andy if Borja could help it.

'Hóla, amigo,' Andy greeted him. Then, with surprise, 'You haven't got a beer. I'll get one for us both.' He sauntered off to the poolside bar – without thinking about it Borja let his eyes follow him all the way – and returned a few moments later with two golden glasses. He grinned at Borja as he sat down. 'You didn't bring your shorts either.' He glanced at the blue water beside them. 'I suppose it would be frowned upon if we went skinny-dipping.'

Borja had not heard the expression skinny-dipping before: it wasn't one of James's. But it was very clear to him, sitting as he was, fully clothed beside a swimming pool, what it meant. 'Have they been giving you a hard time?' he asked.

Andy made a ho-hum sort of face and said, 'Could be worse I suppose. They can't quite believe that so many cock-ups could happen all together like that.'

'No, I don't suppose they can. I don't suppose I could have done this time yesterday. Look, Andy,' he said this very earnestly, leaning forward in his chair, 'I'm not going to let you take all the blame for this. We know now that ATC gave us the co-ordinates for Casablanca, not Rabat. But I compounded that by misreading the chart when I checked it. Heading two one zero instead of two zero one. Same digits, different order. They made the mistake, easy enough to do, but I followed them. What was wrong with the radio frequencies, God only knows, and neither of us is responsible for that, but there's another thing. It didn't look like Rabat as we came in: neither the city nor the airfield. I thought that at the time and I didn't tell you. I should have done.'

'You'd only been to Rabat once before,' said Andy. 'You told me that. You're not expected to have a memory like CCTV. But I should have recognised Casablanca. That was the stupidest part.'

'So should I. I've been here several times.'

'Yes, but on a standard routeing, I should imagine, not arriving the way we did from an interrupted approach to Tangier.'

'Well,' said Borja, 'then the same goes for you. Besides, you had the actual landing to fly, without having to think about the scenery. And the fact remains that I checked the chart too quickly and missed the significance of that radial number.'

'You hardly needed to check the chart at all,' objected Andy. 'Visibility was perfect. You could see for miles. It was like walking along a beach in summer. Follow the shoreline. You didn't need a radial to fly, you couldn't possibly get lost.'

'The fact remains,' said Borja, 'that we did get lost.'

'Well, yeah. One cloud in the wrong place at the wrong time and we missed the whole bloody town. That was just bad luck. It's not been the luckiest of days all round.' Andy took a gulp of beer. 'There's two things I'm glad of, though.'

'Which are?'

'The Air France captain was on a very tight turnaround. He didn't have time to come looking for me. But no doubt,' he assumed a cod-French accent, ''e weel file eez reeport as soon as he gets back home. The other thing … is you.'

Borja gave a snort of surprise. 'This morning you said it must be your lucky day because you'd drawn me in the co-pilot lottery. I don't seem to have been much of a winning ticket.' But Andy's words had touched him all the same.

Andy fingered the misty outside of his beer glass. 'I wouldn't have wanted to be in this mess with any of the others. I couldn't have stood it. With you I'm OK.' He looked down for a moment, his face slightly flushed. Then he looked up again and smiled brightly. 'By the way, I told the cabin crew I'd be buying a drink for everybody in the main bar at about six o'clock. You're included in the invitation, obviously.'

Andy stood his round in the bar at six o'clock. Borja bought a second one, and then somebody suggested going into town for dinner. Martin the purser knew a good French restaurant in the rue de Chaouia, and so the seven of them set off a little later in two taxis, Borja in one and Andy in the other. In the restaurant they found themselves sitting opposite each other and, although they both made a careful point of joining in the general conversation with the cabin crew, they discovered a growing hunger, born out of their conversations earlier in the day, on the flight deck and beside the pool, to know more and more about each other. Where exactly did they both live? Where had they trained and when? Family background? Father's job?

Andy lived alone. He had a mansion flat in London, near Maida Vale: Borja would have to come and see it some time. He was very middle class, he apologised. His father, now retired, had been a doctor. He hailed from Cramond, on the coast near Edinburgh. Borja hadn't been to Edinburgh, but he had heard of Cramond Island – having read The Prime of Miss Jean Brodie: information which somewhat surprised Andy. Borja had to remind him that he'd been a student of English literature and language at Salamanca. Andy had done geography at Durham. That announcement brought the memory of their map-reading, landscape-reading, fiasco of that morning flashing simultaneously into both their minds; they caught each other's eye and laughed, and both knew that they had no need to explain why.

They were sitting at the end of the table, which was rather small for seven. Four sat on Andy's side and Andy's left leg did not fit under the tablecloth but was stretched out at the side. The trouser-leg of his dark uniform had ridden a little way up and exposed a band of bare flesh above his black sock. In its dark frame the exposed skin shone a warm magnolia. It was spangled with light-reflecting blond hairs. Borja caught himself looking at this several times during the meal. He had never thought of this part of the male anatomy as a particular turn-on before, but it was the only piece of Andy-below-the-waist that he had ever seen and he found it strangely compelling, almost teasing his senses, just as – he had tried not to admit this to himself earlier – the sight of Andy walking away from him to get a beer at the poolside bar had done during in the afternoon.

When the meal was done the five cabin crew were in favour of going on to a night club. Would the two pilots be joining them? Borja's and Andy's eyes met and they held each other's gaze for a few seconds, with eyes that were giving nothing away, before they both independently said no. No, they wouldn't. It was a reasonable answer. They were a few years older than the other five; they wouldn't want to cramp their style; they could be assumed to have done night clubs so often in their younger days that the prospect of another night on the town in Casablanca no longer held the attraction it might have done once; and besides, it might have come over as a bit unseemly on a night when their professionalism as pilots was in question and about to be held up for scrutiny. All these things played some part in their decision not to join the general move to go clubbing, it was true, but the cabin crew were unaware of the other reason: that the two pilots were so enjoying the business of getting to know each other that they did not want their continuing researches to be hampered by the presence of other company. Andy was not ready to admit this to Borja, though, and Borja would not have admitted it at that time even to himself.

Andy knew a bar just round the corner in the Boulevard Mohammed V, he told Borja as they all stood up to go. It was just a bar, he added. He gave Borja a searching look to which Borja responded with a curt nod. They all spilled out onto the pavement together, the cabin crew milling around under a street-lamp and talking taxis, while Andy and Borja touched them all lightly on the shoulders, wished them bonne continuation and then faded into the shadows beyond the street-lamp's throw.

In a minute they entered the bar of Le Petit Poucet, where the walls were hung with sketches of the writer and pioneer aviator, Antoine de St. Exupéry. The significance of this was not lost on either of them. St. Exupéry too had got lost flying over the North African desert. They reminded each other how he and his co-pilot had tried to drink the dew collected overnight on an outspread parachute and had turned the unexpected discovery of an orange in a coat pocket into a celebratory feast. 'No restaurant meals or drinks in a cosy bar for him,' Borja pointed out rather too obviously.

'No nearly fatal encounter with a jumbo-jet either,' Andy retorted.

They drank two large whiskies while they took in their surroundings and paid homage to their famous predecessor, after which Andy said, 'Well, what next?' It seemed natural to them both that he should continue to take the lead in planning the evening. They were both, of necessity, still in their pilot's short-sleeved shirts and Andy conspicuously had the four stripes on his epaulettes, Borja just the three.

'I don't know,' Borja said. 'What do you suggest?'

'Well,' said Andy, thinking carefully and articulating the results with corresponding deliberation, 'there is the Centre 2000 down by the port. It has bars and stuff.' He looked at Borja who said, 'Hmm,' non-committally. 'On the other hand,' Andy went on in an even tone, 'we could simply take a taxi back to the hotel and down a couple of nightcaps on the terrace.'

'I think I'd like that,' said Borja.

The terrace in question was an open-air but sheltered extension to the main bar area, furnished with pale blue flowering plumbago plants in orange pots. Beyond its low end wall, palm trees stood like shadowy sentinels in the windless night. The lights of Casablanca twinkled distantly between their fronds. The air was warm and spring-scented and the stars shone. Only a couple of the other, distant, tables were occupied: by men in business suits with books or magazines and mobile phones. Occasionally waiters swam like grebes across the still surface of the scene. Borja and Andy were drinking malt whisky with – Andy admitted that this was mildly heretical – cubes of ice.

'You don't socialise a lot with other pilots, I think,' said Andy.

Borja smiled. 'Always the outsider, I suppose. I'm hardly typical. Gay. Spanish – but never been a bullfighter.'

'Well I mean,' said Andy, 'just how weird can you get?'

'I have a very happy home life, I have to admit. With James. And his theatre's a bit like an extension of the family home – for both of us. We've even adopted an orphan.'

Andy's blue eyes widened. 'Are you serious?'

Borja laughed. 'No, not really. And he's only a theatre orphan, not a real one. We've taken in an ASM – that's assistant stage manager to you. He was a bit lost I think. Anyway, he's come to live with us.'

'How old?' Andy wanted to know.

'He's twenty-four,' said Borja, and thought he should add, ' – and straight. He's only staying a short time while he finds somewhere else to live. But he's good company and bright – and helps us feel young. Fills the house up a bit too.' Borja had made a point of astonishing Andy earlier in the evening with a description of the minor palace that he and James lived in.

Andy almost started to say that Borja and his partner would have to be careful about inviting other men into their domestic space if they wanted to safeguard their own relationship, but found that the advice wouldn't sit comfortably with what he was beginning to feel towards Borja, or with the direction in which the evening might, just possibly, be heading. Instead he waved his hand towards one of the waiters who was treading water somewhere nearby and ordered another large whisky.

One of the stars that twinkled above the palm trees began to grow in brightness, then inched its way across the sky towards them. A minute later it had become a blazing meteor, dipping almost imperceptibly lower now among the trees, finally splitting into a whole candelabrum of separate lights before disappearing behind the building. Moments later they heard the roar of the plane's engines for a few seconds as reverse thrust was engaged on landing, then the fade to silence.

'That was a late one,' said Andy. Neither of them looked at their watches. The hour hardly mattered. The fresh whiskies had arrived and Andy clinked glasses with Borja, obliging the ice inside to chink an echo.

'You know something,' said Borja, 'it still gives me a strange feeling, watching those lights appearing in the sky and thinking – that's one of us up there. Us pilots, I mean. Now I think about it I don't think it's true what you said. About me having no affinity with other pilots. Actually, perhaps it's rather the opposite. When you're approaching Gatwick or somewhere busy like that on a very clear night and you see all those circling lights – filling the whole sky between the south coast and London – climbing, landing, threading their way along the STARs – they look like fireflies, lonely in the dark. Lonely, and yet we're all up there together. And it makes me think sometimes… I know this sounds silly but … like Shakespeare said, like he made Henry the Fifth say … 'We few, we happy few, we band of brothers…''

He had to stop. Andy said, 'hey, hey, hey,' very softly, and touched the back of Borja's hand.

'I never told anyone that before,' Borja said, withdrawing his hand, but not rudely or too quickly, across the table. 'Not even James.' That was an ill-advised thing to say, he realised as he heard himself say it – as well as hackneyed. He would have to be careful with his tongue, after all this whisky. Don't fly misleading signals, he told himself.

The idea that came into Andy's mind at that point was something that was quite impossible to act on in pilot's uniform in the bar of a smart and Muslim-run hotel. He refocused his thoughts. 'You're pretty hot on Shakespeare for a Spanish guy,' he said. He was genuinely surprised.

'I told you I practically live in a theatre,' Borja said, 'as well as doing it all at university. And then, James and

I used to have a sort of game, a competition really, when we first got together – to quote Shakespeare, or misquote him, in everyday conversation.' He stopped, hearing himself as if someone else were talking. 'Sounds a bit stupid, I guess.'

'It sounds really nice, actually,' said Andy. 'You make me envious.'

Borja decided to ignore any possible implications of the last remark. He changed the subject. 'What do you think will happen to us?'

Which sobered Andy up somewhat. 'We already said. We get a paid holiday. Then they – whoever they are – trawl through all the information, including the report which I've got to write, and then confront me with the whole lot at some sort of internal inquiry.'

'Me too, of course,' said Borja. 'Don't forget that.'

'Yes, well…'

'I'm not going to let them blame you, you know,' said Borja quite hotly. 'I told you that before.'

'You're a lovely guy,' said Andy, looking at him in something like wonder. 'But in the end whatever happens happens to me. I was responsible. I can't duck that. Nor can you shoulder it for me.'

For all his pile it on me rhetoric, Andy looked troubled and Borja wished that, in trying to change the subject he had not chosen to go back to that particular one. He was becoming keenly aware of a lot of things right now. First, that he was getting rather drunk: something that he was normally careful not to do – or at least overdo – and especially on night stops, when he usually had to fly a plane out again the next morning. Second, that this fact was altering his perceptions quite markedly: the ambient light of the terrace had softened, taken on an expectant character, the way a change of lighting state in the theatre sometimes artfully seeks to – as he had been learning over the last few years. Now his voice, and

Andy's, came strangely, urgently, across the air between them, disjointed, separate somehow from the bodies they emanated from, cut adrift from the thoughts that either of them, until a short time ago, might have expected the other to express. And also Andy himself, whom Borja, when quite sober earlier that day, had decided was good looking, with his fresh complexion, his blue, teenager's eyes and that open smile… He must not think like this, Borja told himself, and took a large gulp of whisky in the vain hope of reining back his unleashed and galloping thoughts.

Yet tonight was such an exceptional one, the day's events so epic – Andy and he together had twice looked death in the face and survived – that the exceptional, out of character, ending to the day that was now unfolding seemed somehow to be called for, almost preordained: the fitting, the only possible finale. He was still a hot-blooded Spanish boy when all was said and done: something which James well knew and, in his heart of hearts, in view of today's exceptional circumstances would make allowance for. Alcohol was not clouding up his vision, Borja felt, but focusing it, guiding him like the automatic direction finder along the pathways of his STAR, to this day's journey's end. When Andy at last broke in on his meditation with, 'Looks like they want to close the bar; I've got a drop of duty-free upstairs; what do you reckon?' – it was as if the two of them had taken the last turn onto finals, and Borja had no doubt what he was meaning when he smiled back and said, 'Yes, why not?'

And once Andy had unlocked the door of his room, switched on the light and they were both inside – although it was Andy who, because he still had four stripes on the epaulettes of his white shirt, found it natural to continue to take the lead, this time by taking Borja's head between his hands and kissing him firmly on the mouth – it was Borja who returned the embrace so strongly that he temporarily squeezed Andy's breath right out of him with his enfolding arms as he hugged his captain back.

TWELVE

From the breakfast room window you could see parts of the airport quite well, including, fortuitously, the very piece of tarmac where the 737 they had accidentally brought here yesterday stood: alone, like a naughty schoolchild; neglected, like an abandoned toy; and all the time costing the airline money by its inability to work. Sitting alone at the table, gulping orange juice, Borja wondered if the plane had, in fact, 'gone sick'as they all termed it, its autopilot and radio all screwed up, or was it they, himself and Andy, who had screwed up? An engineer was coming during the morning to check the systems, then another crew would come out to fly it home. Andy and he, plus the cabin crew, all still suspended from duty, would fly back on the first scheduled flight that had room on it. To face the music.

Andy and he. To face the music. The phrases reverberated in his throbbing head. Last night. Andy and he. In Andy's room they had taken off each other's shirt, then stood back from each other like boxers squaring up for a fight, attracted yet wary, each a little afraid of the other, both afraid of themselves. Then they had moved together and stood, chest touching chest, holding each other for quite a long time. Both had been struck by the similarity of their size and build, smallish but trimly muscled; both were fascinated by the difference in their colouring, Andy's cool northern complexion against the warmer, southern tints of Borja's own.

They lay together on Andy's bed, lazily touching each other's chests and faces. Their hands strayed no further, though; for some reason that neither was aware of they'd kept their trousers on. They talked nonsense: Borja trying to find adjectives to describe the colour of Andy's blue eyes, Andy waxing lyrical about the symmetrical patterns – long admired by James – of Borja's rampant chest hair. Then Andy remembered suddenly that Borja was supposed to have flown the plane back to Gatwick the next day: in so doing he would have clocked up the requisite number of landings to make him eligible to be a captain. That would now not happen, and this was his, Andy's, fault. Tears welled up as he started to tell Borja all this and how sorry, how desperately sorry he was. To magic the tears away, Borja kissed him repeatedly on the cheeks and nose. Andy stroked Borja's dark hair. Time stood, while whirling madly, like a gyro resting on a pin. Then very slowly, as gradually as the dawn began to break beyond the curtained, shuttered, window, they both came to the knowledge that sex, if it had been going to happen between them at all that night, would have happened already, some time before they reached this present point. At last they both sat up. 'We didn't have that nightcap after all,' Andy said.

Light was prying at the chinks in the curtains. Sparrows chirped outside. Borja grimaced. 'I think I'd better go.' Andy knew that this was true and didn't really try to stop him, though there had been a few moments of affectionate contact in the minute or so that it took Borja to find his shirt and make his way to the door, like the last flaring of a dying bonfire before the embers soften to white ash.

Borja turned the memory of this scene over in his mind, somewhat grimly, as he continued his breakfast-table task of rehydrating his system with orange juice. Only a few hours ago he had been thinking that having sex with Andy would have been a right and fitting end to the previous day, and something to which James would have no objection at all. Now in the bright light of an African breakfast time, he wondered if, by not actually having sex with his captain, he had redeemed himself to any measurable degree. Last night he had trodden the thinnest of thin lines. The difference between having sex with someone and not doing so could be as fine and insubstantial, he thought, as the silvering on the back of a pane of glass that makes that world of difference between a window and a mirror.

Andy appeared at that moment, looking round the room, spotting Borja, then weaving among tables to come and join him. He looked less lovely than Borja had thought him the previous night, seeing him through eyes unduly influenced by alcohol and sentiment and lust. Nevertheless he was wearing a braveish face in the circumstances and Borja wondered doubtfully if he himself was doing anything like as well. A waiter arrived with precision-timed coffee just as Andy sat down. Without speaking, Borja poured orange juice into Andy's glass and then refilled his own.

'I've just been on the phone,' Andy said. 'We're flying out around midday.' He took a gulp of juice and then immediately another one of coffee, then looked straight at Borja and said, 'Look…' at the same precise moment as Borja looked straight at him and uttered the same word. They both stopped. The words that were to have come next, from both of them, – 'about last night' – appeared to be redundant.

'We shouldn't have,' Borja said baldly. 'I mean, done what we did.'

'Well actually,' said Andy, peering at Borja warily, 'if you remember at all well, we didn't.'

'I know, but you know what I mean. Anyway, it's not the same for you. You don't have someone else to consider.' Borja tried to busy himself with a croissant.

'Footloose and fancy free?' suggested Andy.

'Which I am definitely not. And because of promises I've made…'

'Your boyfriend. James. OK, I guess I've got to respect that. But I have to say that, if we both behave ourselves in the future – if we do – then, on my side at any rate, it's only going to be because of that. Because I actually think you're lovely.' He reached quickly across the table and firmly grasped the hand that Borja had incautiously left there.

'Don't!' said Borja, loudly enough for heads to turn in their direction. Andy withdrew his hand but without undue haste. Borja was glad that at that moment two of the cabin crew emerged into the breakfast room, peering about in urgent search of juice and somewhere to sit.

'James is lucky, having you. I suppose I'm jealous of him. Jealous of you too, in a way – for having someone else. I had that chance. I blew it.'

Borja smiled wanly. 'That was with a woman. I don't think you gave yourself a sporting chance, if you see what I mean. You might be more lucky with a man. Settling down I mean. You're still young, no?'

Andy looked down at the table. 'If only we'd met years ago,' he said quietly. 'I don't know how not to wish it could be you.' He paused and his face seemed to break and fragment, like a reflection in wind-ruffled water. 'I shouldn't have said that, should I?'

'Dear God, no you shouldn't have,' said Borja wretchedly. He was appalled, but at the same time thrilled by Andy's declaration. He could not lie to himself: something had happened between himself and Andy during the last twenty-four hours; whatever you chose to call it, it hadn't needed any expression in sex or any other physical contact to make it real. Andy raised his eyes. His gaze met Borja's. Between them the table seemed to grow in size, thrusting them apart, and in each other's eyes they both saw their own raw pain reflected and magnified: reflected to infinity as when two mirrors face each other across a single candle flame.

Andy could not use the cockpit jump-seat on the flight back: a senior captain was doing a line-check, so Andy sat at the back of the plane near 'his'cabin crew and just across the gangway from Borja. Perhaps that was the optimum seating arrangement in the circumstances, Borja thought: they could still talk but didn't have to rub shoulders or knees. Casting around for other crumbs of comfort, he fastened on the fact that the flight crew were relative strangers. He had feared that their captain might turn out to be Amanda Symons; even if you credited her with the saintliest disposition it would be hard not to imagine her feeling some degree of Schadenfreude at the downfall of Andy. And any hurt that Andy experienced, Borja had discovered, would from now on be shared, in some almost organic way, by him.

There would be a debriefing when they got to Gatwick. They talked about this, when they talked at all. It was easier to deal with than the feelings they had so painfully exposed to each other over breakfast. For the fourth or fifth time they ran through the events that had led up to their arrival in Casablanca, exchanging snatched sentences across the aisle in undertones: they had no wish to broadcast the whole story to their fare-paying fellow passengers. 'Just tell it as it happened,' Borja said when they got round to discussing what they would say at the debriefing. 'Then we won't contradict each other. There's no possible way things'll get better if we seem to be telling different stories.' Andy agreed and they fell silent.

'Anything to see?' the passenger next to Borja asked his companion in the window seat beyond.

'No, nothing,' she reported back. Borja glanced briefly towards the porthole. It was grey outside: they were flying through a thin veil of cloud. But there were two different shades of grey as Borja, even from his gangway seat, could see. The light grey was the sea, the dark the land; the line between them was the southern coast of Spain. There was Cádiz, lonely on its jutting isthmus, then the estuaries of the Guadalquivir at Sanlúcar and the Rio Tinto further west. In the furthest distance he could see the Guadiana marking the border with Portugal and the sweep of the Algarve beyond. Nothing to see? He had the advantage, he had to admit, of knowing the route and being able to work out approximately how far they might have got, but all the same. Nothing to see. How could people be so … so unsighted, so unaware of what was going on around them, so plain dull? The flight captain came on over the PA system and told them what Borja had already guessed for himself: that if passengers on the left cared to look out and down they would see Seville. Andy and Borja exchanged the ghosts of smiles.

Borja didn't have his car at Gatwick, Andy did. James had reminded Borja when they spoke on the phone after breakfast that he would be interviewing in London until quite late that evening. They could meet in London perhaps, James had suggested, and travel home together. Borja would have preferred not to make his ignominious homecoming in a car with, presumably, Guy and James's assistant Linda, but it was a practical idea and in any case all those Other People would have to be faced in the future at some stage. Andy could drive Borja into the centre of London on his way home to Maida Vale. Then James said, 'Why not bring your pilot friend with you and we can all go for a drink.' Borja's heart sank. 'Guy seems to have developed a curiosity to meet him.' Borja could find no way to explain that it was the last thing in the world he wanted right then. Flustered, he had agreed instead. But when he rather doubtfully explained this arrangement to Andy he was surprised when Andy, unfazed, said he thought it was a nice idea.

Borja knew the way to the church hall near Earls Court where the auditions and interviews were being held; this rendezvous arrangement had served its purpose before. Even so it was quite late when they got there. 'Look,' said Borja as they finally drove up, 'I know the parking round here. Let me take the car and park up; you nip in and tell them we've arrived. Ask for James Miller. I'll join you in one minute.' He slid across into the driving seat as Andy got out of the car.

Nick was sitting at the reception desk, feeling the cold now it had got dark outside, and looking forward to getting home. There was one more candidate for the stage manager's job to be seen – if he turned up; he was already late – with the improbable name of Butch Holness. 'The names some of them have,' James had said earlier. 'We almost didn't shortlist him for that reason alone.'

Andy walked in just then. He had a pullover on now and so was not immediately identifiable as a pilot. Nick was certainly not going to ask him, 'Are you Butch?' He settled for, 'Mr Holness?'

'Holmes,' Andy automatically corrected, while being simultaneously disconcerted by the manner of the greeting and by the fact that the eyes of the pleasant looking young man who confronted him looked – despite their sheltering behind a pair of not very strong spectacles – extraordinarily like Borja's. He was now an authority upon that particular pair of eyes: he had spent about half of the previous twenty-four hours gazing very intently into them. This couldn't be James, surely: Borja's partner of fourteen years. ...Unless Andy had failed to catch a vital part of Borja's life story. Fourteen years ago this person would have been about ten.

'I'm looking for James Miller,' Andy said.

'Would you like to take a seat?' invited Nick. 'They were expecting you about half an hour ago.' He wasn't going to say, 'You're late,' to someone who might end up becoming his boss. 'But they're running late themselves.' Nick thought the new arrival seemed likeable. Perhaps it would nice if he did become his boss. Except for that stupid name. He imagined himself having to say things like, 'What's next, Butch?' or 'Butch, can someone give me a hand?' No, it was unthinkable. Pity.

Andy realised at once what had happened. He grinned. 'I'm not here for an audition, though I am late. I've driven Mr Miller's partner up from Gatwick. He's just parking the car.'

'Borja?' Nick stood up. 'I'm so sorry. I thought…'

'No, I understand. It's OK.' He gave his hand to Nick. 'I'm Andy by the way.'

'I'm Nick.'

Was this the lodger who lived with Borja and James perhaps? Andy could not remember if Borja had given him a name. But there was no time to find out. A door opened and a young woman came through, smiled vaguely at Nick and disappeared out into the street. Then James and Guy materialised. Guy looked sharply at Andy. 'Are you Butch Holness?' he asked a little testily. The street door opened and Borja walked in.

The nearest pub was about one minute's walk away. Although Borja was inwardly squirming at the thought of James and Andy in sudden close social contact, he suffered this discomfort alone. Andy was loth to let Borja go till the last possible minute; besides, he had just met Nick and was curious about him. Guy, once he had been put right about who Andy was, decided that the youthful-looking blond pilot was really rather attractive and that, although he was usually quickly bored by non-theatre people, his earlier hunch that twenty minutes in his company might not be too much of an ordeal had not been wrong.

It was a noisy pub, loud with piped music, full of dark corners in which gaming machines flashed and chuntered, and with carpets of such dark deep pile that they could only have been filthy. Nevertheless they found a table at which they could all sit comfortably and installed themselves. Borja failed to spot the signs of self-conscious, over-polite, awkwardness in the interaction of James and Nick: he was too busy trying to behave as if everything was perfectly normal between himself and his captain. For the very same reason, James failed to notice those very same tell-tale signs of tension between the two pilots. Guy decided to take the lead in the conversation, and started questioning Andy. He was still in interview mode after the day he had just spent, and following the non-show of the oddly first-named Mr Holness. 'So,' he began, leaning forward with an earnestness that was only partly given the lie to by the twinkle in his dark eyes, 'what made you want to become a pilot?'

By the time Andy had given a public recitation of a substantial part of his curriculum vitae the atmosphere was noticeably more relaxed and Nick felt able to bring up the subject of what had happened to Flight BN 437 to Tangier.

'We're all still alive at least,' said Borja. 'They gave us a rather unsmiling interview when we arrived at Gatwick but they didn't try to put the blame on anyone. That'll be left till the enquiry – still some weeks away, I imagine. In the meantime we're suspended from all duties except picking up our pay cheques.'

'And the plane,' James wanted to know. 'What's happened to that?'

It had still been sitting on the tarmac at Casablanca when they flew out. Engineers were examining the computerised systems.

'Just to be sure it doesn't decide to fly out across the Atlantic instead of coming back,' suggested Nick a little too flippantly.

'That's not as funny as you think,' Andy told him.

'Nick's very keen to hear the whole story,' James came to Nick's rescue. 'He was asking me last night all about navigation systems and so on.' This was quite true. It was the evening after the debacle of that kiss and its repercussions, and it had been useful to have such a topical subject of conversation. By fastening onto it James and Nick had saved themselves from the twin perils of further post-mortem and repeat performance.

Borja and Andy together embarked on an account of what had happened on the Tangier flight, so far as they understood it, and tried to answer Nick's technical questions, beginning to relax at last. There were Andy and James talking together and quite at ease in each other's company; the world had not fallen apart quite yet and that was something to be thankful for. To be thankful to whom, though? Maybe – it was not the first time Borja had had cause to think this – maybe to Nick.

Borja had to show Andy where he had parked his car. As it happened it was literally just around the corner from where James had put his. Guy was talking to James as he turned to unlock his driver's door, so Nick's were the only eyes that followed Borja and Andy to the other car. Only he saw them stop, stand facing each other stiffly for a few seconds, then, still rather awkwardly, hurriedly embrace one another while Andy gave Borja a quick peck on the cheek. Nick at once turned back to where Guy and James were getting into James's car, leaving Borja to make his way back to them unwatched. Did it mean something in particular, that hug and kiss, Nick wondered, or did airline pilots – like theatre people, whether gay, straight or in-between – traditionally behave like that?

They threaded their way out of London and up the motorway. Arriving in the city they bought takeaways and ate them around the table in Guy's town-centre flat with a glass or two of wine. By the time that James, Borja and Nick had driven back out to Sevenscore it was bedtime.

Once they were alone together again between their own sheets James and Borja made love with a passionate intensity, each surprising the other but not himself. While Nick, preparing for bed three closed doors away, found himself considering the idea that, if you did happen to be gay, sharing your life with a handsome pilot was not the worst thing that could happen.

THIRTEEN

The weekend which followed was a quiet one at Sevenscore. Nick went away to spend some of it with his parents. Borja and James, both somewhat subdued, spent the time catching up on domestic chores and being very careful of each other's feelings. Neville was nowhere to be seen, presumably spending the time in town with Rita in her flat somewhere near the cinema.

On Monday morning James and Nick, who had returned late the previous evening, were up at dawn. It was a fit-up weekend at the theatre. The set of the previous production had been struck and got out overnight on Saturday. Today the large and elaborate set for Kiss Me Kate, currently in pieces in the workshops, would be assembled on the stage. The stage management call was for seven a.m. Nick's job, not James's. But since his arrival in post as general manager several years ago James had taken it upon himself to take part in these early morning fit-ups, in jeans and T-shirt, and working boots which he borrowed from the costume-hire department for the day. He saw it as a way of encouraging the team, showing them that if they had to stir from their beds so early on a cold Monday morning, then he knew all about it – knew about it by virtue of being there and doing it with them. And if, as was always necessary, he had to drift off and leave them mid-morning in order to attend to affairs in the office, well, his point was made by then. So this morning he was up and snatching a coffee in the kitchen with Nick before six o'clock, and Nick, whose feelings of awkwardness in the company of James had faded more quickly than he had imagined possible the previous week, was more than happy that he would not have to brave the morning cold on his unreliable motorbike but could cadge a lift in James's car.

Borja was gentleman enough to stir from bed and join them for coffee in the kitchen, wishing them a good day from the comfort of his dressing gown. But then he went back to bed and surprised himself by sleeping on till ten.

He had a leisurely bath and dressed. Alone in the house he was possessed by that strange feeling that the temporary invalid knows so well: that the world has gone on without him, setting off to work and play, while leaving him, as it were, beached, beyond the rush and noise of time, on an unfamiliar shore of stillness. He was totally free. He could do anything he wanted, within reason.

One thing he could do, and it would seem perfectly natural to James when he told him later, would be to pick up the phone, call Andy and say hallo. They had swapped address cards while in the Earls Court pub the other day as a matter of course. It would also appear perfectly reasonable to James or anyone else if he were to arrange to drive down to London and meet his colleague today, or some other day this week, for lunch.

But Borja would do neither of these things. Andy had ceased to play the role of a mere colleague for him some days ago. Andy kept turning up in his thoughts when he least expected him to. It was not something he wanted. He had moved as near to Andy in Casablanca as he was ever going to. Now he was on the retreat from him and no phone-calls under the easy guise of polite concern for his captain's welfare would make that process easier. Quite the reverse, Borja realised only too well. No phone-call then, hard as this decision was to make, and so no lunches either. Borja took the key of the West Pavilion from the hall table and walked out into the garden, away from the temptations presented by the phone.

The apple trees were just coming into blossom, and blackbirds sang to celebrate this April morning from which the sun was just beginning to lift the chill. Borja crossed the wet lawn, walked round the colonnade where white narcissi now nodded among the old stone pillars, and entered the pavilion, the old ballroom, whose inside temperature still stung with winter. Optimistically, though knowing well what a futile gesture this was, Borja left the door open while he went inside, as if this might have some effect on the indoor micro-climate in the short time he proposed to spend there.

Not only wall-high mirrors and the Broadwood piano that Nick was growing to love furnished the West Pavilion. One wall of it was lined with books. Some had belonged to Neville's father, some to his grandfather even, and had somehow survived the estate's temporary use as a military headquarters during the Second World War. A number of them were some of Borja's oldest friends. There was Washington Irving's Tales of the Alhambra for a start. Borja had lived in Granada for a month or two, just prior to moving to Seville with James, and still clung to fond memories of the town and its fabled castle on the hill above. Even the experience of having had once to travel there with Rafael to secure the release of James – and the appalling William – from police custody had failed to tarnish the image he kept in his memory of the beautiful city. He knew Irving's stories almost by heart, had only to leaf through the pages now to bring them to life once more in his mind, though he stopped for a few seconds at each of the nineteenth-century engravings that illustrated this edition: engravings of the Patio de Leones, the Salón de Embajadores, the Torre de las Infantas… He returned the leather-bound volume to its shelf.

Nearby was Stevenson's Travels with a Donkey, another traveller's tale that Borja knew nearly by heart.

Now he glanced only at the book's dedication; he thought it one of the most beautiful he knew: ... Every book is, in an intimate sense, a circular letter to the friends of him who writes it. They alone take his meaning; they find private messages, assurances of love, and expressions of gratitude, dropped for them in every corner. The public is but a generous patron who defrays the postage... Thoughtfully he returned the book to the place whence he had pulled it.

A complete set of Dickens was there, and Shakespeare too, Jane Austen, P.G. Wodehouse and Evelyn Waugh. The collection was about as eclectic as anyone had a right to expect. Spoilt both for choice and for leisure time, Borja at last selected the English translation of Antoine de St. Exupéry's Terre des Hommes.

On returning to the relative warmth of the garden, his pensive mood was joltingly dispelled by the sight of Neville sitting at a small table right in the centre of his path around the colonnade, with a bowl of water, a bathroom mirror and a lathered face, in the middle of giving himself a shave.

'Qué?' he said, forgetting for a moment which language Neville might expect to be addressed in, then, quickly putting this right, 'What on earth are you doing?'

Neville turned towards him with round but un-startled eyes. 'Shaving, as you can see. I thought you'd all gone into town, or I might have chosen a more secluded spot. The electricity's gone in the East Pavilion.' He jerked his head towards it. 'The bathroom's too dark for safety.'

'Oh no,' said Borja, genuinely sympathetic. 'Haven't you paid the bill?'

Borja had an awkward relationship with Neville. But the awkwardness was entirely on Borja's side and in his own head. Neville's feelings toward Borja were without complexity: he thought him a charming and likeable young foreigner whose occasional flashes of darker temperament puzzled him, but only briefly. On Borja's side, however, the relationship had deeper roots. In the nineteen-sixties, when Borja was a child, Neville had had a major success with a children's story which was made into a TV series and shown, dubbed into the various languages, throughout Europe. Borja had watched it, in Spanish of course, enchanted and wide-eyed. It was the story of three children who ran away from home, borrowing a boat, setting off downstream on a great river, and of the adventures they had. Rivers of Eden, it had been called. It had stayed with him, influenced him even, into adult life, as the best children's stories always do.

Then, years later, he had met its creator. Become, bizarrely enough, his tenant in that foreign country that had become his home. And Neville – in the flesh, as opposed to mediated through the magical adventures of three children – was frankly, perhaps inevitably, a disappointment. There was no sign that Neville might ever have been the kind of child his story told about: one who would take a boat out at night and travel hundreds of miles along a vast waterway, confronting dangers as he went; Neville's biggest adventures these days seemed to consist of protracted visits to local pubs and occasional, not too deeply felt, affairs with forty-something local women. Nobody else, except Borja, seemed to remember Rivers of Eden. Even Neville himself, when Borja questioned him, seemed to have little recollection of what it was about. It must have made him quite a bit of money way back then, but there was no sign of it now: it had presumably been divided between the upkeep of his father's legacy, Sevenscore, and the tills of the various local pubs. And then that flash of early success had not been repeated in anything like the same degree. Borja did enjoy the light comedies of Neville's that were occasionally performed at the Regent, and his pantomimes and his adaptations of the classics were professional and workmanlike. But Borja could never find in them the special something, the will-o'-the-wisp of wonder, that shimmered in that childhood memory.

It was simply that he had grown up, he told himself; that was all. And it was himself he should have been cross with on that account: unreasonable of him to blame Neville for that. And in the end, he told himself, he had to like Neville. How could you not like a man who, when you telephoned him, apologised for his delay in coming to the phone with, 'I was just drawing a bath but, never mind, I can colour it in later.'…?

'So,' Borja repeated, 'the electricity bill?'

'No, it isn't that,' said Neville in a faintly injured tone, 'I think it's something mechanical, a fuse or something. I had the kettle, the toaster and the oven all on at the same time and all the lights went out.'

'Then that's easy,' said Borja, knowing full well that for Neville it was anything but. 'Come on. Let's go and get it fixed.' He waited a minute for Neville to finish off his shaving routine, and then they walked together among the stone pillars and the narcissi to Neville's open front door.

In the kitchen the mains switch and fuses were housed in a small box high up on the wall. Inside it was not only a coil of fuse wire of the appropriate ampage, but even a helpfully stationed pair of pliers. Without much difficulty Borja, standing on a chair, identified the fuse that needed attention, fitted a new wire and then re-set the trip button. The lights came back on. How could anyone be quite so impractical? Borja asked himself as he dismounted from the chair. The children in 'Rivers of

Eden'would have got the problem sorted in no time at all.

Neville was lavish in his expressions of gratitude. He had some letters to write, he said, but after that he would be wandering down to the Rose and Castle for a beer or two, and why didn't Borja join him?

Borja, who knew what lunchtimes in the pub with Neville could be like, hastily invented an errand that would take him and his car to Milton Keynes, a destination chosen because Neville was unlikely to have any reason to want a lift there himself, and then politely took his leave.

It had not been such a good idea to select Terre des Hommes as reading material, Borja discovered after thirty minutes of getting into it. He had forgotten quite how much of the book was about male bonding among airmen flying to and from Casablanca, and getting lost among the airways of North Africa. As a strategy for putting Andy out of his mind it had spectacularly backfired. Borja gave the book up and, accepting defeat, walked down the old carriage drive to join Neville in the pub.

It would be the last time, he thought to himself later, experiencing the unpleasant sensations of a slight hangover at five o'clock in the afternoon. Weeks on end of rattling around the house and gardens, trying not to think about someone, trying at the same time not to find himself playing chauffeur, general handyman and companion in bars to Neville, would send him mad. He had an idea. Whether it could be put into practice or not would depend on James.

James returned in the middle of the evening, Nick would not be back till later, this time on his bike. James was not in the best of tempers. 'They're running way behind,' he said as soon as he came through the door. 'The design's so bloody complicated. At this rate half of them are going to have to work through the night to get the set built. Technical rehearsal at ten tomorrow morning… We'll be lucky.'

This information actually chimed, to Borja's surprise, with what he had been going to ask James about. 'Are you short of hands?' he said simply.

'They didn't book enough casuals, if that's what you mean. Either for the fit-up or for running the show, by the look of things. Not Mike's fault, exactly. Nobody knew just how big it was all going to be. Except Guy, and Terry the designer. And they're both famous devotees of the art of the big surprise… '

'…Because I was thinking,' interrupted Borja a little diffidently, 'that if you needed an extra person, a backstage casual, and the work wasn't too specialised, you know, well, here I am with nothing particular to do at the moment…'

'You?' James was astonished at Borja, yet at the same time, conscious of the timeliness of his offer, relieved at the way it might help get his production department out of a difficult predicament. 'But are you sure you'd really be happy doing that? You'd be in a very junior position, you know. Even Nick would be senior to you. It might not be easy for an almost airline captain to swallow. You know, Beaudelaire's Albatross: His giant-like wings impede his walking.'

'I could start in the morning. Or even during the night, if they're working through in shifts.'

'You amaze me. They might give you a hard time, you know. Things like sending you up to the workshop for a 'long weight'and that sort of thing.'

'Don't worry. I know all about that.' Borja grinned. 'They tried that one on me at flying school.'

James's expression froze. 'Who did that to you? When? Why did you never tell me?' He suddenly found himself furiously, absurdly, angry with some unknown person from Borja's training time ten years ago, all his protective feelings towards his lover called forth in an instant, as if Borja had been a child rather than a thirty-five-year-old airline pilot, a mere six months younger than he was himself. There were times though, like this one, when those six months caught him out and mattered enormously.

Borja laughed. 'It was years ago, for God's sake. It didn't matter then and it doesn't now.' All the same, he was deeply moved by James's concern.

The social centre of backstage life, if you didn't count the two nearby pubs, was the green room. Theoretically this was a place of quiet repose where actors might make themselves coffee and escape for a few minutes from the tyranny of their dressing-room mirrors. But the Regent's green room formed part of the corridor between the dressing rooms and the stage. It also lay along the main route between the paint-shop and the stage as well as between both of these and the carpenters'workshop. Below ground level as it was, the stairs from the stage door above decanted into it and it had all the appearances, as well as the lively atmosphere, of a slum kitchen. It boasted one comfy armchair with, intermittently, fleas in it, and some hard wooden benches which were usually piled high with old overalls and trainers, sometimes empty, sometimes with people in them. There was a notice-board for messages. When Borja arrived, down the stage-door stairs, to start his shift at six o'clock the next morning, there was only one message on it. Jeremy, phone your agent.

Sally, the stage manager, was the only occupant of the green room at that precise moment, her black sleeves wrapped round a steaming mug of coffee. 'Good to have you,' she said. 'Though it's going to feel strange at first. For you too, I imagine. I must admit, everyone thought

James was winding us up when he phoned last night and said you'd be coming to join us. But here you are, so it must be true. Nick'll be pleased. You're his big hero, you know. Don't tell him I said so.' Nick had returned to Sevenscore to sleep at two that morning. He would be returning to work backstage at midday.

'I expect we'll all get used to it: having me here, I mean.' And to his own surprise as well as to Sally's, Borja picked her up and swung her round the room – something he didn't often do with women – coffee and all.

'OK,' Sally said, when Borja had put her down, 'I'm going to arm you with a hammer and a pump screwdriver and send you in there with the lions. I'm afraid it's all at maximum chaos just now, with four hours to zero hour, and Terry and Mike stopped speaking soon after midnight. But don't worry too much. It'll be there at ten o'clock. It always is.'

'Sounds like the airline business,' said Borja.

The big pieces of scenery, rostra and flattage, had already been manhandled from the paint-shop onto the stage the previous morning. That was no mean feat, since the stage lay eight feet below ground level and the paint-shop eight feet above, as well as being on the other side of Friars'Way, the narrow street that bizarrely separated the theatre from its own stage door. (Human traffic moved more easily, under the street, via the green-room tunnel.) By now only the smaller pieces were still being relayed out of the high paint-shop doors, trundled across the road and then more or less hurled through the open dock doors down onto the stage below. At first Borja's job consisted mainly of dodging these incoming missiles, but after a while he found himself slotting in to the team effort of assembling rostra and a variety of things that moved: trucks and other strange sliding things on castors, and curtains on runners that would actually work. Looking in through the dock doors on his arrival a short time ago, he had seen the theatre's interior alight like a furnace in the darkness, with a foreground of dust and debris and sweating labour, and beyond all that a baroque world of red plush and gilt and moulded plaster that seemed unaccustomed to exposure to the rude gaze of the outside world. It was as if a bees'nest had been unexpectedly revealed behind a blank wall, full of light and life.

Now here he was in the midst of it, hammering, screwdriving, accumulating splinters, developing blisters on his palms. In the course of the next few chaotic hours the technical rehearsal was postponed twice – by an hour each time; somebody accidentally dropped a flat on Borja and two other people; and Terry, the chief designer, crowned the proceedings by falling spectacularly off the top step of a ladder after swinging his hammer with rather too much abandon while announcing, 'I'll get this bloody thing to work if it kills me.' It didn't kill him in fact, but he needed hospital treatment for his elbow just the same.

Borja would hardly have been conscious of the moment when the fit-up metamorphosed seamlessly into the technical rehearsal, but for the sudden materialisation of Nick at his elbow. 'We're both down to work on the same side,' Nick said. 'Stage right. You, me and another casual I haven't met yet.' Borja could see from his face that Nick was delighted with this arrangement. For his part, Borja had not realised that being stage crew meant he would be on one side or the other. He was handed a pair of black jeans and a sweatshirt by the wardrobe mistress. 'See if they fit,' she said. And everyone unselfconsciously stripped down to their underpants just where they stood, and tried on their new, standard-issue, blacks.

There was a roll-call of props to be done – like a pre-flight check, Borja could not help but think. He said as much to Nick.

'You should have seen the check-list for the panto, then,' Nick told him. 'Seriously surreal. It went something like this. 'Nail varnish?''Check.'Unmissable: the pot was three feet high. 'Magnifying glass?'Also three feet wide. 'Dog's tail on stick?''Check.''Six broomsticks and witches'hats?''Check, check.'Crash trays? Tea-bag? The size of a cushion. One dozen gold eggs? Check, check, check, and the eggs would go rolling everywhere.' It put the modest check-list for Kiss Me Kate into perspective, Borja thought.

It wasn't until the technical rehearsal was over, a fact that was signalled by James arriving with a boxful of packages of fish and chips, that Borja thought to look at his watch. It was seven o'clock in the evening and he had worked without a break for thirteen hours. 'Good,' said Guy, doing a rapid tour of the battlefield, high on adrenalin and rubbing his hands together. 'Dress run to go ahead at eight as planned.'

'Tomorrow'll be dead quiet, you'll see,' said Nick.

At five minutes to eleven, thoroughly exhausted, the whole of the stage crew including Borja trooped into the Post Horn opposite the stage door and thirstily ordered pints. And while they sat enjoying them, each and every one removed the day's accumulation of splinters from his fingers. James and Guy arrived a few seconds later. 'Thank you, Borja,' Guy said, slapping him on the back, and James said quietly, 'Well done, Boyee.' He hadn't called his lover that for years.

FOURTEEN

Crewing the vast elaborate set of Kiss Me Kate, with its open plan, atmospheric backstage gloom and mobile trucks took some getting used to. Handling the trucks during scene changes that were, intentionally, carried out in full view of the audience required skill and a steady nerve. The trucks were large and unwieldy and it was not possible to see what was happening to the person manhandling the other end: whether he had collided with an obstacle, for instance, or was pushing the wrong way. Guy had said, during one particularly dark-night-of-the-soul moment during the technical rehearsal, 'It's like docking in bloody space.'

Borja had added, in an aside to Nick, 'Or like parking jumbos at Heathrow without a radio link.'

But Nick had been right. In time the whole operation, plus the days that framed it, settled into a routine. Once the first three mad days of fit-up, technical and dress rehearsals and first night had come to an end, life quietened down, at least for Borja, quite a lot. Everyone got used to steering the trucking, found that, without intending to, they had learnt all the songs in the show by heart, and discovered that splinters, if left unattended, usually went away of their own accord.

Two young men worked overhead on the fly floor, practising the fine art of hemp-line flying. This was the muscle-wrenching, rope-hauling method of changing painted scene cloths that had remained unchanged since the days, centuries ago, when it was carried out by sailors on shore leave. You had to try and do it without garrotting yourself, amputating another's legs or making an unlooked-for but spectacular appearance in the middle of the action on stage, twenty feet below.

On either side, at stage level, worked a team of three: one ASM and two casuals. On Borja's side, he, Nick and a college drop-out called Smut would sit together in the dark on a laundry basket behind the proscenium arch when not actually doing the scene changes. Then Smut took to doing pull-ups from a beam that crossed their hidden corner. Not to be outdone, Nick started to do the same and Borja, who did not consider himself too old for such things, followed suit. In due course the male members of the cast joined in too. The competitive aspect of this did wonders for everyone's muscles and soon everyone was notching up fifteen pull-ups at each performance – which made thirty a day when there was a matinee.

The weeks passed. When there was no matinee Borja had his daytimes more or less free, but at least he had a job to go to when the evenings came. He got used to evenings that finished over a pint in the Post Horn around ten o'clock, picking at splinters along with the rest of the stage management, driving Nick back to Sevenscore and, if everyone was lucky, finding that James had got something together for a communal evening meal.

Neville was usually pottering somewhere in the gardens on those spare spring mornings, doing something ineffectual with secateurs, and one such day he gave Borja some alarming news. 'Remember Rita?' Borja sort of did. Didn't she live somewhere near the cinema? Neville nodded. 'It seems she wasn't altogether unattached. There's been another man in her life all along. A fellow from the Republic across the water who works all over the place on building sites. He'd been away for over a year. No contact made at all. Now he suddenly reappears again.' Neville looked down at the secateurs in his hand and snapped them firmly shut. 'He's broken her left thumb.'

'Jesus Christ,' said Borja. 'Because she was seeing another man?' A shiver ran through him.

'And he says he'll do the same to the other thumb if…' He broke off and looked at Borja miserably. 'What am I to do? She needs protecting, don't you think? But if I…'

'You'll have to stay out of it.' Borja remembered with a small involuntary twinge of pride how practical he had managed to be in the matter of Neville's fuse box the other week. He must approach this in the same businesslike way. 'You see that, no? You must call the police, or she must, and let them deal with it. He sounds like a madman. She's in real danger.'

'The thing is – and this is the difficulty – she doesn't want the police involved because…'

Borja sighed. How difficult other people's lives were; how impossible they were to help. Obviously this woman had something to hide, something she didn't want the police to know about... A phone rang in Neville's pocket, which startled Borja no end. Neville had never had a mobile up to now. Or if he had, no-one had ever rung him on it.

'Sorry,' said Neville and fished the instrument from out of his heavy cords. The caller was none other than James, phoning from the theatre office. Borja half heard the conversation, saw Neville's startled look turn to astonishment, then to something different again, something that contained an element of fear mixed with delight. 'Good God,' he said, when the call was finished. 'Do you think you could possibly run me into town – in about ten minutes? I've got to take over a role in Kiss Me Kate. Starting tonight.'

'Singing?' Throat asked incredulously.

'Dancing?' queried Hand.

'I didn't know he'd even been an actor,' put in someone else. The stage crew, half the acting company and the electricians had been called in for an emergency rehearsal during the afternoon. Neville was to be rehearsed in the role of Harrison Howell in order to be slotted into that night's performance, taking the place of an actor who had gone sick. The stage crew were having coffee in the green room before the rehearsal began.

'He's actually a very good actor,' said Mike the production manager, 'and he's done Kiss Me Kate loads of times before. That's why Guy thought of him first.'

'I don't know why they don't have understudies,' said Smut, adding a supplementary spoonful of greyish sugar to his already supersaturated coffee.

'Because we're in the Regions and not the West End,' Nick explained.

'I always understood that actors never got ill,' said Borja. 'Doctor Footlights takes care of them. That's what James has always said. And I don't remember it happening here before.'

'There's a first time for everything,' said Sally, who then added – because she was leaving on Saturday, and because Borja had picked her up and swung her round this very room on his first morning, just three weeks ago – 'like getting lost in Morocco, I suppose.' Borja made a face at her and then joined in the general laughter. He had made a point of not standing on his dignity since coming to work backstage; that had been a shrewd tactic: he found that he was fitting in better than he had ever imagined. By now he could begin to see to the end of Kiss Me Kate, three weeks away, and realised that he would miss it. He glanced up at the message board beside him; it's single message read: Wanda, phone your agent.

'I heard that Guy had to employ Neville for financial reasons,' said the assistant carpenter.

'How do you mean?' asked Smut.

'Well, from what I heard, when the office added up all the advances he'd had on the last pantomime it came to more than the total of all the royalties, and he ended up owing the theatre money. They've had to put him on the payroll to claw some of it back.'

There was a general gasp of laughter, half shocked, half admiring.

'Trust Neville,' said Throat. 'Who else could drink seven per cent of a pantomime before it even opened?'

Nick opened his mouth to say something but Borja, who was sitting next to him, stopped him with a sideways look. 'We know none of that's true,' Nick said to him quietly.

'I know we do. But don't let's be the ones to spoil a good story. There's no malice towards Neville in it.'

'When he was in the Scottish play in York once,' said Mike the production manager, 'he had this line…'

'Don't quote it…' warned Sally.

'It's OK. I'll leave the room afterwards and turn round three times. It's supposed to go, 'Let's after him whose care has gone before to bid us welcome.'His version was, 'Let's after him whose car has gone before to pick up Malcolm.''

Laughing, the crew bundled the most senior member of the gathering out into the corridor to pay his forfeit for quoting from Macbeth.

There was a more than usually triumphant feeling among the gathering in the Post Horn after the show that night. Neville had fitted into the show as neatly as if he had been in it from the first day of rehearsal and had delivered a performance of such quality that even the youngest members of the backstage crew quietly applauded him as he came offstage at the end of the curtain-call. Guy bought a vast round of drinks out of sheer relief.

The subject of Neville's woman, Rita, and the ex-lover who had broken her thumb inevitably surfaced during the conversation and cast a slight cloud over the celebration, but it had been dealt with firmly, if temporarily, by Guy who told Neville, 'Have nothing more to do with her. Or him. It's not only not worth it. It's dangerous. You're out of your depth.' Nobody else was old enough to speak to Neville like that.

It was not until the party was nearly breaking up that James was able to deliver a little piece of news of his own. Since it concerned Borja, domestically, and Guy, in connection with work, he brought it up now while they were still all together. 'I was talking to Alexa on the phone today,' he told them. 'Things to sort out about her concert in June. She reminded me – which I'd rather forgotten in the heat of everything else – that I'd volunteered to sit on her committee of trustees.'

Guy wasn't sure if he'd heard about this. James reminded him about Eulogio's legacy: funds for young musicians and so forth. Borja had not forgotten, though it had not been in the forefront of his mind either just lately. As for Nick, he had certainly not forgotten Eulogio's recording of the Schubert Impromptus at any rate; he knew now that he never would.

'The thing is,' James went on, 'the first meeting is in Seville next week. Alexa wants me to go, she and her boyfriend will put me up, and the trust will pay the flight and expenses. But I don't know if I…'

'I don't see why you can't go if you want to,' Guy said very positively. 'Everything's up to date on the forward planning front. You deserve a break. A quick word with the chairman in the morning…'

James turned to Borja. 'The other thing … is you. I was thinking that if I went at all we'd be going together – make it a sort of holiday. I'm sure we could get another casual to replace you. We've got a whole week to find one.'

'Actually, I'm really enjoying my time backstage,' Borja answered. 'It'll be over so soon. I really don't mind if you want to go.'

'Yes, but, when you're grounded like you are, it seems a bit…'

'Oh, Christ Almighty, you two,' Guy broke in. 'After you, Claude, after you, Cecil! It drives everybody mad. James wants to go, and Borja's quite happy to let him: it's as clear as day.'

'It's a change for me to be grounded, so that's OK,' Borja said. 'And, if Alexa and Mark are putting you up, then the two of us might be rather more than they're bargaining for. Besides...' He laughed, and looked at Nick who was standing beside him. '...Someone's got to look after the Kid here. I tell you, though,' he turned back to James, 'when things are more settled again, we'll have a proper holiday in Seville together. Won't we?'

James looked relieved. 'I'd love that,' he said. He meant it.

In the morning James phoned the chairman of the board to ask for permission to take a few days away from his post.

'They tell me young Borja's joined the stage crew,' said the chairman. James imagined his voice as a steel wire. 'Taking a break from flying. Is that correct?'

James wondered who 'they'were. He could picture the chairman's gimlet eyes at the other end of the line. 'More or less,' he answered.

'Well in that case, perhaps we can spare you for a few days. Leave things in his capable hands, don't you think?'

The chairman still didn't make jokes. Had he done so, that would have been another of them.

FIFTEEN

It did cross James's mind as, floating over the sunlit Sierra Morena, his plane began its descent into Seville, that they might be diverted … and then lost, ending up at Málaga, say, or foggy Tangier. But nothing of the sort happened and presently, as the plane came ever closer to the ground, it scooped a wide left-hand turn around the sun-washed city, a sprawling street-spoked cartwheel, as if to show it off to its admiring visitors. James had no doubt about where he was by the time they touched down at the familiar little airport. It had been the gateway to his home once, for three whole years. He walked down the disembarkation steps into the remembered embrace of warm, dry, Sevillian air.

Stepping into the arrivals hall James was met, accosted even, by that three-tone tide of aromas that proclaimed, as for him it always had, you are now in Spain. Olive oil, cigarette smoke, and the orange-flower scented coloña de baño that all the men – and Borja himself – always wore. Beneath that heady wave there was an undertow of floor polish and cleaning liquids responding to the contrasting conditions of strong sunlight and deep shade. He headed into the shadier regions towards the baggage carousel. The plane had stopped off at Santiago de Compostela on the way, where everybody had disembarked and gone through Customs. But James had rather forgotten the implications of this and so it came as something of a surprise to him, as he bent down to retrieve his modest backpack, to be slapped on the shoulders and to hear Mark's voice, still American accented after all these years, saying, 'Hi, guy. Welcome home.'

James picked up the bag and swung round in one startled movement. There was Alexa alongside Mark. He kissed them both.

They looked … well, older of course, but also somehow, indefinably different. The last time he had seen the two of them they hadn't been an item or anything like one. They had belonged to the same circle of friends as James and Borja had, but it was not until some time after they had left Seville that Mark and Alexa began to think that life had been plotting to bring them together. Ten years on, there was no doubt about that now. No, James suddenly realised, there was nothing indefinable about the way in which they looked different. They looked like a couple.

They drove a small battered Séat. Between them they were not too badly off, James knew, but he could also surmise that, even if they had been really wealthy it would not have occurred to either of them to spend large sums of money on a commodious or flashy means of transport. Still, it was an improvement on the rust bucket of a Vespa that Mark had buzzed around the city on in earlier times.

Remembering that old Vespa brought his mind back to Nick's rusty motorbike in England. Would he be riding it home to Sevenscore this evening, or would Borja take pity on him as he so often did these days, and drive him home with the infernal little machine lashed to the boot? Thinking about that made him feel uneasy, for a whole complex of reasons, though none of them was easy to pinpoint or explain on its own. But thinking about all that here, eleven hundred miles away… There was no earthly point to that.

The ever so familiar road from the airport into the city. Only some of it was not quite so familiar. That vast bulldozed expanse, waiting to be built on? That, Mark explained, was to be the site of the new Santa Justa station, which new train tracks would approach through tunnels from all directions and which would eventually offer a high speed rail link with Madrid. The old stations of San Bernardo and Plaza de Armas would soon be closed.

But not just yet. The old hummocky railway bridge still marked the beginning of the city proper, and there it was, just as James remembered it, unchanged since he had last seen it ten years before. Across the main boulevard, Menéndez Pelayo, narrow streets cut their way into the very heart of the city. Down each one ran lines of white and yellow houses that looked like carved cubes of marzipan and icing, pristine and sharp-focused. Orange trees, tight tidy pompoms of glossy dark green foliage, made neat rows along each pavement.

'We'll make a detour,' said Mark. 'For old times'sake. Fancy a beer in the Bodegón?'

'We'll never be able to park,' objected Alexa. But James's spontaneous noise of enthusiasm, a sort of exhalation of yeahwhynot?!, together with the fact that it was Mark who was at the wheel and therefore he who would have to drive round in circles looking for a space, overruled her and so Mark turned left along Meléndez Pelayo, then right, past the huge tobacco factory that Bizet had immortalised in Carmen, towards the Puerta de Jerez and the river. Jacaranda trees... James had forgotten the effect of them, at full dazzle in mid-May. The intensity of that blue made him gasp. He thought it was as if the sparkling sky had got entangled in the branches of the great trees – there were dozens upon dozens of them – and now shone out from among them in a blaze of blue. Mark turned in among the narrow streets near the Torre del Oro and, almost miraculously, found a parking space at once in Calle Temprado. They walked past the toffee-coloured house on the corner of Calle Santander where Alexa and her piano, then later

James and Borja, had lived. The house with the roof terrace. It was a shock to come upon it so suddenly like that, within minutes of arriving: an accidental result of the random distribution of parking spaces. James glanced up at the shuttered windows. 'Who lives there now?' But Alexa and Mark had no idea.

The Bodegón Torre del Oro now had smart new weather-doors in addition to its original set, but its cavernous interior was relatively unchanged. Relatively. 'The lapwing's gone,' James said. A stuffed one had previously peered beadily down from a high shelf behind the long bar. The same smoke-blackened hams – though surely not the very same? – hung from the beamed ceiling; only now, in a more health conscious age, it had been decreed by someone in Brussels that little plastic drip-cups should be pinned into the bottom of each one. A younger generation of white-aproned staff now attended behind the counter. They greeted Mark and Alexa by name. James, on the other hand, was to them just another tourist. That this barn-sized bar had been an extension of his home for years, that this place had been the scene of his emotional reconciliation with Borja after their break-up, played no part in their knowledge of it and would have no meaning for them even if he had been so foolish as to tell them. But for James, looking silently around him for a moment, the white painted pillars and arches, the high dark ceiling and the grave framed photographs of historic corridas still rang with an epic resonance.

Alexa ordered an orange juice, the two men a glass of draught San Miguel each. James stole a surreptitious glance at Mark's waistline. There was just the hint of spread, a faint convexity in the stomach region that had not been there before, but no suggestion of a gut or waistband overhang. Instinctively James tautened his own stomach muscles. He reckoned that he too was still in good shape in that department; but in his own case he felt that luck played a considerable part: he was pretty sure that Mark did not drink as much as he did.

'Remember how we planned that concert in here?' Alexa said.

'The one you didn't even play in the end,' James reminded her teasingly.

'I think I'd turned myself into a chrysalis at that point,' Alexa said. 'Having stopped trying to be a pianist, and not yet hatched out as a performing guitar player.' Talk turned to Alexa's concert giving. 'Playing's one thing,' Alexa said. 'Doing concerts is quite another. I don't think I could ever get tired of playing the guitar, ever explore its limits, ever stop developing. But it's all the other things, the travelling, the grotty little provincial theatres… Oh God, James, I didn't mean…' She put her hand to her face, though her eyes still smiled mischievously over her fingers.

James laughed. 'I know you didn't.'

'It's just that some places here are so badly organised. You must know the sort of thing. Contracts that don't make sense, having to set up lights yourself, making the platform look presentable, even having to go looking for a chair – can you imagine? – and then they pay you late and you have to keep hassling them for a cheque. At least I don't still play the piano. That would be even worse. I bring my own instrument, thank God, and do my own tuning.'

'Well,' said James, 'I can promise you an easier time when you come to the Regent. Professional lighting people and stage management. Do you know something?' He laughed as the bizarreness of this struck him. 'Right now, Borja's doing it. Stage management. At any rate he's working backstage, crewing a show.' Mark and Alexa's faces were matching pictures of amazement. It had been too complicated to explain over the phone. James told them the whole story that had led up to it: the flight to Casablanca, Borja's suspension from flying…

'Perhaps,' said Mark, when James had outlined Borja's present responsibilities, 'you should have assigned him to the fly floor. Made him feel at home.'

They drove back to Virgen de la Luz, one of a skein of threadlike alleys that tangled their way between the Barrio Santa Cruz and San Esteban. It was the same address that Mark had had when James first knew him: the raffish, stylish slum where James had lived as a temporary lodger twice. He had very contrasting memories of those two periods. The first time: he had been living there when Borja first arrived in Seville – to join James, it turned out, though Borja hadn't exactly realised that in advance. In this house they had made love for the first time. But then he had gone back there under very different circumstances three years later: homeless, and dependent on the kindness of Mark and Pippa, Mark's girlfriend at the time, during those desolate, anguished weeks – they were few in number but seemed unending as he lived through them – between the end of his affair with William and the moment in the Bodegón when Borja took him back.

How different the house was now, though. Mark and Alexa had bought the freehold and had the run of the whole building. The lorry drivers who had lived on the ground floor had long since departed on a cloud of cigarette smoke for the great truck-park in the sky, and their old room had become Alexa's studio. Their living space consisted of the two floors above that, just as it had done in the old days, but now all was clean and painted. Decent furniture had replaced the decaying bamboo cane arrangements that James remembered from his last stay. The kitchen and bathroom windows now had glass in them, not just iron bars for the wind to blow between, and the bathroom itself now seemed worthy of the name – no longer a chamber of horrors with mushrooms sprouting from the walls. But even as James looked round the house admiringly and commented on his hosts'good taste in the manner of its refurbishment, a part of him – a useless, nostalgic and sentimental part, no doubt – could not help remembering it as it was and regretting it just a little.

They took an early evening walk in the sun-filled Jardines de Murillo, on paths of gold sand that meandered among dark shrubberies and tall date palms, their crossways furnished with blue and white tiled benches and trickling fountains; they stopped off here and there for a visit to one bar or another, to drink a copita of chilled manzanilla and nibble at olives or lubinas, talking ceaselessly about old times, old friends. They finished the evening on the roof at Virgen de la Luz, still talking under the stars, while below them canaries sang from cages outside windows, wakeful with the streetlamps and the warmth.

What, James asked, of Karsten, Alexa's first guitar guru? At the time some had believed him to be her lover too, but they had been wrong. Was he still carving out a life in the hard stone quarry of the priestly calling? Yes he was, they told him. Still in his tough little parish in Gijón in the north. It was a tough and ill-paid living, and along with it he also taught the local school. James shook his head in respectful wonder at what other people were capable of.

But there was someone else James knew he would have to ask about, and at last James came to it as to a confrontation with himself that could no longer be put off. He had no reason to suppose that Mark would have the smallest idea what had happened to William – but at the same time, now that he was here, knew that the question could not go unasked. He felt uncomfortable introducing that particular name into the conversation: that two syllable word encompassed a whole world of events and emotions that had gone on to shape the subsequent direction of both his own life and of Borja's – before it had been firmly shut away for everyone's benefit in one of the past's closed boxes. Opening it up rendered him suddenly vulnerable and exposed, he discovered, not only to the reactions of his friends – curious, surprised, judgemental maybe – but to those of his own emotions. And yet he could do nothing against the primal urge to know. 'I suppose neither of you … ever heard anything of what became of William?' He had done it. He told himself it was a moment of catharsis. Mark and Alexa would say no, of course they knew nothing about what had happened to him. Then the name of William could be dropped for good, like a pebble into a well, where it would disappear for ever, and James need never think of him again. But this devoutly wished neat closure was denied him.

There was a moment's pause during which Mark glanced at Alexa. Then he answered. 'William lives in Seville.' There was another short pause, then he went on, trying to sound as if it were rather inconsequential, 'Quite funny, really. He teaches English at the British Institute. I run into him from time to time.'

James could not disguise his shock. His eyes widened, and his mouth opened, but for a moment he did not know what he was going to say. The others looked at him, not without sympathy, and waited. James could not get his mind round the idea of William teaching English classes – doing what had once been his own job; still less was he comfortable with the idea that he might himself run into William during the course of his stay in Seville. The British Institute was just a few hundred yards away from where they now sat. Involuntarily he looked across the rooftops in its direction. If they met –

heaven forbid – whatever would they say? William had been remarked by everyone all those years ago to be almost James's double. What would he look like now?

But when James's mouth at last framed the next question, it turned out to be quite another one. 'What about Paco?' he asked.

Mark's answer was the biggest surprise of all. 'They're still together.'

Paco was the older but richer man for whom William had left James. At that time James and William had thought of themselves as very young while Paco, already approaching forty, had seemed to belong to a different generation. Now, with the passing of the years, that age difference had telescoped, becoming something that signified far less. Paco would still be merely middle-aged by the time the rest of them attained the same distinction. James looked up. Above him spread the same Spanish sky, the same eternal moon-and-star-scape he had shared and meditated over, at different times, with both William and Borja. He felt dizzy. 'I think it's time I went to bed,' he said.

But bed offered no sanctuary from his thoughts. Quite the reverse. He was in the one room that had changed hardly at all since he had first slept in it. He undressed and got into the very same narrow bed in which he and Borja had had first made love, tumbling onto it together, tipsy from the Gypsy Bar; he discovering Borja's nakedness like a new thing, the wonderful palm tree pattern of hair on his chest, his sturdy, eager cock, the firm buttocks and thighs…

Every detail of Borja came before his eyes just then, every physical aspect at every stage of their life together: a lifetime's photo album of the memory. But not just snapshots, not just the visual, not just the physical. Everything they had experienced together gathered all at once into his mind just then, jostling for place, like the fast rewind of a life that the dying are said to see. What was all this about? he just managed to ask himself, what was happening? He must have drunk more than he'd realised. To his astonishment he was starting to cry. Borja was miles away, hundreds of miles away, at home alone with someone else, someone he, James, had nearly ended up in bed with on the comet-tail of an evening, not very long ago, when both had drunk too much. James tried to see Nick's face. Unlike Borja's, though, it would not come, except in pieces, and those in absurdly accurate detail: the point where the earlobe joined the cheek, the bridge of his spectacles and nose, the lashes of one eye.

Now Borja and Nick were together at Sevenscore. He was in Seville, and William's workplace just a hundred yards away. Without his noticing it, still less meaning it to happen, his world had turned itself upside down. He turned his face towards his pillow, and snuffled at it, animal-like and desperate, as if trying to catch the youthful Borja's honey-and-milk scent upon it after all the years.

In the morning Alexa had to practise. She was doing Rodrigo's Concierto de Aranjuez. It was not a new work for her: she had performed it many times before. But practice was an activity without end. It could no more be said ever to be done than the Forth Bridge could ever consider itself painted. The meeting of the trust would not be until the afternoon – Andalucían afternoon, that is; in Britain its starting time would suggest early evening. This left James free for most of the day to re-explore Seville with Mark. The only child of wealthy parents who were both dead, Mark was in the enviable position of not having to work too often or too hard – hence his freedom to spend time with James this morning.

'I still do a little teaching,' Mark told him, as they set off, somewhat randomly, into the familiar maze of streets with their mesmeric names: San Esteban, Aguilas, Almirante Hoyos, Virgenes... 'A couple of private students. One very rich, charming lady. I call her the Infanta. She loves her lessons, which is fortunate, as she makes no kind of progress whatever. I think she might stay a student for ever and ever. I do the odd lecture at the British Institute – on topical American issues, which is weird because it's a country I know less and less about as the years pass.'

'And no doubt talk about with ever-increasing authority and confidence?'

'Too right.' Mark gave a snort of laughter. 'Oh, and I write a monthly Letter from Spain for what used to be my local newspaper back in Oakland.'

It was on the tip of James's tongue to ask him if he still wrote poetry, but he decided to leave the question unasked for now. They were turning into Calle Federico Rubio just at that moment. There was the very front door of the British Institute where Mark sometimes lectured and – incredibly – William now taught. Would they bump into him on the doorstep? James felt his muscles tense. He even peered through the wrought-iron grille, which was standing open, into the airy, elegant patio that lay like a cloister court at the heart of the old building. He saw no-one.

The narrow streets opened out at last into the broader Calle Mateos Gago, which wore an orderly row of orange trees down each side of it: viewed down the street the rows of trees looked like two strips of green braid along the frontages of the marzipan and sugar-icing houses. At the bottom end of the vista rose the end wall of the cathedral and, towering above, the pink filigree brickwork of the Moorish Giralda. 'I'd forgotten how magic it was,' said James.

They climbed the Giralda together, glancing through key-hole windows at the tracery of the cathedral's roof buttresses as they passed them. The little russet and blue kestrels that James remembered were still in residence, peering from holes in the masonry, and hunting, mewing and screaming in their darting flight, among the spires. On the platform at the top, just below the massed ranks of bells, they marvelled at the cityscape spread out below them. No longer white and yellow, the centre of Seville was a red ochre acreage of tiled rooftops that hotly returned the sun's fixed stare. A little way off, the gardens of the Alcázar were an oasis of green behind their Moorish, pointy-hatted, battlements. The view slid away towards hazy suburbs, beyond them the flat expanses of the Guadalquivir basin, and finally the picture came to a stop against its moulded frame of distant mountains, half seen, half imagined in the blue distance. He would come back here with Borja, James told himself. He felt the need to do so with an urgency that hurt.

Later they loitered along the way to the María Luisa Park, pausing once for a beer as they came across a kiosk and tables under the trees. Then they sprawled in the sunshine on the brick and blue tile benches along the great colonnade of the Plaza de España.

Above and behind them a voice called suddenly in accented English, 'Hey! You speak French?'

Looking up, James made out the figure of a young man who looked as if he might have been North African. Proud of his ability to do so, he answered in French that, yes, he did.

'Ah, c'est bon,' said the young man and went on, in French: did James know the Museum of Murillo? Was it far from here?

James wrestled with the questions for a moment. He knew the Gardens of Murillo, of course. They had crossed them to arrive here, as well as taking their evening stroll through them the previous night. But as for a museum…

'You're sure you mean a museum, not the gardens?' he queried.

The young man began some convoluted answer. Then Mark yelled suddenly, 'Your bag!'

James spun round where he sat. A foot away from him a second curly-black-haired youth was in the act of lifting his backpack from the other side of the brick bench. Although startled, the boy nevertheless followed his action through, turned away from James and began to run, the bag clutched to his chest. The bag contained nothing at all of any value: a couple of oranges, sun-cream, a comb and that morning's edition of El Pais, yet it suddenly mattered more than anything, equally to James and to its new owner. In the same moment in which the boy had picked up the bag and begun to run, James, without reflection, had sprung over the bench and was in high-speed pursuit. He was conscious of Mark sprinting along behind him, half a second away. And in another half second James had caught up with the thief, laid hold of him, both arms around his neck, had seized the backpack and thrown it back to Mark. Who said that playing rugby would never come in useful in later life? Now Mark held the bag and James found himself with a very young man in his arms, and an extraordinary tangle of feelings to try and make sense of. First was pure rage. Though it could hardly be on account of the near loss of a comb and two oranges. It could only be because he had let himself be tricked so easily. He found himself rooting, almost automatically, through the boy's pockets, as if his subconscious suspected the youth of having picked the wallet from James's own pocket during his split second of opportunity. He did this roughly, finding for the first time in adult life that his fingers itched to clout another person about the head. The next thing, and again it took less than half a second for this to happen, was the realisation that the boy felt wonderful to hold. Now Mark was at his side, shouting something. For the first time in three seconds James made a conscious decision. He let the boy go. Otherwise… The two alternatives his body seemed to be getting ready for might have come to appear disproportionate when viewed in retrospect.

'You let him go,' said Mark superfluously, as the youth went sprinting off towards the sheltering shade of the colonnades and his now vanished accomplice.

'Yeah, well,' said James.

They returned to their place in the sun and resumed their interrupted moment of indolence. The only thing that was noticeably different was that James now kept one strap of his newly precious backpack wound tightly around his hand.

Then Mark said, 'I've been waiting for the right moment to tell you that Alexa and I have decided to tie the knot.'

James was stunned into silence. Then, after a few moments, 'Wow,' he said. Then, 'I meant congratulations actually.' He rumpled Mark's hair. Then he thought of something. 'But I haven't seen any sign of a ring. I mean, I'd have noticed if…'

'Fair enough.' Mark smiled a bit awkwardly. 'She always takes it off to practise, and then she forgets to put it back on again.' James thought that the Freudians would have had a field day with that, but he let the thought pass unspoken.

The first meeting of the Eulogio Pérez Cabrera Memorial Trust took place in the office of a lawyer in Calle Cuna – 'Cradle Street', the site of a long-vanished orphanage. Although the office James and Alexa were shown into was quite spacious, by the time all the trustees had arrived it was decidedly cramped. James had not given much thought to the meeting in advance; he had really come along for fun, to offer moral support to Alexa in case she should need it; and the most obvious fact had not crossed his mind: namely that the meeting would be conducted in Spanish. His own Spanish was very rusty. He was introduced to the trustees'lawyer and to a selection of Spanish pianists and conductors whose names were unknown to him. One silver-haired man introduced himself as the principal of the music college near Seville where Eulogio had taught the piano at the beginning of his career and again at the end of it. Another man who was with him said, looking a little flushed, that he was an amateur of the piano – 'You must not, absolutely must not, suppose a professional' – who had long ago been a pupil of Eulogio's. James looked at the two of them a little more carefully and guessed they were a couple.

The meeting proper kicked off when the lawyer, a large and jowly man with sleepy-lidded eyes, squeezed himself into the small space between the wall of his office and his extremely large desk. Everybody else sat on chairs around the walls and – these seats the last to go – in the middle of the room. The lawyer thanked everyone for coming and explained that he only expected to take the chair for this first meeting. By the end of it they would, he hoped, have elected a more permanent presidente, as well as a tesorero and secretario. He smiled a bit effortfully. It was a weary smile that seemed to say that he did not really expect his hope to triumph over his experience of similar situations. They would also need to agree on a constitution and the aims of the trust.

James suppressed a groan. He had long experience of how business was conducted in this part of the world.

The meeting would go on for ever. But, to his considerable relief, Alexa spoke up. 'There are more important things to discuss, surely. Everyone knows the trust has two simple aims. First, to keep Eulogio's work and memory alive by re-releasing his best recordings in a memorial edition.' James's mind went back to the unlistenable tape of Schubert that Nick had played him – and the events that had set in train. 'The other,' Alexa went on, 'is to continue his work of encouraging new talent by funding scholarships and whatever other schemes the trust may agree on.' She paused and looked round. 'Obviously none of us should expect to benefit personally.' Heads nodded in agreement. 'As for a constitution,' she turned to the lawyer, 'couldn't you just draft the simplest, simplest form of one – you must have templates of these things – and let us agree it at the next meeting? If all of us unqualified people start discussing it now…' She didn't need to finish. Again everyone agreed. More volubly this time.

The music college principal spoke. He asked all those present who knew Eulogio's discography to submit some proposals for recordings to be included in the new collection. 'Perhaps we could all spend some time between now and the next meeting with our headphones on?' he suggested. James, who was feeling decidedly out of his depth and possessed neither recordings of Eulogio nor the informed musicality to assess them – nor even headphones – nevertheless nodded his head along with everyone else.

The discussion now moved on to the scholarships and other schemes that the trust would endow. The principal of the music college wanted the trust to fund two scholarships to the college. A concert pianist from Toledo wanted to set up a summer school in that city, to be funded by the trust and taught by himself. Another pianist from Murcia had been planning an almost identical scheme for Murcia. 'Absurd,' said the man from Toledo. 'Murcia gets far too hot in August.' The lawyer, together with another man who had not spoken till now, proposed a piano competition, to be named in honour of Eulogio and administered jointly by themselves...

Eventually James was asked if he had a proposal to make. He hadn't expected to have to say anything much at this meeting; now he regretted not having discussed any kind of strategy with Alexa in advance – there had been too many other things on his mind. 'Look,' he found himself saying in a sudden rush to the head of Spanish, 'I really have no suggestion to make. It's not at all my field. I'm here to give Alexa my support, that's all. I suggest we give my turn to speak to Alexa and listen twice as carefully to her.' To his astonishment, this unplanned speech was given a round of applause. That never happened at board meetings of the Regent.

So Alexa spoke again. She got to her feet, she spoke, and took command of the room. A competition bearing Eulogio's name would not honour but insult his memory, she insisted: he had been a fierce opponent of competitive pianism; did nobody remember that? As for training courses, what would be the point of them if Eulogio were no longer around to lead them himself? And, although a scholarship was an excellent idea, wouldn't it be better to fund one scholarship at the prestigious London college with which Eulogio had been associated for most of his working life, rather than two places at an obscure school in Andalucía? She sat down again.

At first James could do nothing except sit back and observe the storm that followed. Even Alexa was content to let the others deal with the fallout from her intervention, adding only an occasional footnote to what she had already said. Yet after only a few minutes James was astonished to find himself rising to his feet and calling loudly amidst the tumult for Alexa to be given the position of chair of the trust. He was even more surprised then to hear other voices taking his proposal up. 'Alexa. Presidenta. Si! Si!' The meeting did not go on much longer after that. But it broke up surprisingly amicably and everyone, James and Alexa included, headed for the nearest café-bar.

'You were amazing,' James said to Alexa. He had never seen that side of her before, only guessed at it, deduced it from the events of her life and career as seen from outside. 'As for me, I don't know what I was doing there.'

'I'll tell you a secret,' Alexa told him. 'I don't think I could have gone through that performance, or agreed to become presidenta if you hadn't been with me. I told you at the outset I needed moral support.'

'And I thought you were joking,' said James.

The bar was a dark and atmospheric place: the kind of Andalucían bar that has remained almost unchanged in a hundred and fifty years, whose walls are lined with time-blackened barrels, and behind whose counter – because no woman's hand has been allowed to touch the hallowed place – bunches of rusty keys, and rags, and screwdrivers, and dead light bulbs all jostle for space among the dusty bottles. It was the kind of place in which James had always felt at home.

Because the meeting had been short and the evening was still young it was no surprise to find the bar almost empty when they arrived. Only one person stood at the bar, his back to them as they came in. But even from this angle, and despite the passage of years, James knew at once who it was – recognised that back view with a shock that was like a thump in the stomach. The standing figure began to turn its head towards the large incoming group. William.

SIXTEEN

The new stage manager had started at the beginning of that week, overlapping for a couple of days with Sally before she finally left on a tide of goodwill, promises to keep in touch, and drinks in the Post Horn. The following day Mike the production manager had hung around the theatre during the evening show just in case the new man might need any shepherding – which he did not – but had discreetly faded from the scene by the end of Thursday's matinee. Thursday was the day James had left for Seville. And it was just before Thursday's evening show that the new stage manager, a bulky, ginger-haired man with a decisive manner and answering to the name of Adrian, decided to move a piano.

The show was now running very smoothly. The turnaround of the set could be accomplished quickly and easily at the end of the matinee, instead of forming a major assault course to be embarked upon at the half-hour call. This meant that the stage crew, assembling for their official call at five minutes to seven, had nothing very much to do until the first scene change some forty minutes later. They were available, numerous and muscular, and meanwhile there was an upright piano which needed shifting down from the rehearsal room, which was on the fourth floor of the next-door building. The building was due for major refurbishment, starting the following week.

Accordingly all the boys in black – including Borja and Nick and Smut – found themselves marching out from backstage, through the pass door, into the auditorium, then through the foyer, against the tide of the arriving audience, and out of the front doors into the street. It was while elbowing his way through the scrum of playgoers in the foyer with his seven black-clad comrades that Borja began to realise that Adrian's plan, which had looked intelligent in theory – using a rare over-supply of manpower during a quiet period to deal with an otherwise problematic heavy-lifting exercise – might be prone to execution risk. The second intimation of this came when they entered the next-door building, pressed the light switch and nothing happened. The contractors had stolen a march on them and cut off the power.

Having brought his men this far, and being very new in the job into the bargain, Adrian felt unable to call the expedition off, and so urged everyone onwards and upwards – to move the piano down the stairs in the dark. There was some muttering and swearing as everyone bumped into everyone else on the way up. There was a lot more swearing once the piano had been located and had begun its descent, pinning people against groaning banisters, threatening to separate limbs from bodies. But at the bottom of the first flight of stairs the instrument stuck fast in the angle and refused to budge another inch. From below somebody called up to say that the banisters on one of the lower flights were only partially attached. And now Borja suddenly found himself bellowing, in a voice of fury that nobody present had ever heard before or even imagined him capable of, that the whole scheme was complete lunacy and should be abandoned, together with the piano, there and then. Adrian, invisible in the dark, did not try to gainsay him: seven pairs of boots went crashing down the stairs and there were murmurs of appreciation for Borja's having voiced out loud everyone else's unspoken thoughts.

Having reached ground level those seven pairs of boots headed towards the dim light of the street. All blundered through a deep pile of swept-up rubbish and somebody kicked over a large tin of something. Nobody stopped to investigate. It was fifteen minutes to curtain-up. No time to walk round the building to the stage door. The crew shouldered their way through the packed foyer like storm troopers, creating ripples of apprehension as they went, then trekked round the horseshoe corridor behind the dress circle. Finally, like genies disappearing back into their bottle, they filed through the pass door and – from the audience's point of view – into the oblivion of backstage.

Borja and the others arrived in the green room. Microseconds later so did Jack the front of house manager, in full dress shirt and a crimson bow tie which tonight was almost exactly matched by his face. He was beside himself. From the front door to the pass door ran a hundred feet of red carpet, and it now bore the imprints of seven pairs of feet, etched in white paint. Furthermore, the audience was now in the process of spreading it all over the rest of the front of house areas, the way ants will obligingly spread a drop of poison throughout an entire nest.

Borja looked down at his boots, taking in his black jeans on the way. He was piebald to the knee. Uncharacteristically, he swore. In Spanish. First at Jack. Then at Adrian. Then at the whole assembled company. Shaking with rage he climbed the stairs up to the stage door (Maria, phone your agent) and exited into the street. Having got that far, he looked about him, uncertain where to be angry next. Almost opposite stood the open door of the Post Horn. It would do as well as anywhere else. To his momentary surprise he saw Guy, alone at the bar, drinking a whisky. Storming up to him, and only just remembering in time to put this in English, he shouted, 'Your new stage manager's a fucking idiot. He needs his head looking at. Or better still, removing entirely. There's paint all over your bloody theatre!' He looked down at himself for a second, then added bathetically, 'And over me.'

Guy had every right to ask him what he was doing off theatre premises after the half-hour call and order him back to his post. Of course he did no such thing. He turned to the barman and ordered a large whisky for Borja instead. 'They can handle the first scene change without you by now, I expect,' he said placidly. 'It's not quite the same as handling take-off in a Boeing. Strictly between you and me, though. Don't tell the others I said so. And talking of the others…' he put the glass of whisky and ice into Borja's hand, '…have you made young Nick yet?'

'Oh for God's sake,' said Borja, appalled. 'Surely you don't think… Surely people aren't saying…'

'Get real. Of course they are. You must know about theatre gossip by now. Nick adores you, everyone can see that. And people aren't judgemental, you know. All the same, if I've put two and two together and made sixteen I sincerely apologise.' He took a swallow of whisky. Borja took two. 'Not an obvious beauty, young Nick. Not a centre-fold. And yet he somehow grows on you, don't you think?'

Borja couldn't deny that he had made the same discovery. He had also discovered that his surprising volcanic outburst of temper had subsided as quickly as it had arisen. He managed a smile. 'I like him, it's true,' he said. 'But please don't read too much into that. If people need something to gossip about, that's up to them. But they'll have to invent their own plot-lines and script, because Nick and I will not be providing them.' Borja flashed a grin that Guy had not often seen before.

'Well, again, I'm sorry if I got that wrong,' said Guy. 'And I'm sorry about the new stage manager too. I'll get Mike to rap his knuckles.'

'I think that Jack may be doing just that right now.'

'Anyway, Adrian was more your beloved James's appointment than mine, so you can talk to him about it when he gets back from Spain.' Guy smiled mischievously. 'Maybe we should have given the job to your handsome captain since he turned up so obligingly, if confusingly, at the interviews. What was his name again?'

'Andy,' said Borja. The name came out awkwardly. He hadn't pronounced it out loud for nearly a month. 'Anyway, you may have the chance to employ him after all. If the enquiry goes against us, you may find both of us coming after you for jobs.'

At that moment a figure appeared in the doorway, looking anxious and breathless. It was Nick. He stopped where he was, wide-eyed at the sight of Borja calmly drinking whisky with Guy in the pub three minutes before curtain-up. Guy beckoned him over and then checked his wristwatch in one follow-through movement. 'Relax. Have a whisky. You've time for just one. First scene change is still thirteen minutes away.' He called across the bar for a drink for Nick, and then took a phone from his pocket and called the stage door to report their position.

'Shit,' said Nick quietly to Borja while Guy was doing this. 'I walked right into this. I was just worried about you and where you might have got to. I didn't mean to…'

Borja cut him off. 'It's all OK. The storm is over. No windows broken. No-one's in trouble, and certainly not you.'

'I've never seen you angry like that before,' said Nick, wonderingly. 'I hope I never find myself on the receiving end, that's all.' He sounded quite impressed. And something in Borja was deeply stirred, because Nick had broken one of the strictest rules in the book to come and look for him. Nick adores you, Guy had said. Everyone can see that.

After the show Borja drove back to Sevenscore with Nick. He had been expecting to have to chauffeur Neville as well but this evening that proved unnecessary as Neville had been invited to spend the night in the dangerous vicinity of the cinema. When Neville announced this in the Post Horn, Guy had caught Borja's eye and raised his own in a some-people-just-won't-be-told sort of way. And Neville asked Borja if he'd mind feeding his cat in the morning.

Nick had volunteered to cook something – which was generous of him, since he was generally working longer hours than Borja was. Borja accepted the offer, knowing that he would give Nick pleasure by doing so but privately deciding to invite Nick out to dinner in a restaurant the following night. It was the first time they had arrived home alone together at the Court House: something neither of them had given any thought to until they went in through the kitchen door and the suddenly switched-on light caught them peering, blinking, at each other, surprised and self-conscious at finding themselves in this new situation. Borja dispelled the self-consciousness swiftly by pouring them both a glass of wine.

Nick's dish was a sort of pilaff, with chicken livers, sliced pigeons'breasts, rice, mint and peas. Slightly exotic but mercifully quick and simple once the initial cutting up had been done. Pigeons were not a rarity at Sevenscore. Locals at the Rose and Castle would sell them, dead but still fully clothed, for a pound or two a brace and it was the work of a moment to rip away their pink and grey feather coats.

As they sat at the kitchen table and talked over their glasses of wine, Nick occasionally rising to adjust the gas flame on the hob, Borja was conscious, not for the first time, of the broken stitching in one side-seam of Nick's jeans. He had to overcome an embarrassing urge to offer to do a quick repair with needle and thread, unaware that James had had to fight off the same over-protective urge a month before.

'I think there's rats in the attic above my room,' said Nick conversationally as he washed some lettuce leaves for a salad.

'No there aren't,' said Borja authoritatively. 'It's only birds. They're nesting. Starlings and swifts. Birds sound like rats. If it's mice it sounds like spaniels. You've only got rats if it sounds like a football match.'

'I suppose I have to take your word for that. You being a farm boy and all that. Funny, I never think of there being farms in Spain.'

'Funnier that you don't.' Borja was both surprised and amused.

'Of course James is a country boy too,' Nick went on. 'The Sussex Downs.'

'Cuckmere Haven. High and Over. Alfriston.' Borja spoke the place names as if he were trying them out for inclusion in a poem. 'Yes, it's one of the things we were surprised to find we had in common when we started getting to know each other. We discovered we'd both spent our childhoods wondering what town kids found to do in their spare time.'

'Most of us,' said Nick unnecessarily, 'asked the question the other way round.'

Borja began to set cutlery on the plain scrubbed kitchen table, but then Nick said, 'Oh come on, let's eat properly,' and took a cloth into the big living room and spread it on the polished mahogany table there, the way they did when all three of them, James, Borja and Nick, were eating en famille. 'After all, it's the first time the two of us have had dinner alone together.'

Borja made no comment, only reflecting privately as he helped to set the table that he would not have dared to come out with the innocent remark that Nick had just made.

He would have to choose tomorrow night's restaurant with care, he thought, as he began to swallow forkfuls of Nick's pigeon pilaff. He himself was an OK cook, James too. But Nick's cooking was in a slightly higher class: Borja had been forced to admit it a few times before. Tonight he had excelled himself. Borja did not suppose it was by accident. 'Tomorrow I'm taking you out for a meal after the show. OK?' The invitation had been easier to make than he'd expected. And Nick repaid him at once with an uncalculated smile and a faint pinkening of the cheeks.

As they were finishing their meal, a sound started in the silent room that made them look up. It came from not far away, loud and brisk, rhythmic and insistent, like the ring of a phone. After a moment's puzzlement Borja relaxed with a little snort of a laugh. 'It's the cricket. First time this year. Now we know spring's arrived.'

'A cricket? Are you having me on? A cricket on the hearth like they have in books?'

'Why not?' said Borja. 'Life's not unlike what happens in books, after all.'

'Only if the books are any good,' said Nick.

'No. Only if the lives are any good.'

'I think you may be talking rubbish.' Nick had consumed just the right amount of wine to say this sweetly.

'You may be right. Let's go and look for it.'

They crawled on hands and knees around the inlaid Dutch chest towards the empty fireplace and were rewarded with the sight of a shiny brown insect, the size of a small cigar and bristling with whiskers and pistons, bustling away towards a dark recess behind the fire-back.

'That's something,' said Nick, getting to his feet. 'But I think I can beat him at his own game. Leave the washing-up. There's something I want to play to you on the piano.' He led the way towards the garden door, picked up the big key from the hall table, and led the way out into the garden.

It was a clear night and surprisingly warm for mid-May. The last few days had delivered a steady rise in temperature and so when they unlocked the West Pavilion and went inside they found it quite pleasantly warm for the first time since Nick had arrived at the end of winter.

Nick chose to play one of Beethoven's shortest and simplest Bagatelles. He chose it carefully as it was a piece in which he could demonstrate his capacity for sensitivity and depth of feeling … just in case Borja had not yet perceived the extent to which he had those things in him. The simple melody was adorned with a trill, first in the treble and then echoed in the bass, that Nick knew how to make as poignant and tender as the heartbeat of a fledgling bird. The piece was finished almost as soon as it had begun. Nick's audience of one was moved, just as Nick had intended him to be, and as Borja realised Nick had intended. That realisation did nothing to diminish the moment: rather the reverse. 'I've never heard you play better,' Borja said simply. Then, 'Could you play some Bach for me?' He didn't know why he said that. He wasn't a particular fan of Bach's keyboard music; the request just seemed to come from somewhere.

'Bach?' Nick was slightly taken aback. 'At this time of night? After beer and wine… Wait a minute, though. Here's something I might be able to manage.' He rummaged among the pile of music on top of the piano: the pile had been growing slowly with each of the weekend returns to his parents'home that he had made over the last few months.

'Italian Concerto, slow movement,' Nick announced. Then he played it. The left hand began with muffled funerary drumbeats, but then the right hand picked up a tune and started to fly it like a kite: it rose uncertainly at first and then began to soar, diving down unexpectedly from time to time in strange swirls and twists before sailing aloft once more. It might have been, to the listener whose thoughts so tended, the progress of a soul, released from earth's dull gravity, making its faltering, wayward, but in the end triumphant way into the beyond. Borja listened in a state approaching shock. It was the piece Alexa had chosen to play to him all those years ago just after Rafael's death. He was sure he hadn't heard it since. But the harmonies and the memory of Alexa's playing, and the atmosphere of that moment had, in the intervening years, chiselled themselves into the depths of his being. Swirls of emotions, memories and thoughts had engulfed him by the time Nick finished. It was as if he were descending through turbulent cloud, direction-finding needles and compasses flicking wildly, uselessly, to and fro. 'Thank you,' he said finally, when he'd broken cloud and the gauges were starting to give normal readings again. 'I never need to hear you play better than that.' He felt a powerful urge to rush Nick into his arms, hold him and kiss him: an urge he only withstood by some complex conjuncture of accident and will. Then with a shock that was almost physical, and almost terrifying, he realised – or was his imagination playing a trick on him: one navigation aid still giving a false reading? – that Nick was expecting him to do just that. 'Come,' he said, turning to the door, overcome but still faintly aware of absurdly echoing Hamlet's uncle at the play,'We'd better go.'

Once outside the pavilion, 'You're not OK,' said Nick. 'I'm sorry.' Then he came out with what Borja would remember for ever as the epitome of Nick's endearing Nickness. 'Did I play the wrong thing?'

They turned down the steps that led to the bassin and walked slowly around its rectangular stone surround. The water gleamed softly like a bath of mercury from which the statuary fountain that was its centrepiece reared up in stark black silhouette. Borja told Nick, as they walked, about Rafael. How they had been at school and university together but never spoken in all those years. How they had met again when Rafael was a steward and Borja on his first ever flight. Had become lovers when James ran off to William. How quickly that had ended with Rafael's death in the Valencia air crash. How he and Alexa had talked a few days later – when she played to Borja the piece that Nick just had – and how Alexa's words had led him to take James back.

'Oh wow,' said Nick. He was wise enough to leave it at that.

'And that, more or less, is how I became a pilot. STARs. They join the dots and show us the ways – which are far from obvious.' Then he had to explain to Nick what STARs meant, as they ambled up and down the lawns among the silvered cypresses and marble statues. After that he felt the need to turn the conversation away from himself. 'Tell me what STAR led you into the theatre then.'

'I never thought of it as a star. But it was a light of a sort. It was just after I left university, and I'd been turned down for every job I'd applied for, and I was beginning to think I'd never get any sort of a job at all. I was walking round London with some old university friends. Exploring really, I suppose, because we didn't know London very well, any of us. It was about pub chucking-out time and the streets were dark. Suddenly a huge door in a black wall opened and light flooded out – a warm, golden light. Through the door – I didn't know it at the time but it was the dock door of Wyndham's Theatre – I could see the stage, and a set being struck, and beyond that the gilded dress circle and the warm red velvet. I looked at all that and … sounds silly I know, but … it looked like … home. I think a home was what I wanted. The friends I was with hardly noticed anything. At least, not till I shouted through the doorway to ask if they had any jobs going. Then they noticed. They thought I'd gone mad.'

Borja too found it difficult to imagine the rather quiet bespectacled young man at his side bawling, Give us a job, into a West End theatre's scene dock at midnight. But, 'I suppose I'd had rather a bit to drink,' Nick explained, and the scene became slightly easier to visualise. 'The amazing thing was, somebody shouted back. It was the theatre carpenter. He said if I was serious I had to come back and see him at ten the next morning – which was Sunday – when I was sober. Then there'd be a few days work. They were short of casuals for a get-in and fit-up. I didn't know any of those words but I could guess. And the next day I went along and started…' he gave a bit of a laugh, '…doing what you're doing now.'

Borja remembered now the impression the sight of the open dock doors at the Regent had made on him when he'd started work there in the small hours of a chill morning a few weeks ago: the warm light spilling out into the night-dark street.

Nick continued. 'It was a home I wanted. Not so much a job: a home. I suppose I've been looking for one ever since. All the time. Only sometimes now I feel as if I've found it – here – with you and James.'

Borja didn't attempt to say anything.

'I shouldn't have said that, of course,' said Nick, feeling the need to backtrack and trying to sound tough and matter-of-fact. 'That wasn't fair. It's your home and

James's. I've no right to take advantage of something you've worked at for years. …I'm not talking about the material side, obviously.'

'I know,' said Borja. 'I understand. But you're not being unfair to us, to me and James. What you said is actually very flattering – to both of us, and James would say the same if he were here.' If he hasn't already done so, Borja half thought, but he suppressed the thought as unworthy and didn't pass it on to Nick. 'No,' he went on, 'it's yourself you're being unfair to. I know you split up with your girlfriend not so long ago. And I know – because I can see it – that that's left you very bruised, much more so than you'd ever admit to me or even to yourself. But listen. It's time to start again. Get out there. I'm not saying: get out of Sevenscore; only, find a new girlfriend; get back in the…' He interrupted himself with a snort of laughter. 'I won't risk any grotesque metaphors.' And they both laughed.

They steered their way between old brick walls into the orchard. 'It's a beautiful place,' said Nick, using the remark to bounce the conversation off in a new direction, 'but why are you still renting after all this time? I mean, you and James have been together that long and you can't exactly be short of money, being a pilot.'

'Well,' said Borja, charmed rather than affronted by Nick's directness, just as James had been a few weeks before, 'the first thing is – look around you – we'd never be able to buy a place like this. The second thing is – which you so tactfully reminded me – I earn rather more than James does. That sometimes causes difficulties when partners decide to buy into property together. And the third thing is my Spanish family. Whether I like it or not, I'm part of an old-fashioned farming family. I had to fight hard to exchange my share of the farm for the money to train as a pilot. Funnily enough, if I made a lot of money and lost it in the casinos they might be more comfortable with that than if I spent it on a property that wasn't part of the farm. Farms are firms, you see, and families are funny about them.'

'Well then,' said Nick – and Borja could sense one of his bright ideas coming along, 'why don't you and James go to Denmark or somewhere and get married? If you were an officially married couple, your family could hardly object to your wanting to get a place on your own.'

'Nick, Nick, for God's sake!' Borja couldn't entirely suppress a laugh. 'You haven't seen my family, or met my mother. They're not just old-fashioned: they're very religious, observant Catholics from rural Castile. That doesn't make them saintly – far from it – but my mother could no more come to terms with her youngest son marrying a man than with his eating babies. She just about tolerates the idea that I live with James … but even that's only on the unspoken condition that she never has to meet him.'

'That's very sad,' said Nick.

'OK then,' said Borja combatively. 'Imagine yourself in my position. No, not even that. Imagine yourself in yours, with your own, presumably, liberal parents. Think very hard and try to imagine the scene if you were to tell them that you were engaged to be married … to another bloke. Just … try.'

There was silence for a moment as Nick exercised his imagination as per Borja's instructions. Then, 'OK, you win,' he said. 'If I was gay, I mean if I was – then yes, that might be very hard for me too.' He looked at Borja. 'I was being silly, wasn't I?'

'I'm not sure if you were,' said Borja. 'Maybe the wine was. Anyway, have you looked at your watch lately?' Nick did. It was two-fifteen. 'And you're in at what time in the morning?'

'Not until you are, for once, so ha-ha. There's time for a lie-in for both of us.'

'Good. And I'm pleased for you. They work you kids very hard.'

'Talk to James about that,' said Nick cheekily.

They had come back, at the end of their meandering circuit, to the door of the Court House and it seemed to both of them the right moment to go inside and part for the night. Inside the door they stopped in the small hallway where their paths would diverge, Nick's to the right and the Chinese bedroom, Borja's to the left, across the living room and into his and James's 'master'bedroom. And then, before he had had time to consult his better judgement, Borja found himself giving Nick a goodnight kiss after all – a platonic peck on the side of his neck. He did not wait to see if Nick would return it – or not return it; neither possibility was without awkward implications – but departed for the safer reassurance of his own bedroom and his own particular side of the four-poster bed.

SEVENTEEN

'Hallo William.'

It was a far greater surprise for William than it was for James. James at least had had twenty-four hours to digest the fact that William lived in Seville and might be run into just like this – had even half-looked for him when passing his place of work earlier that day. William had had no such warning. 'Jesus Christ,' he said. 'I can't believe it. Jacobite!'

'Orange.' Years ago they had called each other by those names; they hardly remembered why. Now they both stood rooted to the spot. How did you greet a former lover after all this time? Someone you'd slept with, lived with and then broken with entirely. Someone you'd betrayed your partner for. Did you embrace, shake hands, or what? Neither of them knew what the etiquette was, any more than they knew what they felt. Slowly, stiffly, they shook hands, staring steadily, silently into each other's faces, while around them the rest of the committee chirruped and chattered and ordered beers and coffees, oblivious – except for Alexa – to the gravity of the moment just then unfolding in their midst.

As far as James was aware, he had not changed in the slightest in the eleven years since he'd last seen William. William on the other hand had. He no longer looked like James's double, as he once had done. Furthermore, he looked all of his thirty-five years and ten months. James didn't even need to do the calculation. And, as he gazed in rather troubled wonder at the face before him, James felt quite certain that identical thoughts were passing through William's mind with regard to him.

'What are you doing in Seville?' William at last spoke again. James told him, indicated the people around him, introduced Alexa. Had they met before? They didn't think so, they both said, as they shook hands with the wariness of people who know each other by sight and have heard a great deal about each other but are not going to say so. And then, as if suddenly remembering simultaneously that they were British, all three of them said in chorus some version of What do you want to drink? and were then relieved at the excuse for laughter that the subsequent impasse provided.

Moments later a perfectly normal social situation had developed in which people who knew each other were exchanging banalities with people who didn't, and James found himself contemplating – in the part of his mind that stood apart from the small-talk he was engaged in – the extraordinary, mysterious fact that in the middle of this group stood two people, William and himself, who had once been madly, stupidly, in love and now were not.

William already knew, through Mark, that James still lived with Borja, in England, that he managed a theatre there, and that Borja was a pilot. James likewise knew, and from the same source, where William lived and what he did for a living. But they went through all this again as a kind of ritual and all because – apart from exchanging a little more detailed information about the houses they lived in, and William was genuinely interested and impressed when James described Sevenscore – they found that they had no idea, after all this time, what else to say.

Night after night, in a different, shared time, they had lain naked in each other's arms and then joined more intimately than even that. Now they stood talking together, so very separate, so very clothed. There came into James's mind the image of the tombs of Ferdinand and Isabella, in the Capilla Real in Granada. Together William and he had seen them during their visit to the city that calamitous weekend. They had commented on the cold separateness of those two plain coffins, oblivious to the fate that awaited their own, shortly to be ended, heedless joy. That lead-encased separateness would soon be for them.

James answered William's questions about the future viability of the subsidised theatre in Great Britain and wondered how and why he had ever wanted this man so much. The emotions of that time were inconceivable now: as impossible of recapture, even in the form of memories, as forgotten dreams. He had no doubt, as he listened to William talking about teaching – William teaching English! – that William felt the same.

Alexa found the right moment to ask, social antennae most delicately deployed, if William would like to join Mark and James and herself for dinner a little later. To no-one's surprise he said no; he was meeting Paco later. The party began to split up; Alexa and James were going to move on to the Bodegón to meet Mark. James said he would catch them up in a few minutes if Alexa wanted to go on ahead, which Alexa had no difficulty in interpreting, and a few moments later he was alone in the bar with William.

'And Paco?' James asked. The question sounded almost brutal. He added, 'Mark tells me you're still together.'

William gave a surprised little laugh. 'You didn't expect that, did you?' He looked up at James challengingly. 'To tell you the truth, neither did I at first. Not for a long time in fact. It wasn't like you and Borja, planning a lifetime together from the day you met. But the years went by and, amazingly, there we were, together still, and liking it that way. It was never a love affair, exactly. Not at all like with…' He aborted the sentence. For both their sakes, he could not say, with you. 'It's something quite different. It's on its own terms. It's good. You can't compare one relationship, one way of finding happiness, with another.' James nodded a silent agreement. 'We're not going to leave each other now.' He shrugged. 'Es la vida. That's life.'

'You must give Paco my love,' said James. 'In those words, I mean. Not just 'James says hallo'.'

William smiled wryly. 'If he'll have it, you can say the same to Borja. I have a clear memory of what he looked like and sounded like. He was a very, very beautiful young man.'

'Still is.' James kept finding himself staring at William and having, for politeness's sake, to relax his gaze. He could not quite believe that this conversation was taking place. 'I guess I'd better go and join Alexa and Mark,' he mumbled awkwardly. He didn't really want still to be here when Paco arrived. 'Did you know they're getting married?'

William showed his surprise. 'No!'

'Well, keep it under wraps. Mark'll want to tell you in his own time, no doubt.'

'Tell them I'm very happy for them. No, I'll tell them when the time comes. Very happy indeed.'

'And you are for yourself?' It was a very intimate question. James was sure he had no right to ask it.

William smiled. 'I am. Just as you are, only in a different way, I guess. But don't doubt it.'

They said their goodbyes with a handshake and James turned to go. From the door the scene looked the same as when he had first entered the bar, as if the clock had been turned back twenty minutes – or twelve years: William leaning on the counter, idly exchanging a word with the barman, waiting for Paco, his back to James in an empty bar. James remembered how the loneliness of William had so touched him at the time of their first meeting. For the first time this evening he remembered – was again in touch with – the reason why he had fallen in love with him. He paused for a second in the open doorway. Then he walked out through it. It was one in a long line of uncomfortable partings from William, only this one, James thought now – with the kind of certainty that had used to be the preserve of Borja in his second-sighted youth – would really be the last.

He walked out of the bar and made his way along the palm-lined riverfront paseo towards the Tower of Gold, now lit broadside by the evening sun.

EIGHTEEN

In the time that followed the traumas of Casablanca, the first thought that had flashed into Borja's mind on waking, whatever he might or might not consciously wish, was the thought of Andy. Not any particular memory, or image of his face, but simply the fact of his existence, which seemed somehow to want to reassert itself with the dawn of each new day. But over the last few days Borja had begun to win that particular battle with his unconscious. His new job, with its new preoccupations, then his unexpected growing friendship with Nick, all had helped to put thoughts of Andy and one highly-charged day and night into perspective. At Casablanca something had happened – something which had a place, a reality, in the patchwork of experiences that made up his life, but it was something he had now drawn away from and, without diminishing the experience itself, put in its appropriate place behind him.

But now, this morning, what should happen? Borja's first thought on waking was of Nick. Nick's face flashed upon his inward eye just as his bodily ones opened to the brilliance of a May morning with birds singing outside his window. Nick, presumably snoring soundly, was a living room and a hallway distant. Had Nick really been giving him a come-on last night? Borja wondered. That offer, so late at night, to play the piano to him; that look that seemed to expect a kiss? He could not be sure. It was the easiest thing in the world for the older of two people to read into the actions of the younger one what simply wasn't there. Borja remembered two occasions during the last few days when he had turned away from Nick in the normal course of to-ing and fro-ing at work backstage and had had the feeling – eyes boring a hole in the back of his head – that Nick was watching his departing figure with a particular intensity. He hadn't dared, either time, to turn round to check. If any of this were true, unlikely though it might be, and bizarre in view of both Nick's youth and his self-proclaimed heterosexuality, Borja could not deny that it would be very flattering. With a spartan effort of will he hauled himself from the bed and headed into his bathroom to take a shower.

A few minutes later he was surprised to find Nick already in the kitchen, cooking scrambled egg for them both. He did it the Irish way, with masses of butter, and chopped chives from the herb garden stirred in at the last second. They took their breakfast out of the garden door on trays and ate it at the table, unused since the previous summer, that stood just beside the door in the sun-trap created by the sheltering southern wall. It was going to be a hot day, the first of the year: the start of one of those mini heat-waves that occur in May in England – which collapse inevitably back into another trough of late spring cold and disappointment, but which are joyfully welcomed while they last.

Consciously putting off the task of doing the last night's washing-up, which was still sitting, piled-up and reproachful, in the kitchen sink, they let themselves into Neville's pavilion and fed the cat, then did a daytime tour around the grounds, approximately retracing the steps they had taken late last night. They wandered the lawns, relaxed in the knowledge that with Neville away in town they would not be intruding on his privacy, circumnavigated the bassin, meandered through the orchard, leaped from paving-slab to slab in the checkerboard herb garden like animate chessmen, and ploughed their way through a small section of the wood. And nature, as if it had been locked in a box all winter, came spilling out to present itself to them all at once.

A kingfisher, a blue spark, flew whistling from the statuary centrepiece of the bassin as they approached. The giant gold carp, nicknamed Bismarck, who hadn't been spotted since last November, showed his portly battleship shape just an inch or two below the unfurling water-lily leaves. Not one but two cuckoos flew out of an emerald-leaved apple tree in the orchard, almost into their faces, and showing them their striped breasts: the male cuckooing triumphantly, the female giving a quiet, liquid chuckle. Then, in the wood, a ginger-tailed bird rose up vertically almost at their feet, mounting slowly for a second like a rocket from its launch pad, then suddenly accelerating with a whir of wings to vanish completely among the trees. 'A partridge?' hazarded Nick. His stay in the country had been a steep learning curve.

'Not among the trees like that,' said Borja. 'You've just seen a woodcock. Maybe the only one you ever will. So don't forget it.'

'You'll tell me all about woodcocks sometime, won't you?' Nick teasingly adopted the tone of a much younger person as they walked back towards the house. It was no fault of Nick's that this should blow a moment's chill across Borja's morning.

Back indoors and about to embark on the washing-up, they both together spotted a flashing light on the telephone answering machine. 'Why don't you and James get mobiles?' Nick asked.

'Why don't you?' retorted Borja.

'I can't afford one. I'm an ASM remember. You're an almost airline captain.'

'At the moment,' said Borja with mock hauteur, 'I'm not even an almost ASM. Remember that.' He pressed the playback button.

'Guy here. I need your help. Something's come up. I need you to be James for a few minutes. Be my manager. Can't really go into it on the phone. Can you be in the Seven Stars at one o'clock? Oh... Might as well bring Nick too if he happens to be with you.' Borja looked at his watch. It showed twelve o'clock. Nick had already started on the washing-up.

Borja did not visit the Seven Stars at lunchtime all that often, but he was familiar enough with the look of the place at that time of day to notice at once that something was missing. Or rather someone. There was no sign of Neville.

Guy was sitting by himself at one of the small round tables, an untouched half pint in front of him. He rose to his feet as soon as they entered. 'Thanks for coming, Borja. I just need someone to talk a rather serious problem through with and...'

'Perhaps I ought to leave you both to it,' said Nick.

'No, stay,' said Guy. 'Here.' He took out his wallet. 'We may need one of your off-the-wall solutions in a minute. In the meantime, make yourself useful and get Borja and yourself a drink.' Help, thought Borja. For all I said to him yesterday, he's treating the pair of us like an item. Guy looked pointedly round the bar like an actor in a melodrama. 'I think you can see for yourself what the problem is.'

'Neville isn't here.'

'Right. But that's just a symptom. He rang me from High Wycombe early this morning. He took a taxi there in the middle of the night.'

'High Wycombe? It must be fifty miles.'

'An ex of his lives there. Maya. Remember? Oh no. You were away that famous weekend.'

'I heard about it,' said Borja.

'It seems the Irishman's threatened to kill him. Hence the moonlight flit to High Wycombe. According to the other woman, Rita, he's got hold of the fact that Neville's appearing in Kiss Me Kate and he plans to join the audience tonight and shoot him when he's on stage.' Guy delivered this perfectly deadpan.

Borja stared at him, round-eyed. 'You have to be joking.'

Guy relaxed and chuckled. 'I'm perfectly sure it's nothing but empty words.' Then his expression became very serious again and he leaned forward across the table. 'But Borja, supposing I don't take it seriously and then, unbelievable though it appears to us now, someone gets shot at tonight's performance… What then? Don't you pilots find yourselves assessing just this kind of threat from time to time?'

'Captains do,' said Borja cautiously.

'Consider yourself promoted,' said Guy.

Nick rejoined them. Borja was surprised to find himself more than ready for his drink. Guy went on. 'Neville says that Maya's quite willing to drive him over here and back to High Wycombe both tonight and tomorrow, providing there's some sort of guarantee that he'll be safe. And just to complicate things further, I then had Harold on the phone.' Harold was the indisposed actor whom Neville had been replacing. 'He rang to say he was OK to do the show tonight and tomorrow. I told him there was a slight risk that he'd be shot in mistake for his understudy and then he wasn't so sure any more. I haven't told anyone else yet, by the way. Not Mike, not Linda, not the cast even. I needed to…'

'I understand,' said Borja. 'Have you contacted the police?'

'Not yet,' Guy said.

'Well that's surely the next thing, no?'

Guy smiled wanly. 'You think they may have a standard procedure for maniacs in theatre audiences threatening to kill actors on stage?'

'No,' Borja admitted, 'but they must have more experience with slightly similar situations than we have.'

Nick had a question. 'Does this Irish bloke know what Neville looks like?'

'I asked that,' said Guy. 'They've never set eyes on each other. Of course Rita could have been pressed into giving a description.'

'Then how will he know which one he is on stage?'

'The same way the rest of the audience does,' said Guy. 'By looking at the programme.'

'But his name isn't in the programme,' said Nick. 'It's only on a photocopied insert. I've seen the usherettes slipping the programmes with them before the doors open.'

Borja and Guy looked at each other. 'Glad I brought him?' said Borja. He couldn't resist that.

'We just have to get the usherettes to un-slip the programmes,' Nick went on excitedly. 'Or we can do it ourselves – Borja and me, I mean,' he clarified quickly, but then got caught up again in the onrush of his thoughts. 'The front of house staff could listen out for Irish accents…'

Guy stopped him. 'Perhaps that's where the police come in, don't you think?'

There was one other thing, and Nick spotted it first. 'It's all very well Neville decamping to Buckinghamshire. What if this nutter misses him at the theatre and comes looking for him out at Sevenscore?'

A catchphrase that had once been Mark's, years ago in Seville, came unbidden to Borja's lips. 'I think we can handle it,' he said calmly.

The meeting ended quickly. Guy thanked Borja and Nick effusively for helping him talk the problem through. He would call the police as soon as he got back to the office. Then he emptied his still untouched glass in one go, and walked out of the pub across the church square in the direction of the theatre.

'So why did he ask us?' Nick asked Borja as they drove out of the town. 'We didn't actually do anything – or say anything – that Linda or Mike couldn't have suggested themselves if he'd only asked them in the first place. He only needed a sounding board.'

'Sometimes it's not just a question of hearing the right noises being made,' said Borja thoughtfully. 'It's hearing them from the right people. Often, for Guy, that right person is James. That's why they get on so well. Guy appreciates him very much. But today James wasn't here – and so he wanted it to be me. And you. Learn to take these things as compliments.'

'I've been learning to take a lot of things as compliments during the last few months,' said Nick enigmatically.

It was Borja's idea to drive out of town. If Nick hung round near the theatre, Borja knew, someone would be sure to collar him for some task or other and his well-earned day off would have simply disappeared. On the other hand, he didn't want to drive back to Sevenscore. They had had their idyllic country walk there that morning and he was unsure what they could do to pass the time there this afternoon that would not seem an anticlimax after the radiant morning.

So they drove out in the other direction to a point on the canal where boats climbed the green hillside by means of a flight of locks so steep that they formed a staircase. They played for a while among the locks, lending their weight and leg-power to the beams of the great wooden gates as the tourist craft and narrow-boats went up and down the stairs. They had a sandwich in the sun outside a café, and Borja told Nick all about woodcocks, or at any rate all that he knew. 'We have them in the winter, in Castile, as well,' he told him. 'We shoot and eat them.' They were shy, inland-living, wading birds, he told Nick, with short legs and long beaks, eyes like frogs'and feathers the glowing russet colours of the forest floor. They travelled from place to place at night when the moon was full. 'The full moon draws the earthworms up towards the surface, you see, in the boggy places where the woodcock go to find them.' ('Wow,' said Nick.) 'They spend their daytimes resting, camouflaged, under trees in woodlands, like the one we saw. Then in the evening they fly out, on regular airways like the pilots use. They have their departure and arrival routes like us. Only…' he paused for effect, 'they're better eating than airline pilots.'

'Not that you've tried one of those, I suppose,' said Nick. 'Perhaps we could go out tonight with one of the emergency torches, dazzle one and catch it for breakfast.'

'A pilot or a woodcock?'

Nick gave him a mock punch.

'It's the close season, actually,' said Borja, now sounding very British. 'They're supposed to be nesting. And besides, it's more difficult than it sounds.' He didn't want to encourage Nick's fantasy to the extent that he really would have to spend the night roaming the woods with him and a lamp on a futile hunt.

Arriving back at the theatre in time for the half, they noticed an end-of-term feeling in the air. Tomorrow, not tonight, was the actual end of the run, but tomorrow would be an exhausting evening: the show would be followed by a strike of the set that would go on into the small hours. It would then be goodbye to all the casuals including Borja. The next few shows would be quite small-scale ones from the technical point of view. The next big musical was months away.

'Ever been up the fly tower?' Nick asked.

'Years ago,' said Borja.

'Well, come on up again.'

Of course Borja had been over every square inch of the theatre. When James had been appointed general manager seven years ago, one of the first things he had done was to show off every nook and cranny of his new kingdom to Borja. Together they had crawled through the roof space, inspecting the still visible evidence of the fire of 1891 among the rafters and purlins; together they had ascended the fly tower, the cavernous space above the stage, climbing slender ladders up to the grid where the pulley wheels on which the flying system depended were attached; on up still further to the smoke vent at the apex of the roof. Here James had pulled off a coup de théâtre by switching off the electromagnets that kept the louvres shut. Opening with a bang, they had given them both a spectacular rooftop panorama of the town. Now Nick was going to give him the guided tour again. And after all, why not? Borja thought, as Nick scampered up the vertical wall-ladder to the fly floor, looking unexpectedly strong and muscular from Borja's viewpoint as he followed upon his heels.

'Well, hallo boys.' This was Hamish, the flyman, checking his hemp-lines, adjusting his figure-of-eight tie-offs around the wooden cleats. Overnight changes of temperature or humidity played about with the hemps in the same way as they did with a sailing ship's rigging, or the strings of a musical instrument, so that a scene-cloth whose bottom batten had been spirit-level straight the previous night could be hanging at an odd angle the next day, and if not checked and corrected would fly in, swinging from side to side and creating havoc in the dark of the scene changes. Hamish, who drew one of the smallest salaries of anybody on the staff was one of the most diligent when it came to ensuring that everything would be right on the night every night. Borja, who as a pilot was paid rather more for attending with assiduity to similar small details, had been humbled on first meeting Hamish.

'Just a flying visit,' said Nick. Hamish and Borja looked at each other, ritually rolled their eyes and groaned.

'Thought you might have come to avoid flying bullets,' Hamish said drily. The threat to Neville was public knowledge by now.

The ladder up to the next floor was on the other side of the tower. They crossed by the gantry at the back. Already they were looking down on the lighting bars where row upon row of square black lamps peered down, barn-doors agape.

'I like this floor best,' said Nick, when they had reached the next level. They looked about them. Up here, forty feet above the stage, on this narrow ledge, the chorus girls and dancers of a century ago had changed their costumes, applied thick make-up and gossiped. The evidence was still here, despite successive renovations. There, screwed into the brickwork, sad and neglected, were the wire coat-hooks where gaudy costumes had once hung. Here was the black, strangely menacing, iron sink in whose cold comfort those young chorus girls had washed greasepaint from soft skins. Thinking about it…

'Gives you the creeps, doesn't it?' said Nick. He was enjoying himself, being in command. He scampered up another flight of ladders, then two more, zigzag, past the grid; the forest of ropes and pulleys now lay below. Finally they stood together on the small platform inside the smoke vent. Nick looked suddenly deflated. There was nowhere else to go. 'Well, here we are. That's it.' He shrugged and grinned. 'Nowhere else but down, I suppose.'

'No, wait.' Borja had had no intention of doing this on the way up, but it seemed now that something more was needed. He didn't like to see Nick looking at a loss like this. The switch was just beside him. He reached for it and cut out the electromagnets. Bang.

'Oh, hey,' said Nick. Around them the city showed itself in long thin strips as if through a Venetian blind. The evening sun slipped slanting in. Outside it glinted on the orb and cross of All Saints'Church, it bled into the trees of Racecourse Park. River and canal flashed coded silver messages one to the other. And the sun's last flames licked at distant gentle hills beyond Sevenscore and onward, south and east.

But it was some time since the smoke vent shutters had last opened and the louvres harboured quite a quantity of dust and grit. Which soon began to make its presence felt on stage some sixty feet below, where actors were limbering up and running through dance steps, and stage management were setting props. Murmurs of surprise and discontent soon floated up. Borja switched the current back on. 'You close them manually with a cord,' he said.

'I know,' said Nick. He reached forward for it, which brought him face to face with Borja. 'You're special,' he said, and pulled the cord and kissed Borja on the lips.

Borja was stunned for a moment. So was Nick. They faced each other, silent and still. Then Borja said, 'Time to go down and face the firing squad?'

There wasn't a firing squad as such. Just a number of plain-clothes policemen mingling with the audience in the foyer, and two more of them in one of the theatre's two boxes – which formed elegant little bridges between the enfolding arms of the dress circle and the proscenium arch. This news had been soberly and seriously communicated to all company and staff; but that had done nothing to prevent rumour inflating the police presence to Special Branch or the Flying Squad and a pair of marksmen in the box. The self-evident fact that marksmen would probably not be employed to take out a gunman hiding in a capacity theatre audience of six hundred people was not allowed to get in the way of the more interesting version. In the circumstances, as Borja and Nick were relieved to discover, a little dirt falling from the top of the fly tower onto the stage was quickly forgotten. And in spite of everything, the curtain went up dead on time.

The first half of the show was without incident. The competitive element in the company, still including Borja and Nick and Smut, did their usual fifteen pull-ups on the beam in the corner and the scene changes ran smoothly. But after the interval, during one front-cloth number, Smut just happened to say to Borja that young people like himself never learnt to waltz; nobody ever showed them the steps. 'They're easy,' Borja said, and demonstrated them. Then, in a businesslike way he took hold of Smut and danced him up and down the back wall of the stage, within the shady colonnade that formed the rearmost part of the set. After a couple of turns Smut had got the hang of it. He said a delighted thank you, Borja released him and that was the end of the lesson. Then Nick arrived. 'Nobody taught me either,' he said to Borja. He sounded slightly piqued. 'You showed Smut. Show me.'

Casablanca, thought Borja, and then that the silly boy was actually jealous because he had danced with Smut. He was incredulous, but also flattered, and aware at the same time that the latter reaction was no less foolish than Nick's jealousy. He didn't share any of this with Nick; he just laughed. Then matter-of-factly he took the floor with him just as he had done with Smut. Up and down the colonnade they went, in and out of the vaulted arches. Despite a promise to himself not to let his feelings get involved where Nick was concerned, Borja had to admit that he was enjoying the sensation of dancing with him. Nick seemed to be getting the hang of it remarkably quickly, and moving quite gracefully…

Out of the corner of his eye Borja saw actors waiting in the wings for their entrances as usual, but they were not standing still as they usually did; instead they gesticulated and mouthed at him. At the same moment Nick and he, still clasped together, both stopped and looked downstage. Then Borja saw something that every actor sees nightly and takes for granted but that he had never experienced before. The front cloth had been flown out while they were engrossed in their waltzing, the scene had changed and the full depth of the stage was in use, a new lighting state rapidly brightening the gloom like a tropical sunrise. The proscenium arch was the frame for a view, like something seen through a deep dark mirror, of the dress circle dimly gleaming, exit lights glowing dull green in the farthest distance, and everywhere a blueish sea of faces, indistinct as boulders underwater, but each one focused on the strange spectacle of two young men in black waltzing together in and out of the shadows.

'And not only that,' said Nick when they had at last unfrozen, unclasped and faded into the wings with as much invisibility as they could muster, 'but one of those faces belongs to somebody with a gun.' It crossed Borja's mind for the first time – he who had daily faced the theoretical one in a hundred thousand chance of a hijack at gunpoint – that actors too could be routinely brave.

When the final curtain came down and the huge iron safety curtain wheezed to a stop on its hydraulic buffers, the sudden realisation that nobody had been shot after all came inevitably as something of an anticlimax so it was fortunate that there was something else to talk about in the Post Horn afterwards; and that something was, of course, the public dancing display that had been provided by Nick and Borja. The ribbing was unrelenting but delivered with good, if bawdy, humour and Borja and Nick had no choice but to take it in equally good part. Eventually the crowd broke up. Maya bundled a reluctant Neville into her car and set off towards the Chilterns and High Wycombe. Maya had spent the show sitting in Neville's dressing room. Although she had been offered a complimentary ticket to see the musical she had declined; she said she didn't want to find herself in the role of a second Mrs. Lincoln.

And at last Borja and Nick found themselves alone together, just as they had done the previous night. But the ground had shifted so much beneath their feet since then that they had even less idea than twenty-four hours ago what the evening would be like.

'There's a new French place,' Borja said. 'I haven't tried it yet, nor has James I think. But Guy says it's good. What do you think?'

'Por qué non?' Nick, by some process of osmosis, had started in the last couple of weeks to lace his speech with Spanish interjections.

The restaurant was spacious, minimally furnished and fashionably free of clutter. The attention that other diners were paying to their food was a good sign, and so they took their seats with already a feeling of relaxed anticipation.

'You've never told me,' Nick said, once they had ordered and were sipping prematurely, like naughty children, at their glasses of Crozes-Hermitage, 'why you and James eventually chose to make your home in England and not Spain.'

Borja looked at him. Nick was not wearing his glasses tonight. That was not unprecedented, but still unusual enough for Borja to focus his mind on the fact for a second or two. His eyes looked rather splendid without them, Borja thought; they were large and a lustrous brown: almost Spanish looking, and there was something oddly familiar about them – familiar in a reassuring sort of way. It was clearly not a matter of chance or carelessness that had caused Nick to remove his optical extras: after all the little signs and incidents of the last twenty-four hours, Borja could have no illusions about that. Nor about the fact that Nick was wearing his open-necked white shirt in a way – half the buttons undone – that displayed quite a lot of his smooth chest. Nick's chest was not all that impressive – the athletic, muscular part of him all lay below his waist and, although much in evidence on the climb to the top of the fly tower, was now invisible beneath the table – but it was no doubt the thought that counted. His mouth was slightly open in a smile that showed the tiny gap between his top front teeth. His cheeks were faintly flushed. Borja had tried quite hard up to now not to think the word beautiful in connection with Nick. Yet beautiful he was.

Two customers arrived, came towards them: two women.

'Oh no,' said Nick quietly, half annoyed, half amused. 'Not them again!'

Borja looked up quickly. The women were Sammy and Chris, bowing slightly, saying – was there something a little arch, a little knowing, in the delivery? – 'Hallo,' and, 'Bon appétit,' and, 'Enjoy yourselves,' before moving on to find a table for themselves at a tactful distance.

'Jesus,' Nick said. 'Why does it have to be them, of all people?' He stopped and very slowly began to blush.

Borja felt suddenly cold. His feeling of well-being collapsed like a punctured, bright balloon. 'What did you mean, not them again?'

'They were here … I mean there … when we … when I…'

'When what?'

Nick took a breath and told the truth. After all, he had nothing to hide. 'When James took me out for a meal a few weeks ago.' Telling the truth and having nothing to hide did not save him from turning completely red.

'Oh,' said Borja flatly. Then, 'I didn't know you'd had a meal out together. Obviously neither of you thought it was anything worth mentioning.'

'Sorry,' said Nick anxiously, 'but it wasn't a major event...'

'Like this evening,' said Borja coldly.

'Look, I didn't mean…' Nick had the sense that there was nothing he could say that wouldn't make things worse. He felt like someone floundering on a steep slope of loose shingle: whichever way you moved, the same thing happened. 'It was just that it was the weekend you and Andy got lost in Morocco and upstaged us all.' That did at least put a wan smile back on Borja's face, even if he was slightly startled to hear Andy's name come so easily to Nick's lips. 'Anyway,' Nick volunteered a bit more brightly, encouraged by the smile, 'nothing happened.' And was back on the shingle, sliding down.

'Oh really,' said Borja, icy again. 'And what might have happened?'

'Look, nothing. I mean nothing. Please don't go on like this.'

Borja didn't. At least not just then. Their starters arrived at that moment and both men were relieved to discover that the atmosphere had not deteriorated to the point at which appetites were lost. Dealing with his warm salad with toasted goat's cheese and walnut dressing Borja had time to reflect that he was hardly being fair on either Nick or James in objecting to their having dinner together. After all, he was doing exactly the same, in inviting Nick to dinner tonight, himself. Was not his irritation simply a cover for disappointment? And jealousy of James, if he were honest with himself, for beating him to it. But that nothing happened still rankled. People only said that when something had. Plus, there was Nick's extraordinary behaviour over the last two days – which could only be interpreted as flirting. Had Nick let all that loose on James too? Nothing had happened, exactly, between Nick and Borja either, except that each had, at different moments, been surprised into giving the other a kiss. Borja decided to let the matter rest – at least as far as Nick was concerned; he would have questions for James later. He looked up from his croustillant de chèvre. 'Look, I'm sorry about just now. I was being a bit pathetic, no?'

Nick didn't think Borja or his apology pathetic at all. 'You're just great,' he said soberly – the last utterance of his that evening to which the adjective could be applied. Relieved that the moment of awkwardness was past, his tongue began to loosen by the glass. He told stories about his home in Oxfordshire and the dog he'd had as a child. He related a scary story from his time in fringe theatre, when something had gone wrong with the electrics and the circuit breakers kept tripping, plunging the stage into darkness. In the end, he and another ASM had stood by the fuse-boxes, each of their fingers holding down a separate trip-button, while smoke coiled out in slow sinister wreaths. It was a gamble as to whether they would make it to curtain-down before the whole lighting box exploded in a shower of sparks. The two boys had silently dared each other to keep their nerves, and the day had been won.

Borja found he was quite content to let Nick talk. In spite of himself he was falling under his spell, listening, and watching his animated face. James had travelled this road before, he remembered at one point, but determinedly pushed away any troubling thoughts about where the road might lead. When the main course arrived Nick had the idea to order a second bottle of wine, and Borja did not try to stop him.

'You're so lucky to have James,' Nick said. 'Of course, he's lucky to have you. You're both so … you know.' He found an example to clarify his meaning. 'You know how James always comes and does the fit-up with us on the Monday morning before a new show? That means such a lot to people. It's not that he's actually all that useful. You're much better with a hammer and a pump than he is. But it's the fact of him being there. People go the extra mile for a boss like that.' Despite his present annoyance with James for taking Nick out to dinner without telling him, Borja was pleased to hear this. Somehow, when people praised his partner, he felt taller by an inch or two.

When they left to go home they were the last customers by a long way. Borja left an appropriately generous tip. He was pleased that Sammy and Chris had faded from the scene without feeling the need to revisit them at their table. Driving back to Sevenscore, he found for the first time since he was a teenager that it was necessary to shut one eye in order to make the two centre-lines in the road merge into one. He told himself it was due to fatigue rather than alcohol. But whatever the cause, it also prevented him from noticing that Nick was considerably more drunk than he was himself.

It was still warm when they got back to Sevenscore. When Nick uncorked a bottle of wine and insisted on taking glasses outside Borja did not try to stop him. It was too late to be sensible. They took their drinks to the steps that led down to the bassin, between the two pavilions and their colonnades and sat down on the cool stone slabs.

'Maybe I really am gay,' said Nick, à propos of nothing. 'Do you think I am?'

'Cielos,' said Borja, suddenly exasperated with him. 'You do choose your moments. I honestly don't know. How am I supposed to know, if you don't? What does it matter what I think, anyway? And besides, do you really think that's a wise question to a half-drunk maricón, when his boyfriend's away, and you're sipping wine with him in the moonlight?'

Whether Nick had any answer to that, Borja was not about to discover. The next thing they heard was a crash of breaking glass near at hand that startled them both out of their wits.

'It's that Irish maniac come to get Neville,' said Nick, jumping to his feet, alarm in his voice.

'Take it easy.' Borja caught him by the arm. 'Neville's not here, and the man's got no quarrel with us. We'll walk round quietly and have a look.'

Fright subsided quickly. No car had followed them up the drive, and it would not have been an easy walk through the time-warp wood in the middle of the night. In a businesslike way they made a circuit of Neville's pavilion. On the far side was stacked a collection of large panes of glass, the legacy of a demolished greenhouse, which were waiting for Neville to make some decision about them. The moon highlighted the head and back of a small deer which turned and looked at them for one startled second before turning tail and running, then vanishing with a leap over the balustrade into the fields beyond.

Relief found its expression in laughter: loud, drunken, rib-aching, tear-wrenching. Nick clutched at Borja's sleeve. 'We'll go and find woodcock. Catch one in the wood and cook it for breakfast. How much cooking would a woodcock want cooking if a woodcock…?'

'Stop it. You're pissed.' Borja tried to take charge of him. 'We are not going to look for woodcock. Claro, amigo?' All his life Borja had been a younger brother, then James's slightly younger lover. Even Rafael had been older than him. It was a welcome novelty, with Nick, to be the senior one for a change. He put his hands on Nick's shoulder. 'Let's go back, finish our wine, and then it's bedtime, don't you think?' He had not chosen his words carefully enough. He certainly hadn't meant bed together. But Nick might have taken it that way. It wasn't altogether clear from his reaction, which was to interpret Borja's hands on his shoulders as an invitation to dance. He seized them and began a kind of mad, hopping jig around Borja, turning him in circles until inevitably he fell to the ground with Nick sprawling quite happily on top of him. 'Why don't we,' said Nick, presumably inspired by the naked marble statues all around them, 'get naked and climb the vacant plinth? The Draughtsman's Contract lives.'

Years ago, when they were younger and more puppyish themselves, Borja and James had done exactly that; had even taken photos of each other, and then had to persuade friends with a darkroom to develop the film: they hadn't had the nerve to go to Boots. But Borja was not about to share this information with Nick now. 'You might look very nice up there,' his voice came muffled from beneath Nick's left arm, 'but you'd catch your death.'

'Why can't I come inside a woman?' Nick asked suddenly, wildly. He ran both hands without discrimination over all the bits of Borja that he could reach without getting off him. 'I don't know why, but I never can.'

'I don't know.' Borja felt suddenly miserable. Had something in him changed this year, something that made him suddenly the object of other people's sexual curiosity as never before? The better part of him still did not want to have sex with Nick, but the chances of that not happening seemed to be falling away. 'I really don't know. Maybe you're gay, maybe you're not.' He tried to reassert control, over Nick, over himself. 'Look, can we stop this? Get off me. Now.'

Nick was still just capable of picking up from Borja's tone that he meant what he said. He got unsteadily to his feet, and in spite of himself Borja found himself perversely wishing for a second or two that he hadn't.

They meandered back to where they had left their wine bottle. 'How fast the moon goes,' Nick said. 'It was only there just now.' He pointed imprecisely at the sky between the two pavilions. It was true. The moon now stared across the dark fields at them from the other side of the fountain in the bassin. 'Is that how life goes when you get older, do you think? Faster and faster, like the moon across the sky, when we used to think it would be like the stars'slow journey – when we were younger, I mean – and take forever. Of course, I suppose I am still young. Up to a point.'

Borja smiled involuntarily; it was not directed at Nick. 'You're an extraordinary boy,' he said. But the words came out in the tone of voice that is usually reserved for other words, and Nick caught it easily.

'I love you,' he answered.

The silence that followed was a long one. Borja could have sworn he actually saw the moon slowly move, like the hand of a watch. Eventually Nick said, 'I mean I love both of you. James and you. Together.' As a damage limitation exercise it was better than nothing.

Resignation was the feeling that was uppermost in Borja's mind as he reached out a hand and started to stroke Nick's hair. Nick didn't react at all and for some time nothing happened. Then Nick said, 'You're more cuddlesome than James, perhaps. But only slightly.'

Borja withdrew his hand. 'You're not supposed to be in a position to make the comparison. You told me nothing had happened between you. Remember?'

'I know, but…'

'But what?'

'But nothing.'

Borja wondered if he was being stupid: too heedful of the voice of his own tender conscience to consider the possibility that James and Nick had slept together; perhaps they did so regularly when he was away; and now Nick, drunk though he was, seemed to be indicating that he thought it only natural that he should be having sex with Borja too. Nick wondering if perhaps just maybe he was gay: that was a pretence. Nick was as gay as he and James were; he slept with men as a matter of course, without batting an eyelid.

Borja would never discover what he might have done next. Because Nick suddenly stood up, swayed around a bit and then said, 'Oh fuck, I'm going to be sick.' And then he was, all across the nearest flower border among Inigo Jones's fastidious Corinthian pillars.

By the time Borja had mopped Nick up and taken both him and the abandoned wine glasses indoors with him, the sexual static that had been building in the atmosphere had been dissipated as conclusively as real static gets discharged in any thunderstorm. And when he undressed him and put him to bed in the Chinese room he found he was quite free from any desire to climb in beside him – something which, a mere ten minutes before, had seemed such a probable end to the evening that he had been shivering uncontrollably. He observed the naked Nick quite dispassionately, and saw that he was not only beautiful but impressively equipped as well; but Borja simply took in the view in the same objective spirit in which he might have contemplated a Michelangelo statue. As for Nick, he was no longer a candidate for sex with anyone that night: he hovered in the twilit zone between drunken wake and sleep.

'James…' Nick began, as Borja was about to leave the room. Borja turned back to him, sat on his bed and cut Nick's sentence off by pinching his nostrils shut, which forced him to keep his mouth open in order to breathe.

'I don't want to hear any more about what didn't happen between you and James,' Borja told Nick sternly. 'If it was so uneventful that he didn't remember to tell me, perhaps you shouldn't be going on about it either. And if you don't see the wisdom of that just now, you'll see it in Technicolor in the morning.'

Nick was making inarticulate gurgling sounds like someone at the dentist's. Borja released him. 'And now goodnight.' Nick burped once and fell asleep.

NINETEEN

The birds failed to wake Borja the next morning, but the telephone did. He looked at his watch. Nine o'clock. He pulled a dressing gown around him bad-humouredly and scrambled into the living room. 'Hallo?'

'Borja? Hóla.' Female, Spanish. 'Soy Marisa. Escuchas…' Marisa, phoning from Salamanca, phoning from a crisis. 'It's Borja, young Borja, Rizo…' She went on, delivering bad news in a shrill rattle of pain.

'Missing?' Borja was aghast. 'Since yesterday?'

For some extraordinary reason Marisa was saying she thought Rizo might have gone to England – to find Borja.

'Why? Why me?' Borja's heart as well as his head was pounding.

'He idolises you. No, not just that, not just you. We're trying everybody. The police…'

'The police?!' Borja tried to calm Marisa: a hopeless endeavour when he was panicking himself. 'I don't know where he might be. But let me think. Give me a little time.' What time could do to help, except slow his racing pulse, he had no idea. 'Do you want me to fly out – fly over to you? Just say it and I'll do it.' He was ready to promise anything.

'No,' Marisa said. 'Not yet at least.'

'Just let me think. I need time.' He needed air. Or a drink. Someone to hold onto. Talk it through with. James… No, not James. 'I'll call you later in the morning. By then you may have news...' He put down the phone.

Not James. That was impossible. Nick? No way. Other workmates from the theatre? No to them too. Colleagues in the airline… Andy? Yes, Andy. Only Andy. He picked up the phone again and dialled his number.

He was just putting the phone down when the far door opened and Nick, dressed but dishevelled and chalk-faced, ghosted into the living room. He looked fragile and as much in need of comfort as Borja did himself.

'I'm so sorry.' Nick struggled to put words together. 'Things I may have said last night. I don't know if I…'

'You said plenty of things you shouldn't have. But all of us do that. Don't worry about last night. Listen. Something's come up. A family problem. I've got to go to London. But I'll be back in time for the show. If you want to go into town I'll drop you off.' He thought of something. 'Hell. Can you do some shopping for the weekend? Or James'll skin me alive. I'll give you the money. And go to the off licence if you can face it.' He stopped and looked at Nick more closely. 'You're not looking your best. I'll make us some tea and you'll feel better.' He moved towards him and rumpled his hair, as much for his own consolation as for Nick's. It was a gesture of relief too; he was glad that he hadn't slept with him last night. At least he had got that right in the end.

'Don't,' said Nick plaintively. 'My head hurts.'

Borja had arranged to meet Andy in his local pub. Andy had said, come to his flat, but Borja, flustered, had said a pub would be easier to find. In reality he wanted the neutrality of a public space for this potentially difficult re-encounter.

Andy's local turned out to be easy to find: it was just off the main approach to London from the north. It was called the Warrington Hotel and Borja, entering it for the first time, was quite taken aback by its grandeur. Marble pillars and stained glass partitions, panelled niches and dark, carved ceiling mouldings were the order of its Edwardian day, and Borja could imagine its spacious saloon peopled by monocled colonels on leave from

India, reading newspapers and quaffing pink gins. Now the sub-Beardsley ladies, etched in russet and black on the friezes, mingled with a Saturday lunchtime crowd of … they looked like the kind of people that James had used to call yuppies; to be honest, they looked like James and he had done just a few years ago, although with keener edges than they had ever shown; but perhaps that was just London. He looked up at the ceiling, papered with red-brown intertwining leaves – he half-expected to see woodcock hiding among them – then looked round for Andy … who came up unseen from behind him and announced himself with a clap on the shoulder, the way James would have done.

It was the first time they had seen each other in casual clothes and there was a half second during which they found themselves surprised by what they should have been expecting: the other person looking youthful and only partly familiar in jeans and coloured summer shirt. Momentarily their faces registered a certain innocent pleasure in this novelty, though nothing was said. Instead, Andy ordered drinks in a businesslike way, shepherded Borja to a gleaming mahogany table, placed the glasses on it and sat down. 'You're lucky I'm free today,' he said. 'Though it's great to see you. I can't pretend I haven't noticed your silence over the last couple of months. So what's upset you so much that you want to come rushing down here?' He paused for a split second to remember Borja's partner's name. 'James?' Then, which surprised Borja somewhat, 'Nick?'

'James is fine,' Borja said. 'And Nick.' Unbidden by anything conscious, his hand gave a tiny automatic wave of dismissal. He did not want to talk about Nick just then.

'Then it's you that's in trouble.' Andy frowned. 'You haven't got ill, have you?' Aids was rarely mentioned, but it lurked just below the surface of even the sunniest conversation like a pike in a mill pool.

'No. It isn't that. It's the son of a friend of mine. In Spain. He's disappeared. He's sixteen.'

'I see. When?'

'His mother – my oldest friend – phoned me this morning.'

'And you're upset. I understand.'

'You don't. That's only part of it. His mother thinks he might come looking for me.'

'Why would he do that?' Andy asked.

'He seems to have developed a bit of a crush on me. It all got a bit awkward one night.' Conversations in the vicinity were loud and energetic. Nevertheless Borja lowered his voice as he went on, a little haltingly. 'We had a conversation that got a bit too frank, that's all. And he seemed to get the wrong end of the stick.'

'Uh-huh,' said Andy, when he had finished. 'I think I see where you're going with this.'

'Well, don't go too far down that route. Nothing ever happened between us.'

'In the way that nothing happened between you and me that time?' Andy asked carefully.

Borja drew in a breath. Then he said, 'Even less than that. Give you my word. I'm not even supposed to be mentioning this to anybody. That's a promise I made to Rizo. So please don't...'

Andy threw Borja a smile, like a rubber ball. Borja recognised it. It was the same smile that he had given Andy, after that take-off and the wasp sting, when he had just fibbed to Gatwick Tower that there had been no problem. Borja knew that smile like his own face in the mirror.

'Don't be anxious,' said Andy. 'A teenager gets the wrong idea about something and months later he goes missing. That's two separate events. There doesn't have to be anything that links them together. There could be any number of reasons for the lad to run away. He has his own life, for God's sake. Just because you don't know very much about it doesn't make it non-existent. More things happen to teenagers in the space of three months than one over-frank conversation with an older man. Think back! Remember? The chances of his disappearance having anything to do with you are about a thousand to one against.'

'You manage to sound very reassuring. I hadn't actually allowed myself to consider that. But the fact remains that he's missing and I'm feeling somehow that I ought to be doing something.'

'I don't know what you can be expected to do. You're in England, he disappeared in Spain. Of course, if he turns up here that's another matter, but then he isn't missing any more and the problem goes away.'

'I just feel I ought to be over there, in Salamanca. Trying to find him.'

'That's because you feel guilty – unnecessarily, I think. Don't let that get in the way. It would look very odd if you turned up suddenly. It's not as if he's a blood relation. All you can do is to keep phoning your friend as often as you feel like, to keep up with events. If she wants you to do anything more she'll ask you herself. There's a father, I suppose?'

'Yes.'

'There you are then. The ball isn't remotely in your court.'

Borja considered this. 'I suppose you're right. Maybe I'd better give her another call now.' He looked around for a pay-phone.

'You still don't have a mobile, do you?' said Andy. He took his own from his pocket. 'Here. Help yourself.'

Even though the conversation was one-sided and Spanish, Borja hardly needed to explain after it was finished that he had spoken to Alberto, Rizo's father, and that there was no news. 'They're obviously both in a state,' Borja finished up.

'Like you,' Andy said, eyebrows raised expressively.

Borja laughed faintly – for the first time that day – and Andy was quietly pleased. 'Listen,' he said. 'I've got some salad and stuff for lunch at home. It's literally a minute away. If we take your car, that is.'

'The thing is,' said Borja, as they drove the short distance, 'I have a feeling, a sense that I know where he is. All the way down the motorway I kept seeing a picture of him – in a theatre of all places.'

Andy took a few seconds to get this. 'Park anywhere along here. How do you mean, you saw him in a theatre?'

Borja began, a bit shyly, to mumble a story about himself, when a teenager, being able – he thought, or maybe he just imagined – being able to see where things were without actually seeing them, if Andy could understand that, no?

Andy thought he had understood what Borja said, he told him. Though that wasn't quite the same as understanding what it meant. Borja decided not to tell Andy that he had had regular visions of death and judgement day at around the same time, and that he had only stopped having them when he was in his early twenties. That had better be kept for another occasion.

'Let me get this straight. – There's no lift; I'm sorry.' They were climbing the stairs inside Andy's mansion block. He lived on the fourth floor. 'When you say you've seen Rizo in a theatre, that means you actually think he may be in one? That that's where he should be looked for?'

'Possibly,' said Borja. For one person, Andy's flat was spacious. It was also airy and bright. Borja was impressed.

'Was he a member of an audience? Acting? Working backstage like you do?' Andy was as sceptical as most about people who said they had visions: he was more than surprised to find himself humouring Borja now, apparently going along with him on this one. He tried to move back to solid ground. 'You're sure your own experience hasn't put the idea into your head?'

'I don't know. It wasn't very clear. There was something odd about the theatre, though. It looked as if it was in the middle of restoration. Seats had been taken out. Doors were missing and plaster had been stripped from the walls.'

Andy sat down at his kitchen table and motioned to Borja to do likewise. 'I can't imagine why any kid would run away to a theatre that was being refurbished. Does he hang out with theatre people? Or interior decorators?'

'I don't know who he hangs out with. Oh, except I know he has a friend called Manuel. Manuel Peñafiel. And I only remember that because that's the name of someone who used to be the mayor of Salamanca. It's an unusual name, and they're a wealthy family. The kid might be the grandson.'

'I'm not sure that this is helping,' said Andy patiently.

'No, but wait. I remember something else. He told me Manuel was always going on about running off to Madrid, to disappear among the drop-outs. All very romantic and teenage and silly. Apparently he liked to think of himself as an outsider.'

'Well that might be something. They could have buggered off to Madrid together. Phone your friends and tell them that at least.'

Borja frowned. 'It's not so easy. Rizo and Manuel were having some sort of affair together. Their parents weren't supposed to know about them. So how am I supposed to have come by the knowledge? You told me yourself it would look odd if I turn up on the doorstep. It'll look even odder if I phone up and blurt out that little lot.'

Andy thought for a moment. Then, 'How many theatres do you suppose are being renovated in Madrid at any one time?'

Borja laughed. 'Not very many, I don't suppose.'

Andy thought for a moment. Then he said, giving Borja a bit of a sideways look, 'You'd like me to be with you, wouldn't you.' Borja nodded. Andy went on. 'Do you want me to come with you to Madrid?' This time Andy didn't even require Borja's nod by way of an answer. 'Lucky in a way we're both suspended. Time on our hands.' Saying the words time and hands caused him inevitably to glance at his watch.'Then what we have to do is clear. I just need to make a call to someone at Heathrow.'

Borja looked uncertain. 'I'm supposed to be working tonight. I can't just…'

'Ring them too,' said Andy. 'An emergency is an emergency, even in the theatre.' A flicker of doubt crossed his face. 'I suppose you've got your passport with you?'

Borja nodded slowly. 'I suppose I have.'

Two hours later they were boarding a scheduled flight to Barajas. The plane was one of the new generation of Airbuses, and as they sat in the two jump-seats behind the pilots they ogled the array of new technology in front of them. Most of the familiar dial-and-pointer flight instruments had been replaced by liquid crystal displays. The navigation displays were the size of small television screens and would show their position as they travelled the route as if on a map. Like children examining new toys, Borja and Andy chatted with the pilots and were able partly to forget the strangeness of their errand and – in Borja's case – the anxiety that had occasioned it.

Though the thought did go through Borja's mind that Andy, as a captain suspended from duty and awaiting the verdict of an enquiry, might not have wished to spend time in the company of other, working, pilots, and was being generous with more than just his time in sharing this adventure with him.

Their SID – the outbound equivalent of a STAR – tracked west to the Woodley beacon on the outskirts of Reading, where a sharp left turn brought them down to Southampton, to join the familiar route that Borja flew so often from Luton or Gatwick. The list of reporting points came up on the navigation display in a familiar roll-call as they threaded a nearly cloudless sky over the Channel Islands and crossed Brittany. Not for the first time in his life Borja found himself experiencing a plane journey as a precious, sun-filled, time bubble, a temporary cessation of hostilities between himself and the real world in the ongoing battle of life.

The Airbus and James's homebound Boeing passed each other over the Bay of Biscay at a combined speed of eleven hundred miles an hour. James actually saw Borja's plane, since he happened to glance out of the window at the particular moment that it sped into view like a rocket, only to disappear immediately beneath the wing of his own aircraft, trailing behind it a feathery thread of white that itself dissolved into the sky within seconds. Ironically, it was one of the very few times since Borja had become a pilot that James had observed a passing aeroplane without at least half wondering whether Borja was on board. As for Borja, he was well aware that James's plane should be passing them at some point on the journey and was half on the lookout for it, but he didn't happen to spot that particular speck against the afternoon sun.

James made his way on foot from the station to the theatre, pack on back. The backpack had taken on a new and almost mythic importance in its owner's mind since its dramatic theft and recapture in Seville. He would find Borja at the theatre, since it was just before the half. He hoped to see him before running into everyone else, if that were at all possible. He wanted to tell him, in the simplest words that he loved him. After all that had happened, all that he had felt and thought, in Seville, he needed very much to do that. He would take him on one side for a moment that would be very private. He hoped – though this was a bit optimistic in view of the realities of backstage life – that he would not find him in the company of Nick. Greeting Nick again could come later, and would be low-key. He glanced down at the front entrance of the theatre from the top of Pembridge Street. The audience was beginning to arrive. He didn't want to go in that way, smelling of travel and shouldering luggage, bumping accidentally into people he might slightly know. He continued on round the block and entered by the stage door, clattering down the stairs into the green room. The new stage manager, Adrian, was there: he looked sulky and gave James only a jerk of the head by way of greeting. James was faintly surprised but gave it no further thought. Throat, and a couple of casuals who were also strewn about on the grubby furniture, smiled more reassuringly and said hallo. 'Where's Borja?' James asked.

Throat glanced quickly at the others and then looked a little uncomfortable as he replied. 'Nick's got a message for you from him. He's in the Post Horn with Guy and Smut.'

James looked at his watch. It was, admittedly, not yet the half. But Nick, Smut and Guy seemed an odd trio to be in conclave in the pub together just before a show. And where was Borja? For a dizzying moment he wondered if something terrible had happened. He put the thought behind him. He had no wish to stay where he was, asking junior members of staff to bring him up to date about important things. He threw his pack down on one of the moulting sofas and clumped back up the stairs. As he exited the stage door, he saw Nick and Smut emerge from the door of the pub just across the way. James let Smut scuttle past him and into the theatre; all his attention was focused on Nick. 'What's happened? What's happened to Borja?'

Nick seemed different: different from the Nick whom James had known before. His face was drawn, his eyes wide and startled. He seemed unnerved by James's sudden materialisation, as if this were one more fright in a day that had been full of them. 'He's had to go to Spain. It's OK about the show. Guy knows. And Adrian. Smut and me'll cope.'

James had noticed before that Nick's habitually well-bred grammar deserted him in times of stress.

'Fuck the show!' James almost shouted. 'Why's he gone to Spain?'

'He phoned from London a few hours ago. A friend's son's gone missing and he and Andy have flown out to Madrid to find him.'

None of this made sense to James. He heard himself reciting a standard rubric of questions. What was Borja doing in London anyway? Who in God's name was Andy? He felt his anger rising – inexplicably, he thought, now that he had assured himself that Borja was safe and well; after that the reasons for his disappearance were surely only a minor puzzle.

Nick did his best to answer James's questions, but seemed more and more distraught in the face of James's growing anger. 'It's all OK,' he said. 'I've been and shopped for the weekend. Borja wanted everything to be just so when you came back. I've been to the offy and got wine and everything.' His voice rose steadily like a wave, then broke and dissolved into a cascade of tears.

'Oh for God's sake!' James was exasperated. As if there wasn't enough already that he couldn't make sense of. But he was himself prone to sudden tearful outbursts, and his defences were quite unable to withstand for very long the impact of anything similar when suffered by attractive younger men. He managed to stay standing where he was, one pace away from Nick, but he did reach out with one hand to touch his forearm. 'Don't be upset. Whatever it is, you can tell me later. I'll stand in for Borja during the show. You can tell me what I have to do. And the first thing I'll need to know is where he keeps his blacks.' He checked his watch again. Five to seven. 'We're on, I think.'

Borja's black jeans were a little short in the leg for James, but they fitted just fine around the waist – which was the main thing. The scene changes were easy enough and Nick, recovering his composure as the evening progressed, was very clear in his explanations of what had to be done at each stage. Even so, the fifteen customary pull-ups on the beam did come as a bit of a surprise to James. End-of-show goodbyes with the actors who were leaving the company were perfunctory, as was traditional, or else non-existent: some people preferred simply to vanish, according to the superstition which held that saying goodbye to a theatre meant never coming back. Someone had written Everybody, phone your agent, rather heartlessly, on the green-room notice-board. Neville was driven away once more to High Wycombe. For the second night running he had not been shot.

The strike got under way at once. It was always a moment of sadness, tearing down a structure in which people had worked, lived and created magic for a month or two, but the pace of the work was hectic and there was little time for anybody to indulge sentimental thoughts. Adrian directed operations. Furniture was manhandled across the orchestra pit, bumped over the carefully tarpaulin-ed seatbacks of the stalls, then carried out of the building via a fire exit which ran beneath the foyer, to end up in the furniture store a few doors down the street. Half the flattage went the same way. The other flats – marked with a P rather than an F – went in the other direction: upstage, out of the high dock doors and up into the paint-shop above the stage door on the other side of Friar's Way. Dealing with each flat was a two-man task, and James found himself randomly in tandem with Nick, Smut or one of the others, but most often with Nick. It was two in the morning and there had been no mishaps – except a minor one when somebody knocked over a fire extinguisher – which went off, and Smut got soaked to the skin … and then somebody remembered something. P on the back of a flat stood not for paint-shop, but for Pembridge Street, where the furniture store was situated, and the F stood for Friars' Way. The two stacks of flats, now a quarter of a kilometre apart, had been taken off in diametrically opposite directions to the ones that the head of design had intended.

'We'll just have to change them back,' said Adrian. 'Sorry folks, but we're not going home just yet. Back on your heads, lads, and let's get the mess sorted out.'

There were muted objections and loud exhalations all round. James stepped up to Adrian. 'A quiet word in your ear?'

Adrian glared at James. For a moment it occurred to James that Adrian wanted to hit him: he could not imagine why. Then Adrian gave in and walked with James a few paces away from the others.

'We don't need to do this tonight,' James told him. 'Quite apart from the overtime bill, everybody's knackered. The stage is clear for Monday morning. Flats can be swapped over as needed during next week in normal hours.'

'But I've just told them…'

'Tell them you've changed your mind. Tell them they can break. They'll love you for it.'

'Just a minute.' Adrian said this just loudly enough to be heard by the others and then stopped.

'Yes?' prompted James.

Adrian seemed unsure for a moment whether to say what was on the tip of his tongue. Then he said it anyway. 'Who exactly is running this strike, James?'

'You are,' said James, deadpan. He felt the muscles of his face and stomach tighten. The crew and stage management, hanging about on the stage and pretending not to listen, were now all ears. James waited for Adrian to speak next.

Adrian was pressing his fists together, grimacing and rolling his eyes. It looked alarming but no longer threatening. 'I've had just about enough. First we have your boyfriend backstage keeping an eye on things, telling me what furniture I can and can not shift…' James was baffled: he had not had time to catch up with events; did not know about the piano-shifting episode. '…And now you turn up, and take personal charge of everything, overruling me…'

'Calm down.' James spoke sharply. 'It isn't like that, and we're not going to discuss it like this, here. Just send everyone home, and you go home yourself – I'll lock up – and we can talk on Monday when we've all had some rest. OK?'

But it was not OK. 'Don't tell me to calm down.' To James's astonishment there were tears in Adrian's eyes, though they did not have the same effect on him that Nick's had had earlier. 'I can't work in a madhouse like this.' He cast around for an example. 'A place where …

where the manager's boyfriend goes dancing on stage in the middle of a show with this little fancy-man.' He gestured towards Nick, who looked suddenly mortified. There was general laughter.

'Go home,' James yelled, and this time he thought that perhaps it was he who would hit Adrian, his reflexes sharpened by his experience with the bag-snatcher in Seville. He didn't know whether he was angry with Adrian or with Nick and Borja. Whatever had they been doing? 'Just clear out. Now.'

'I'll do that.' Adrian was yelling too. 'I'll do just that. I've had enough. Death threats to actors. Police marksmen…' Tears were running slowly down his cheeks. 'I'm off.' He unclipped two large bunches of keys from his belt, threw them to the floor at James's feet, turned and disappeared along the green-room tunnel. Heads turned to watch his departure and then nobody moved or said anything for quite some time, while James slowly bent down to pick up the keys and wondered how he would explain to Guy and the production manager that he had managed to lose them their stage manager three days before the opening of a new show. Then he pulled himself together. 'Go home everybody. It's two-thirty for the time-sheets. Thank you, casuals, and see you again some time. Stage management: eight-thirty on Monday morning. Goodnight.' He raised the palms of his hands in a no-more-questions-tonight gesture. Then he turned angrily to Nick. 'Would you mind telling me what the fuck has been going on?'

When he had been able to talk to Nick during the show James had been preoccupied with trying to piece together the timetable of Borja's departure first for London and then to Spain, and puzzling over the reason for it. It seemed an extreme reaction to the overnight disappearance of a teenager who was technically an adult, half a continent away. James had not even thought of asking Nick for news of the theatre or Sevenscore. Yet he had noticed a change in Nick: it was something indefinable, like the way his car felt different after someone else had been driving it.

Nick did his best to give a toned-down account of the past few days that would nevertheless satisfy James's curiosity. Because of things that had taken place between the two of them in the past, James knew he was in no position to challenge Nick's version of events, and he knew that Nick knew this too. But even with Nick leaving out a number of particulars that he was far from proud of, there was enough to horrify, anger and alarm James in equal measure. And at the end, when Nick had finished and they stood alone together on the empty stage, James quietly fuming and Nick looking sorry for himself, there was another realisation to face: there was no car to take them home; Borja's, on which James had been relying, was somewhere in London, while his own was out at Sevenscore. 'We'll have to get a taxi,' James said without enthusiasm. He was wishing that his homeward way did not have to be the same as Nick's.

'No we don't,' Nick said. He took a gamble. 'I'll take you on the back of my bike.'

James was surprised into a laugh. 'On that rust bucket? We'd never get there.'

'Well let's try anyway. Even if we only made it halfway, we could always walk the rest.'

'I suppose we could,' James said grudgingly. He tossed one of the two bunches of keys to Nick. 'Do you know the lock-up drill backstage?' Nick nodded. 'I'll put the chains on at the front. See you at the stage door.'

James rode pillion with his hands resolutely laid along the sides of his thighs. He would not clasp Nick around the waist. 'It'll take the hills if we both bounce up and down a bit,' Nick said over his shoulder. And so it did.

Until they reached the short but steepish climb up from the canal at the Rose and Castle. Then the bike could be cajoled no longer and Nick rode up on his own, James following on foot to join him and climb back aboard a few minutes later at the top. After that it was an easy run, slightly downhill, through the time-warp wood.

Neither of them had eaten for over twelve hours. James made an omelette, which they ate in the kitchen with a couple of cans of beer, coolly polite but wary of each other. Nick made one attempt to return to their earlier conversation. 'Nothing happened between Borja and me, you know.'

James looked at him in silence for a second. Then, 'Nothing happened, if you like, between the two of us six weeks ago.' All too easily he could imagine Nick making the same disclaimer to Borja about that occasion, and in an identical tone of voice. Nothing happened between James and me, you know. James smiled bleakly. 'Was it the same sort of nothing?'

'Perhaps it was,' Nick said uncomfortably. He looked down at the table and fiddled with his glass of beer. A faint sound came from outside. Nick looked round to where the night was framed in the un-curtained window. 'The birds are starting to sing,' he said. Then, diffidently, 'Come out and listen?'

They stood in the yard at the back where the cars were normally parked among the outbuildings. A thrush was toying with little silver threads of sound, sounds that took their colour from the cold stars that were now beginning to fade against the lightening sky. Shyly, a blackbird joined in.

'People say I lead men on,' Nick said.

'Who says that?'

'People backstage. But it isn't as if I meant to.' He stopped. James did not attempt a comment.

'What exactly happened with you and me back then?' Nick appeared to be asking the question of himself. And indeed it was he who tried to answer it without giving James the time to risk doing so. 'I suppose we just caught each other out. Surprised by the intensity – for a few moments – of the other's emotions.'

'It happens to human beings quite a lot,' said James in an even tone.

'Being older and cleverer, you'd know that, naturally.'

James refused to rise to that. 'You're an extraordinary boy,' he said. It was not so much the words but the tone of voice that made Nick start.

'I might have slept with you,' Nick said. 'It's really only chance, I suppose, that I didn't. It wasn't on my star. Not one of my way-points.'

'Not on your star? What does that mean? I notice you put it all in the past anyway: might have done.'

'Woodcocks have STARs and pilots have them: fixed but invisible ways that zigzag through airspace and bring them home. Maybe we'll see a woodcock flying home in a minute.'

'Crazy kid.' James said. 'You don't know where your home is yet, I think.'

'I don't know the songs of all the birds,' said Nick. 'Just blackbirds and thrushes. But they're all beautiful. People walk through the parks in towns with Walkmans on to shut the birdsong out. Don't you want to pull the plugs out sometimes and say, just listen? But maybe they've lost it – lost the music and just hear random noises that touch them nowhere.'

'There's a wren now,' said James quietly. 'A dunnock and a wood pigeon. Goldfinches…'

Robins and greenfinches, chiff-chaffs and pheasants, chaffinches and skyborne swifts all added their songs, till the silvery sound became fanfares of gold and the stars gave way to the rising sun.

TWENTY

The bus from Barajas airport dropped Borja and Andy at its underground terminal beneath the Plaza de Colón. Where the decision about what to do next was taken for them as soon as they got off by a sign pointing to the Centro Cultural Villa de Madrid and, underneath it, the indication: Teatro. They did not even have to go above ground. Finding the box office in the heart of the 1970s complex, Borja asked the woman on duty if anyone knew of any theatres in the city that were currently being refurbished. She looked a bit surprised at his question, giving a little frown and a shake of her tied-back braided hair. 'Well there is one,' she said. The Teatro Real, the city's principal opera house, had recently closed for a major restoration that was expected to last for some years. 'But it's been dogged by problems,' she added, taking her cue from the signs of keen interest on Borja's face. 'Did you know, the architect in charge suddenly died of a heart attack while he was inspecting the site? Nobody knows when, if ever, it's going to get finished.' Borja and Andy looked at each other. It sounded a most unpromising place to start looking for a runaway youngster. Were there no other theatres being done up? The lady at the desk asked among her colleagues. They were as certain as they could be that the answer was no. Almost as an afterthought Borja asked if they had been approached by teenagers from Salamanca. He gave Rizo's name, and Manuel's. The names meant nothing. But teenagers... The city was alive with them and had been for the last few weekends. You know, he was told, it was the Caretera de Bacalao. Salt-cod Highway? Andy queried, reluctant to trust his Spanish on this. Borja responded with a nod. 'I thought that all happened down at Valencia and Barcelona,' Borja told the woman.

'But now at Madrid it's the same.' She laughed. 'Without, I suppose, the bacalao. May the Second was crazy. Now it's San Isidro.' She raised her eyes. 'Any excuse to have a party.'

'Where does it all happen?' Borja wanted to know.

'The streets around the Plaza de Chueca, and Malasaña too, of course.'

'Both walking distance from here, right?' The woman gave some rapid directions, waving her hands as if directing fast traffic, and Borja said, 'Right. Vale. Let's go.'

Borja explained to Andy about the Caretera de Bacalao. The nearest equivalent in England would have been a rave. Lots of young people. Stolen cars. Ecstasy. Long drives through the night to get to the coast… Andy got the picture but was not entirely cheered by it. 'Are you seriously suggesting we search two whole districts for two youngsters among thousands?'

Borja looked deflated. 'I don't know, exactly. I suppose that's a bit unrealistic. But we seem to have come to the right place. For once.'

They decided to head into the general direction of Chueca, and made their way up to street level. They could talk about plans of action as they walked. To their surprise they found that Madrid had had a short keen shower of rain while they had been underground; now the buildings had a sharp-edged, silver look, and glistened in the late afternoon sun. They tried one or two more theatres on their way, but without any serious expectation of finding news of Rizo and Manuel. Instead, Borja unexpectedly found himself regarding the theatres with a newly expert eye: peering at box office computers, taking in arrangements front of house, comparing things, almost proprietorially, with his own latest place of work.

Nobody in any of the theatres had heard of Rizo or Manuel, but everyone knew about the Careteras. The grizzled stage doorman at the Maria Guerrero said that if they were looking for runaways they should surely go first to the police. A younger man behind him, with earrings and a ponytail, overhearing this, added rather pointedly that if it was two young lads together, they should start looking in the gay bars. And just in case they didn't know where to start – the young man scrutinised the faces of Borja and Andy closely as he said this – here were some addresses, and he wrote them down for Borja, near the Plaza de Chueca once again. 'Refugios nocturnos, night shelters for the homeless,' suggested the box office manager at the Teatro Marquina on Calle de Prim, and gave them an address just a couple of blocks to the north.

'He'd hardly be likely to end up in a place like that,' Andy objected, as they meandered on in the general direction of the Plaza de Chueca, 'if he's come to Madrid for a bit of fun.' Borja agreed. He was beginning to be more relaxed. There seemed to be every probability that Rizo was here in Madrid – whether they managed to track him down this evening or not – and Borja was coming to accept the reassuring probability, put forward by Andy that morning, that the reasons for his disappearance had nothing whatever to do with himself.

It was now dark. The streets here were teeming with young people of Rizo's age and a bit older. Borja tried stopping one or two of them and asking, in a vain attempt at up-to-date Madrid street slang, where the party was. But they laughed in his face. Andy sighed. 'It's as useless as people like us asking where the next rave's going to be back home. Makes you feel old, doesn't it?'

Then they found themselves at the refugio anyway. 'Might as well ask,' said Borja. The warden listened to them politely, but he hadn't seen anyone corresponding to Rizo's description. Had they tried asking around the squats in the area? Many student drop-outs and runaways hung out in such places; they formed quite a community – los paracaidistas; new arrivals would be known about. The warden suggested a couple of addresses. They thanked him and left.

They felt strange and uncomfortable knocking at the door of a building, where the stucco was cracking away from the walls like the icing on an abandoned cake, whose ground floor windows were boarded up and where the entry phones had been ripped out. Nobody came. They pushed at the door and to their surprise it opened at once. They found themselves in a large open space that might once have been a workshop or a bar but was now totally derelict; weeds sprouted from what was left of the old wood floor. They could hear voices from the top of dark stairs. Then a door opened above them and someone came out and leaned over the banisters. A girl with very long hair. 'Qué quieren?'

'Buscamos Borja López … Rizo ... y Manuel Peñafiel,' said Borja.

'Are you the police?'

'No. Family.'

'Nobody of those names here.'

'Newly arrived from Salamanca.'

The girl hesitated. 'Look, come up.'

They followed her up and into a room where missing boards made ankle-breaker traps in the floor, where plaster crumbled from paintless walls, and candles in jars guttered, perched on upturned beer crates, and seemed to make the dark ceiling even blacker with the oscillating shadows they cast up. They found themselves among some six or seven young people in various stages of drug-induced somnolence – whether they were happy stages or not was impossible to guess. Some were sitting half inside sleeping bags on the floor. Others appeared completely comatose. None of them looked more than about seventeen.

One boy glared at them from a large, deep armchair which, being the only piece of real furniture, gave him something of the aura of a young king enthroned. He was painfully thin, plimsoll-ed but sockless, and wearing a filthy pullover so pulled and picked-at that it overflowed his pale knuckles and reached halfway down his brittle thighs. From his seat of power he spoke first. 'You're looking for the kids from Salamanca, yes?' They said they were. 'To take them home?' They nodded. 'You're welcome to them if you can find them.' The boy sank back into the depths of his throne.

'Have they been here?' Borja wanted to know.

'Not here. Little rich kids, porrero wannabes, thinking they want to try the life…'

'How many are they?'

The boy thought for a moment. 'Four or five, maybe. Three boys, maybe four, and a girl. Stupid things.'

'How did they get here from Salamanca?'

'Don't know. Stole a car maybe. That's the usual thing. Everybody comes here now.' He adopted a posh voice. 'We're the height of fashion here, didn't you know?'

'Any idea where they might be now?' Borja asked.

'No idea. In some squat or other.'

'There might be hundreds.'

'No.' The boy considered for a second. 'A dozen maybe. Not more. Not round here.' Then, after another short pause, he said, 'Adios,' and dismissed them with a small flick of his hand. The audience was at an end.

Borja and Andy began to leave. But as they reached the bottom of the stairs someone scampered down and caught them up by the door. ‘Wait.’ It was another young boy, his eyes unfocused and glazed like marbles. ‘Don’t waste all night going round the squats, trying to talk to the gandules. They’ll be at El Draco later, likely as not. Everyone will. Not yet. Much later. Don’t tell anyone I said.’ He gave them directions through a maze of back streets with strange names. Borja willed his brain into memorising the sequence; it was almost certainly the only chance he would get.

They were glad to get out into the open air. ‘Who’d have kids,’ said Andy.

It was ten o’clock and they were both famished. They also realised that they had made no plans for spending the night in the city. They walked a little way and checked into the first hostal they came across. It was rough and seedy but they were not feeling like being particular in the circumstances. It compared very favourably with the squat and the night shelter. They were shown into a room with two single beds. Borja thought that he could just about cope with that.

Coming out of the hostal they passed a doorway in an alley from which the smell of frying chicken wafted out like an invitation. To them in their hungry state it was almost a command. They went in and ordered cheap and greasy platefuls which they washed down with a couple of glasses of wine. Returning to the open street afterwards they saw an old man in a wheelchair, his hands red and swollen, a begging bowl on his lap. He was wrapped up against the spring night in an overcoat, a muffler and a fetid hat. Behind the wheelchair crouched another old man. Ashamed of the squalor of his situation, he was trying to hide his evening meal: a few scraps which he was eating from a paper plate, on the ground, like a dog.

Andy was shocked by the sight. Borja dived matter-of-factly into a pocket and brought out a few coins which he deposited in the begging bowl; Andy was a visitor in Spain, he not.

'Will that be us in half a lifetime, do you think?' Andy asked. He sounded as if he was serious. 'Do you suppose they could be two old queens who used to be pilots and then lost the plot?'

'I'll try not to think about that,' said Borja. The airline's enquiry into the Casablanca incident loomed for both of them. It must come soon now, though neither of them had had any news about it yet. But right now Borja had to concentrate on the directions he had been given through the back streets to El Draco, whatever kind of a place that might turn out to be.

The directions they were following – assuming they had followed them correctly – led them at last to an unlit and hopeless-looking sort of street. If it had been full of shops and cafés once, they were now closed and boarded up. But there were signs of life at the further end. Figures were moving among the shadows, converging on one area of dark wall and then disappearing into … a hole? … a doorway? When they got closer they could see there was a contractor's hoarding across the front of the building, but one section of it had been well and truly broken and trampled. Behind it there was a doorway in the wall, though the door itself was missing. Incredibly – or perhaps it was the extreme darkness of the street that made them temporarily indistinguishable from people nearly twenty years younger than themselves – they went unchallenged as they joined the converging knots of youngsters and made their way through the doorway.

The street frontage of the building was the only one that stood. They found themselves in a rubble-strewn space, open to the sky, its boundaries defined by the party walls it had shared with adjoining buildings, the way the space once occupied by an extracted tooth is defined only by its remaining neighbours. In the centre of this area an enormous bonfire blazed and around it crowded a hundred or more figures, fire-lit on the far side, but near at hand in massed silhouette; the crowd was growing quickly, augmented by a steady stream of arrivals through the doorway behind them, even as they watched. Two guitars were being played in a fairly coherent joint improvisation. Borja and Andy stayed near the entrance for a minute or so, trying to accustom their eyes to the lighting, trying to make sense of the scene.

'What do you suggest?' Andy asked. 'Wander through the crowd peering into people's faces, or make an announcement from the top of the bonfire like Joan of Arc?'

'I don't know,' said Borja. By now a few people had started to look in their direction, then nudged others who also turned to look briefly themselves. Perhaps they were being taken for reporters or police. For the moment no-one came to challenge them, but that could not last for long. They would not have much time.

'Oh my God,' said Borja. 'Have you realised what this place is? I was right all along.' He pointed out the vertical iron girders, rusted and fire-blackened, that had once been hidden inside fluted pilasters and borne the weight of the dress circle tier. And on the walls they could see, now that they looked properly, traces of gilded mouldings and plaster swags where mirrors and ornate lamp brackets had once been. 'It wasn't being restored, it's being demolished. It must have looked like the Regent.' A wave of intense sadness swept over him. It was as if this sight of beauty stripped to the bone – or rather, of bones abandoned by beauty – was a metaphor for the ephemeral nature of all beautiful things, for the futility of all human endeavour.

Andy, who had not just spent a highly charged six weeks working backstage in a beautiful Victorian jewel of a theatre, did not experience Borja's sudden feeling of desolation for himself, yet the shock of sadness communicated itself to him from Borja somehow, like a small electric current. 'What's wrong?' he asked.

'I can't explain,' Borja said, and Andy didn't press him to. Instead – and, he thought, more sensibly – he pulled Borja's head towards him and kissed him on the mouth.

At which Borja protested, 'No don't,' but simultaneously a youthful voice was saying, 'Borja, qué haces aqui?' in astonishment.

'We came to look for you,' said Borja, taken aback. Rizo looked a good inch taller than when they had last met just three months ago.

'James?' the boy hazarded, looking at Andy.

'Andy.' Andy held out his hand. 'Just a friend.'

'Obviously a very good one,' said Rizo innocently. Then, suddenly aware of his gaffe, he added, 'I mean, to have come such a long way.'

'Listen,' said Borja. 'We have to talk.'

Rizo's face fell.

'I'm not going to tear a strip off you. Though I can't promise that your father won't. You need to know that your parents are … well, worried, not to put it more strongly. They need to know – don't you think? – when they can expect to see you again.'

'Did they send you?'

'No,' said Andy, and managed to summon up just enough Spanish, aided and abetted by gesture, to indicate that the search party was Borja's own idea.

'Look,' said Rizo, explaining reasonably. 'If I telephoned them they'd want me back straight away, which would defeat the object of coming here. It's like a party, sort of all night. And if you take me away now the whole point gets lost, see.'

'And if I leave you here,' said Borja, 'what do I say to your mother? To Manuel's mother?'

'How did you know Manuel's here?'

'I sort of guessed. The police are looking for you. Do you know that?'

'Listen,' said Andy to Borja. 'If we let them finish their party or whatever it turns out to be, and we phone the parents to say they're safe at least…'

Borja turned back to Rizo. 'If we do that, and if we tell them to call the police off, will you promise to go back home tomorrow? Have you got the money to do that?'

Rizo shook his head and stared at the ground, suddenly a child again.

'How did you get here?'

'A car. We – one of us – found a car.'

'Found one,' said Borja heavily. 'I see. And where is it now?'

'I don't know. It got lost. I think it was parked in the wrong place and towed away by the police.'

'Like our aeroplane,' suggested Andy.

'I suppose it'll sort itself out,' Borja said, not sounding very convinced. He was remembering how he had got into trouble with the police when he was barely a teenager himself – a bit of a business with some spray paint, and the local bishop had had to be brought in as a character witness... 'Do you want your father to come and fetch you tomorrow?'

'No. That'd make it worse.'

'Then I'll give you the money for the train and take you to the station in the morning. You'll have to come and find us.' He gave Rizo the address of their hostal. 'I'm not going to give you the money now: you'll lose it or get it stolen. And I don't want to know what you get up to at your all-night bash. That's your life to lead, your own mistakes to make, and I want nothing to do with them. You know what I'm talking about. But, if you don't come by midday I'll tell your parents exactly where you are and I'll give details to the police as well. Understand? Don't let me down.'

Someone, a handsome fellow of about his own age, called Rizo's name from a short distance away; Rizo said, 'Hasta mañana,' to Borja and Andy, then turned on his heel and melted back into the fire-flickering throng.

Borja and Andy did a smart about turn too, ducked out of the doorway of the one-time theatre and, despite taking a few wrong turns in the narrow streets, found themselves a few minutes later in the brightly lit Plaza de Chueca. Borja telephoned Marisa. It was a long conversation: Andy had already started on his second beer by the time Borja sat to join him at his table under the painted ceiling in the Ángel Sierra. 'Well,' said Andy. 'All's well that ends well. Do you think they came all this way to check out if they're gay or not – and remember, they had a girl in tow – or just for the drugs and the excitement?'

'To be bloody honest, I'm just so relieved to have found him safe and well that I don't care.'

'And what about you?' Andy asked slyly. 'What do you feel like doing?'

For the crowds all around them, evening in Madrid was only beginning. Unwinding from the stresses of the day they got caught up in the atmosphere, strolled from bar to bar, wandered on to a club, and managed to forget that they were even as much as a day older than twenty. It was after five o'clock when they found their way back to their hostal. 'You know,' said Borja, as they climbed the stairs, 'I think I've been here before. I think this may have been the very place I stayed with James the night we met.'

'Uh-huh,' said Andy. 'And did you…?'

'No,' Borja said. 'And neither...' He realised that it was unnecessary to complete the thought. That particular fire would not ignite again for either of them. Locating their room – was it the actual one that Borja had shared with James? – they stripped and got into their separate beds, hardly able to believe that that was what they were doing. 'Tell me something,' Andy said, a little while after they had put out the lights and said goodnight. 'Tell me about Nick.'

'I thought you might ask me that,' said Borja.

'Did you? Then tell me all about him.'

'All?' Borja pondered this. 'It might be rather a long story.'

'We've got the rest of the night,' said Andy.

'Son las once y media,' announced a young voice, rather diffidently. Rizo was in the bedroom with them, telling them the time: half past eleven.

Borja sat up, woke up – he was not sure of the order of the two events – with a jolt. 'Joder,' he said. Andy began to wake in the other bed. Borja saw Rizo take note of the sleeping arrangements. Through the door he glimpsed the rubbernecking figures of what appeared to be two boys and a girl. He reached a banknote from the muddle on the bedside locker and handed it to the boy. 'Get yourselves a coffee on the terrace downstairs. We'll join you in a minute when we've showered.'

TWENTY-ONE

Nick cooked dinner. It was roast chicken with lemon and tarragon – the tarragon fresh from the herb garden – and it was timed to coincide with Borja's return in the early evening. Nick reasoned that, if the atmosphere was going to be tense, a good meal would at least do nothing to make things worse.

As it happened the scene was not set for a family row around the Sunday table. There was something more urgent on James's agenda than mutual recriminations with his partner over Nick. He came out with it almost as soon as Borja walked through the door. 'Adrian's gone. It's nobody's fault in particular, but you won't be surprised to know that you did get mentioned in despatches. Anyway, I need your help with the fallout. Can you join the stage management team for a week or two?'

Borja had rehearsed several possible conversations with James as he drove up the motorway from London. This particular one had not featured. He sat down at the already laid table in astonished silence.

James went on. 'You'd be jointly responsible with Sandra.' Sandra was the deputy stage manager, Adrian's junior and one grade senior to Nick. 'You'd be on DSM's pay, same as her.'

Borja came to. 'I'm not worried about the pay. Just astonished at the situation. What's Equity going to say? And what about the other staff?'

'The other staff don't get to choose. Not even Nick here.' James nodded towards him. Nick was carving slices of chicken in prudent silence. 'Equity's OK. Guy phoned the general secretary at home this morning. So long as it's not for more than a week or two, and provided we start tomorrow with ringing round the candidates we said no to at the interviews, Equity won't make a problem.'

Borja would not have felt able to refuse James's request, or offer – whichever it most resembled – even if he had wanted to. But he found that, except that he had been looking forward to a rest and a few lie-ins after his hectic schedule of the last few days, he was actually quite pleased to be going back to work in the theatre once more.

'It's not going to be a heavy fit-up,' James reassured him. 'Who's Afraid of Virginia Woolf? is nothing like Kiss Me Kate. We don't start before eight thirty.'

'Well that's something.' Nobody made the crass observation that anyone else looked exhausted. It was only too obvious, and the signs too equally present on all their faces. But for now the practicalities of stage management and the opening of the new production engaged their attention – right through the meal and for the rest of the evening. Eventually Nick made an excuse and said it was time he went to bed. He left James and Borja alone together with a feeling of something like relief, but shamefacedly aware that it was a relief he did not entirely deserve.

'I have to ask you…' James began, as they started to clear up together in the kitchen.

'You have to ask me?! I have to ask you…'

'About you and Nick…'

'About me and Nick?' said Borja. 'Please, you tell me.'

James took a breath. 'I haven't slept with Nick. I haven't had sex with him. That's the short and truthful answer. Now you tell me.' He rattled some knives away into a drawer.

'I haven't either. It's that simple.'

'Then why were you dancing with him – on stage – in front of six hundred people – while I was away? What kind of a statement did that make? It was in the bloody show report, for God's sake! Guy thought it was very funny, fortunately, but that's not the point.'

'You've got it out of context,' said Borja uncomfortably. 'It wasn't the way you think. I danced with Smut too.' Absently he stashed a colander in the wrong place.

'With Smut!? In full view of the audience? What the fuck were you thinking of?' James was chopping up raw liver for Neville's cat.

'He wanted to know the steps, that's all. And it wasn't in sight of the audience. Nick wanted a lesson too, because I'd shown Smut. There was nothing more to it than that. I'd forgotten there was a scene change coming up, that's all. And I'm sorry about that; it wasn't very professional. But that's all it was, or wasn't. Still, I don't see that you're in any position to talk about making statements in public. You took Nick out to a Chinese restaurant while I was away, where anybody could have seen you – Sammy and Chris did – and you didn't think it worth mentioning to me.'

'Now you're being ridiculous. Didn't somebody else take him out to a French restaurant when I was away and was also seen with him by Chris and Sammy? And you didn't think to tell me about that.'

'Cojones! I haven't seen you since then. That was two nights ago. I've only just got back from Madrid. When did I have a chance to tell you? You had six weeks.'

'That all happened when you got into trouble in Casablanca. Which quite simply put it out of my mind. Come on, let's go and give Hodge his dinner.' Hodge was the name of Neville's cat, just as two centuries before it had been the name of Doctor Johnson's. Together the two men crossed the lawn with the glistening plateful and let themselves into the East Pavilion with the spare key. The kitchen lay on the right of the entrance hall. As you approached it you found yourself looking through the open door into Inigo Jones's majestic double cube room, its ornate plaster-work gleaming softly in the evening light. James had time to notice that the half-used bale of hay that had sat spilling itself onto the carpet just beyond the Adam fireplace had gone, and the carpet appeared to have been swept. 'Who got rid of the hay?' he asked Borja as they turned into the kitchen. It was unlikely to have been Neville.

'Nick did,' Borja said. 'Stage management habits overflowing into his home life.'

'Home,' said James with a bit of a snort.

Borja didn't pursue that. 'A donkey, of all things,' he said. He was back on the subject of the hay-bale. A year before, Neville had been persuaded to buy a donkey and trap. The idea had been that Neville would drive down to the Rose and Castle in it, and the donkey would pull the trap with Neville in it back up the hill when it was time to return. Though Neville might be in his cups, the homing instinct of the donkey would operate like a sort of automatic pilot... That the plan was never going to work was so evident that, when it didn't and the donkey and trap had to be sold at a considerable loss, nobody had even felt it necessary to say, I told you so.

'I still don't get,' said James, as Borja rinsed feeding bowls under the tap, 'why you had to disappear to Spain in such a rush, leaving the stage crew one down like that.'

'I didn't,' Borja said, sounding pained. 'I spoke to Guy on the phone and he cleared it with Adrian there and then. Otherwise I wouldn't have gone. I wasn't letting anyone down.'

'OK, I accept that. But why did you have to go to Spain at all? Some teenager goes missing. He's not even your family.' Hodge arrived suddenly from nowhere and put his front paws up James's leg, impatient for his meal. James lowered the plate of liver to the floor.

'Marisa's my oldest friend, that's all,' said Borja. He crouched down and fondled the dining cat.

James looked down and addressed the dark top of Borja's head. 'But Andy isn't your oldest friend. Yet you rushed straight off to him when you got the news about this chap disappearing. I can't see how it all ties up. What's the connection between Andy and Marisa and her son? And what's between you and Andy, come to that? You do one flight together, stopover in Casablanca, then you don't mention his name for a month, and then suddenly he's your confidant and best buddy and you swan off to Madrid with him and spend the night together in a hostal. He doesn't just happen to be gay, does he?'

'As it happens, he does.' Borja continued to stroke Hodge and thought about turning the spotlight on the all in James's 'that all happened when you were in Casablanca', but decided against it in view of what he was going to have to say in a minute.

James went on. 'And you go sharing hotel rooms in Madrid and Casablanca with him and don't think to mention to me the fact that he's a poof. Who is this Andy character?'

Borja twisted his head round and looked up at James with an expression that was hard to read. 'You've met him already.'

'For half an hour in a pub.'

'Well, you're going to have the chance to get to know him better. I've invited him to come and stay with us for a few days in a week's time.' He looked down again and continued to fondle the cat. Hodge could hardly believe the amount of attention he was getting.

'Oh great!' said James. 'Have you forgotten that it's Alexa's guitar recital next Sunday? And naturally I've invited her and Mark for the weekend too.'

Borja looked up at James again. Perhaps this time there was something like relief on his face. 'Well thank you for telling me now. But actually it won't be too much of a problem. Andy can't make it before Sunday afternoon. There'll only be a short overlap.'

'You don't half like to push things.' James sighed. 'Asking someone I've hardly met…'

Borja got to his feet as the cat cleaned around the sides of the plate. 'I'm sorry about that. Honestly.' He wondered for a moment what he was actually saying sorry for. And how honest he was being. Then his lips twitched in amusement as he remembered something else. 'Mind you,' he said, 'I did hear about some other lunch party a couple of months back...' Now he gave James a pleading grin that was meant to say, Look, can we put all this behind us, please? He was cheered when, a moment later, James shyly returned something of the same sort.

TWENTY-TWO

The following Saturday morning found Nick alone in the West Pavilion, assiduously practising Bach's A-minor English Suite. Although the air outside was already nicely warm, the inside of the ballroom still had the early morning's chill on it. Nick hardly noticed the temperature; he was working so energetically that he generated his own warm micro-climate of body heat. He even didn't notice that someone had entered the room and sat down in one of the chairs until she – a woman with red hair whom he suddenly caught sight of in one of the great mirrors that made up a large part of the wall space – had been sitting listening to him for some minutes. He stopped abruptly.

'Do go on,' said the woman. 'It's rather good.'

As the woman could be none other than Alexa, the 'rather good'counted for far more with Nick than a verdict of excellent, or brilliant, from most other people. But it was with some trepidation that he re-engaged with the music and played the massive Prelude movement through to its end.

'I don't know who you are,' said Alexa when the piece was finished, 'but you play Bach very nicely.'

'Thank you. Really, thank you. Because I know who you are at least.' Nick introduced himself. 'James and Borja are in town shopping. I don't think they were expecting you till this afternoon.'

'I know. I'm really sorry. Mark thought it would take the whole day to get here from London. He couldn't quite get his head round the idea that there are motorways in England. He's having a look round the garden. It's amazing here. I had no idea they lived in such a place. Of course James told us about it. I suppose

I must have thought he was exaggerating. Tell me, what else do you play?'

By the time Mark wandered in to join them a few minutes later they were deeply engrossed in piano music: scores were lying open across the piano lid and Nick and Alexa were animatedly discussing points of technique and interpretation.

'It's cold in here,' said Mark, when he had introduced himself to Nick. 'I think of the garden of the Selfish Giant. And that piece you were playing sounded so bleak and wintry. At least your garden's warm. And beautiful. May blossom, crimson chestnut candles, clematis…' He left them to it, preferring to wander in the real warmth and sunlight outside. Some time later he heard the sound of the piano again: something brighter this time; it was Weber's Invitation to the Dance, being played for fun, with Nick doing the left hand and Alexa doing the right.

They arranged to meet Borja and James in the Rose and Castle for lunch. 'I'd better tell you before you meet them,' said Nick as they walked across the fields along the grass-grown carriage drive. 'It's been a bit of a week. Especially for Borja.' He told them about Borja's temporary elevation to joint deputy stage manager. It had been quite a steep learning curve. 'And then, two days ago he had to go to his company headquarters – his airline company I mean – to answer questions at the enquiry… Did you know about this? I'm talking about the Casablanca thing. When they landed at the wrong airport?' Mark and Alexa nodded that they did know. 'He thought they might give him a very hard time, but in the end, he said, it wasn't so bad. Just a lot of very detailed questions.'

'And the outcome?' asked Mark.

'He won't know for maybe another week. In the meantime, his comrade in arms, Andy, has been invited up here for a few days – to take his mind off things, I suppose. I can't think it will though, if he's spending all his time with Borja.'

'Hang on a minute,' said Mark. 'Who's Andy?'

Nick explained. With hindsight he regretted using the expression 'comrade in arms'. It brought back the image of Andy kissing Borja goodbye after they had all been to the pub together in Earls Court. 'Anyway,' Nick concluded, 'he's supposed to be arriving tomorrow, in time for the concert as it happens, so you'll get to meet him.'

'I suppose,' said Alexa carefully, 'that everything is all right between Borja and James?'

Nick looked a little uncomfortable. 'I suppose it is,' he said. He did not want to elaborate much on that either. There had been a degree of tension between the three of them, unexpressed in words but palpable in the atmosphere, during the few days since Borja had returned from Madrid – since James had returned from Seville, since… There were places where Nick didn't want to let his mind go, just at present.

When they arrived at the Rose and Castle and made their way into the top bar, Mark ducking under the beams, Nick was surprised to see Neville sitting there, complete with tweed suit and tie, with a pint of Pedigree in front of him and doing the Telegraph crossword with a smartly coiffed Maya. 'Is it safe for you to be here?' Nick asked him at once, surprising Mark and Alexa just a little.

'Apparently yes,' said Maya. 'The Irishman's gone back across the water, taking a wodge of cash that that woman – for some idiotic reason – kept under the mattress. We heard this – by phone of course – from the horse's mouth.' Presumably the horse was Rita. 'So for better or worse I've brought him back to you all.' The door opened and James and Borja arrived to join them.

'You're in luck,' said Neville, 'I can offer you a drink. They've just installed a new till and it's on the blink – not accepting money just at present.' He turned his head and called across the bar, 'Lily, can you give these good people a drink of whatever it is they're having? I'll pay you next time, when you've got that thing working again.'

In the evening James took Alexa and Mark to the theatre and bought them tickets to the show.

'I'm sorry,' James said. 'Who's Afraid of Virginia Woolf? is not exactly what I'd have chosen for a pair of friends who are just about to get married, but there it is.'

'It'll give me a chance to discover the acoustic,' said Alexa drily.

The next morning Alexa, who had commandeered the West Pavilion for most of the previous afternoon to practise her guitar solos, took some time off to make piano music with Nick. She hadn't played the piano for years, she said: Nick had to excuse her rustiness. Nick thought there was nothing to excuse: her piano playing, rusty or not, was on a level far above his own. They played some Schubert duets, then Alexa asked Nick to play the Bach again. This time he played it all. When he had finished, Alexa sat in silence for a while. And then she said, 'There's something wrong, Nick. I don't mean in your playing. Your playing's very good. Better than yesterday. You have technique, and also understanding and real feeling. I'm talking about something else. There's something in the atmosphere between you and James and Borja. I don't know if it's the effect of that gloomy play I saw last night. And I hear a sadness in your playing. I know Mark said the A-minor was a wintry piece, but it's more than that. Has something gone wrong between the three of you?'

Nick looked round the ballroom and out through the long windows into the shining garden. 'It's so beautiful here. The garden, the buildings, the piano to play on … two friendships … I've been so lucky – and I've messed it all up.'

'What do you mean?'

'I think I've got to leave here. Leave Sevenscore at least. Maybe the theatre too. I told Borja I'd decided that during the show last night, backstage.'

'But you seem to fit in so well. You're such a part of the family here.'

'Maybe I fitted in too well,' said Nick carefully. 'I haven't been very clever in managing my friendship with the two of them.'

'One young man and two slightly older gay ones,' said Alexa gently. 'Is that what you mean?'

'I suppose two gay men's company and three's a crowd.'

Alexa detected an ambiguity in Nick's answer but deliberately refrained from exploring it or asking for clarification. Instead, she said, 'I think it's very sad if you think you have to move. Especially if you end up somewhere with no piano – that would be very bad for you. I'm sure they don't want you to go. Think about it for a day or two. Give yourself time to reconsider. I'm sure the three of you can sort something out.' She laughed as a thought struck her. 'Maybe you should move somebody else in with you.'

'Funny,' said Nick. 'That's what Borja said when I told him I was leaving.'

A snack lunch was in progress when Andy arrived a couple of hours later. Alexa, with a concert just a few hours away, was by now slowly distancing herself from the world around her and the people in it, and there was a strange feeling in the Court House of life suspended, as if people were watching and waiting for an eclipse of the sun. Andy was conscious of entering this strange house from the back. Having parked his car next to Borja's, which he recognised, he saw two possible means of entry: a pair of big gates that led to a kind of Alice in Wonderland garden which was occupied by buildings that appeared to have sailed over from renaissance Italy; or, nearer at hand, what looked like a rather humble kitchen door. He knocked at the latter. It was opened by Nick, whose warm brown eyes, though well remembered, nevertheless gave him an unexpected jolt. 'Come in,' said Nick. 'We're just having cheese on toast.'

Borja, wearing his stage manager's hat, had planned the afternoon in meticulous detail. Only one person would be required to work backstage. Move a chair, pull curtains, escort Alexa to the stage at the right time … that was all there was to it. Nick was pleased now that it would be himself; and Alexa, who had been paying Nick the compliment throughout the weekend of treating him as a fellow, if junior, musician, seemed pleased too. Nick would go into town with Alexa, taking Andy and Mark with him – which meant Mark driving them all in his car. Nick would install Alexa in the theatre to practise, and Throat would be on hand – 'Ha-ha, very funny,' said James – to sort out whatever Alexa needed in the way of lights. Nick would be free to take Mark and Andy for a walk round the city, and everyone would meet up again before the performance. 'Are you sure it's OK for us to abandon our house guests and leave them to entertain each other for the afternoon?' James asked Borja.

'Trust me,' Borja replied.

'Well, it will make a change to have an afternoon all to ourselves for once,' James admitted. One thing that had always been a plus in their relationship, a dependable certainty over the years, was that whenever one of them was feeling like sex, then so was the other.

'Even Paco Peña didn't pull in a bigger crowd,' the chairman of the board told Alexa over drinks in the Regent Room when the concert was over. James had specially asked the chairman to come. He had answered that he would come with joy – which James thought was an unusual way of putting it: people usually said 'with pleasure'. It was not until later that James had remembered, as he shook hands with her in the foyer, that Joy was the name of the chairman's wife.

As it sounded in Borja's lightly inflected accent, 'the bus was good'. Many in that sizeable audience had come out of mild curiosity. The curtains had parted and flown up to reveal a startlingly bare stage, brightly lit but furnished only with a plain oak chair. Alexa, in a shot silk dress of kingfisher blues and greens had walked calmly on, sat down to muted applause – and then electrified the house from the first chord. As she played her own, and Segovia's, arrangements of Bach and Scarlatti, pieces by Villa-Lobos and Fernando Sors, and one piece by her first guitar teacher in Seville, Karsten Bäcker, the audience's mood swung from curiosity to surprise, then to wonder and exultation. When she finally left the stage and Nick had rung the curtain down for the last time the fabric of the building was vibrating with cheers and shouting and the stamping of feet.

Dinner at the Court House was late and the living room table crowded. Neville and Maya were there, Guy too – he wanted a progress report from Neville about his adaptation of Barnaby Rudge. Then there were Alexa and Mark, Nick, and Andy – who was feeling rather overwhelmed by the company of quite so many strange and arty types, in particular Neville – plus Borja and James, the two hosts. Nick had given them instructions, and a recipe by Pierre Koffman, for a dish called gigot à quatres heures, which involved putting a whole leg of lamb in the oven with onions, carrots, herbs and white wine and leaving it there for the whole time they were in town for Alexa's concert. Nick had told them it was impossible to go wrong if they simply followed the recipe to the letter, and he had been right: the guests were suitably complimentary.

Nick was a strange fellow, Andy thought. He'd been alternately charming and oddly spiky during the afternoon when he had tried to engage him in conversation as they walked around the city centre with Mark. Borja had told him that he had revised his opinion: Nick was almost definitely gay; he had certainly flirted quite outrageously with Borja and – Borja had feared – with James too. Whether Nick's behaviour towards Andy could be construed as flirting it was too soon to say. But what Andy was growing more certain of was what he himself felt about Nick. What he had seen of him, what he had optimistically guessed at concerning his personality and character during his first short contact with him in London… No, he did not think he had been mistaken.

'They tell me,' said Neville to Mark, tasting the wine without bothering too much about the label, 'that you're a poet. Is that true?'

'Hell,' said Mark, 'who told you that? It's true I used to write poems – least, what I thought were poems – when these two guys first knew me.'

'You were writing all the time,' said James.

'How wonderful,' said Maya, genuinely impressed.

'It wasn't wonderful at all,' said Mark, more sharply than he'd meant to sound. 'I burnt the lot.'

'You didn't!' said Neville, appalled. One of his spare bedrooms was stacked with typewritten reams of paper that might, just possibly, be considered useable by somebody for something at some point in the unforeseeable future. He certainly had never considered destroying any of it.

‘When I met Alexa,’ Mark explained gently, ‘I discovered what real talent was. Something that I just didn’t have. There was no point going on after that.’

‘Please don’t,’ Alexa said to him; then to the others, ‘I hate it when he disparages himself this way. It upset me so much at the time.’

Maya tried to pluck consensus out of what was threatening to become an intimate domestic discussion between Alexa and Mark. ‘Whatever else, at least it shows Mark in the light of a true gentleman.’

‘There’s no such animal,’ said Neville. ‘He’s as mythical a beast as a unicorn.’ Nick chose that moment to catch Andy’s eye with a smile.

‘All right,’ said Maya. ‘Allow that no man behaves like a gentleman all the time. What kind of actions constitute gentlemanly behaviour? What does everyone think?’

‘Well, I’d exclude burning your own poems for a start,’ said Guy. ‘That’s more like masochism.’

‘Do you mean the way someone lives his life, or are you talking about particular acts of gallantry?’ asked James. ‘They’re two very different things, surely.’

‘Topping up the glasses all round might be a particular act of gallantry just now,’ Neville reminded him, à propos.

‘Opening doors for women, something as simple as that,’ suggested Andy.

‘Not any more,’ Alexa shot him down. ‘These days we construe that as sexist behaviour. We think, what does he want out of this?’

‘Brutality, thy name is woman,’ said Neville.

‘Well, what about this for gallantry,’ said Nick. ‘I heard about an airline pilot who left a female colleague stranded overnight on Gran Canaria without clothes or sanitary towels because he wanted to get home in a hurry.'

There was a moment's surprised silence while those who didn't know the story wondered what it was all about and which pilot was in question, and those who did know it considered their response to Nick's intervention. Andy himself looked stunned. Borja found his tongue first. 'I'd say that bringing that up in a dinner-party conversation runs it a pretty close second in the un-gallantry stakes.'

'Seconded,' said James. 'That doesn't sound like you, Nick. Getting a little bit pissed, are we?' He frowned a shut-up look at him.

'I'm sorry,' said Nick, abashed by his friends'reactions. 'I don't think I meant it to sound quite the way it did.'

Andy, recovered from his surprise, gave a laugh. 'How in God's name did you get to hear about that?'

Borja answered for him. 'Airline gossip, I'm afraid. It travels faster and further than we do.'

'I'd better give you an explanation of my behaviour, then,' said Andy. He was no longer laughing. 'Since I'm obviously sitting in the middle of a group of people who've taken me all along for a total rat. I didn't know till now – how was I supposed to? – about the timing of my colleague's period. Amanda Symons is her name, in case anybody here doesn't know that yet.' He glanced round the table, as if daring someone to challenge him, and wearing a rather cornered look. 'It's true I did want to get home that night. A friend of mine was going for an Aids test the next morning. I'd promised to go along with him for support. But I suppose a real gentleman would have had the honesty to tell Amanda that.'

There was a prickly silence, then Maya said, 'I think you can consider yourself forgiven – by the people around this table at any rate.'

'But tell me about the friend,' Nick wanted to know. 'Was he OK?'

Andy looked at Nick with an expression that was hard to read. 'He's not that close a friend. But thank you for asking. Negative. All clear.'

'I'm glad,' said Nick. Then, more quietly, to Andy, 'I'm really sorry about just now.'

Borja reached for a fresh bottle of wine. The refill so pointedly requested by Neville was overdue.

Ideally Andy would not have chosen to encounter Nick for the second time in the middle of a weekend house party where he knew hardly anyone. But if Borja had forgotten about Alexa's concert when he invited him, well so be it. He was happy to be invited at all, he reflected as he took advantage of the conversational interlude between the end of dinner and bedtime to try to draw the young man out a bit more. Tomorrow the others would be gone. Nick might be more relaxed; he didn't have a call the next morning – Nick had told him that. They would have more space and time at their disposal. In the pursuit of getting to know him better, Andy had time on his side.

People began to drift off to bed. Maya and Neville made their way across the lawn to the East Pavilion. Mark and Alexa were already established in the Red Room, so Guy had to make do with the little one next to it. Andy had been given the Blue Room on the north side of the house beyond the kitchen. On the far side of it he had his own bathroom. He did not visit it until he was already undressed for bed, and was surprised, on opening the door, to find the light already on.

Nick, cleaning his teeth at the washbasin, similarly naked and with his back to Andy, spun round towards him in surprise, toothbrush frozen in mid-stroke.

'I'm so sorry,' said Andy.

'I'd forgotten…' said Nick.

'You look funny,' said Andy. 'And lovely too.'

'You don't look bad yourself.'

Andy was suddenly aware, with a terrifying clarity, that what he said next, and Nick's reaction to it would determine the direction of the rest of his life. There was a moment of silence. Then, 'Spit and rinse,' he said slowly. 'And then come here.'

He had no idea if it would work. Never having had children, or worked as a dentist, he had never told anyone to spit and rinse before, let alone considered using the phrase for a purpose such as this. As a pick-up line it left a lot to be desired. There was a moment while his future hung in the balance. Then, with Andy hardly daring to believe it, Nick obediently cleaned his face and walked the three paces towards him, the lower half of him responding to the summons as unambiguously as if he had been running up a flag.

TWENTY-THREE

Alexa and Mark had already left for London when Nick and Andy arrived in the kitchen for breakfast. Although the unusual geography of the house allowed them to make their entrances from two different directions, their demeanour, facial expressions and body language told the story of the night just ended as clearly to Borja, James and Guy, seated at the table, finishing their coffee, as if they had been holding up the text on placards. But nobody made any remark or even raised an eyebrow.

James and Borja left for work together – James and Borja left for work together: the very concept was a new one for them – taking Guy with them in the car. Conversation during the journey was very carefully orchestrated to avoid the possibly delicate subject of Andy and Nick.

Nick immediately went off to the pavilion to play the piano by himself, pointedly shutting the door behind him and leaving Andy to wander among the glories of the garden on his own. Andy was not sorry to have been given this pause for thought. He felt as though he had caught mercury in his hand: grasp it too hard and it would spurt away from him, relax and it would slip through his fingers. It was not the first time he'd had sex with someone twelve years his junior. But he had not felt, those other times, as he did now. It wasn't just sex they'd enjoyed together, though that had been surprisingly good for a first time: there was a seriousness about Nick that made him different – Andy had sensed that on first meeting him in London three months before. He was very deeply moved. The mercury was a good image, he told himself. Then he imagined another one. He was a fisherman who had hooked a rare, silvery specimen on the end of his line. Now he wondered if that line would be up to the task of reeling in his prize.

He was sitting on a bench in the sunshine when he was startled by the arrival of Neville, in tweeds and a woollen tie and bedroom slippers, appearing through an archway in the orchard wall. 'Hallo,' he said, and then, because Neville was conspicuously alone, 'Where's Maya?'

Neville winced. 'Gone back to High Wycombe, I fear. Another attempt to fix a replay goes west. However,' his face brightened a little, 'there is this filly who lives near the cinema. I don't suppose the others mentioned…'

'Actually they did,' said Andy. 'The Irishman and the shotgun?'

Neville nodded heavily. 'Indeed, indeed. Well anyway, how are things with you, dear boy? Everyone else deserted you?' He cocked his head. They could both hear the distant sound of Nick crashing very loudly through the last sonata of Beethoven at full speed and with scant regard for the right notes. 'Oh dear,' Neville said. 'I do hope Alexa isn't around to listen.'

Andy smiled. 'They left early. The others have gone in to work. As for Nick – I think perhaps I've frightened him off.'

Neville sat down on the bench beside him. 'You do surprise me,' he said in a voice that suggested the surprise was genuine. 'You strike me as a most unfrightening person. I mean that in the nicest possible way. And, if you don't mind a rather impertinent personal observation, I thought last night that young Nick was particularly unfrightened of you. In fact, that he was quite the opposite of frightened – whatever the opposite of frightened is.'

Andy exhaled audibly. 'I think that was true last night. Your powers of observation do you credit. But this morning seems to be a very different matter.'

'Ah,' said Neville meaningfully. 'I see.' He paused for a second. Then, 'Well, maybe that's a good thing?' He studied Andy's face for clues. 'Perhaps? Perhaps not. I don't know, of course, what it is you want.'

'I think,' said Andy, surprising himself vastly by his candour with a near stranger, and astonished by the baldness of the words that came out next, 'I would like to keep him.'

'Would you?' This was the second thing he had heard from Andy that surprised him. 'You can't keep them all, you know.'

'I do know that, Neville. I was married once. I lost that match. After seven years.'

'You lost the match. I do like the way you put things. You're a source of great surprise to me. I thought pilots were such a boring race in general – our friend Borja being the honourable exception – but now it turns out that you have not only a chequered past but a nice turn of phrase. Perhaps you do know what you want after all. I was married too – once or twice actually. But I've never been good at making those things work. Never wanting something quite enough, perhaps. Which is why, I suppose … why Maya is not perambulating the garden with me this morning.'

'I'm sorry,' said Andy. They both watched Neville's cat make his way along the path that led into the wood. Hodge was going birdwatching.

'Listen to that boy in the pavilion,' said Neville, 'banging away at Beethoven with all the wrong notes. If you really mean what you told me – if you want him to know – you'll have to go in and tell him.'

'Not just now, though. Don't you think he wants to be by himself for a bit? All this violent music and the door shut? I'll only screw it all up if I barge in on him now.'

'Only if you say the wrong things.'

Andy managed to laugh. 'Thanks very much.'

'But you won't say the wrong things.' Neville sounded very earnest. 'It's me that's done that all my life: never ever getting it right with women. But you're different from me. You'll do OK. And I think now would be as good a time as any.' He got up to go. 'Good luck.' He patted Andy on the shoulder and ambled off.

Andy felt far from persuaded; rather, he felt like someone shamed into doing something. He walked slowly out of the orchard, across the lawn and round the colonnade. The door of the ballroom made a noise as he opened it that joined the sound of the Broadwood echoing round the room. Nick stopped playing immediately, turned and looked across at him. They both froze, and the wall-length mirrors framed them both, behind and in front of each other's reflections at opposite ends of the great room.

'I didn't think you'd come,' said Nick neutrally.

'Well I did. Do you want me to go away?'

'No.'

'You ran away after breakfast,' Andy said.

'I felt I needed some time to myself.'

'And do you still?'

'Yes.'

A tremor of hurt ran across Andy's face.

'But not right now. Stay.'

Andy moved across the room towards him. 'Tell me what you want from me. Say the word, whatever it is, even if it's disappear, and I'll do it.'

'You're very nice,' said Nick.

'We took each other by surprise last night,' said Andy. 'Maybe there would have been better ways for it to happen.'

'Meaning that you're glad it happened?' Still neutral.

'Yes, I'm glad. Yes. Very glad. If you are.'

'I think I am,' said Nick slowly. 'I think so. And I need time to think. I wasn't sure if you…'

'If I cared at all about you? If it was just a slightly drunken one-off? Yes, to the first. To the second, I hope not. All evening … I didn't know what to think. Peaks and troughs. I wanted sex with you one moment, the next I … I wanted more – but I thought it was too impertinent to think such a thing and threw the thought away.'

'So it was just a drunken one-off? For both of us?'

'I've come to tell you I don't want it to be. I want to ask you…' Andy's fair-skinned face was turning red. 'You'll think me so stupid for saying this: I want to ask you if you could think about turning this into more than just a one-off.'

Nick looked at him in a frozen kind of way, a deer caught in torch-light, a woodcock about to take flight.

'I'd like to see you again,' Andy went on gamely. 'Shit, I'm going to scare you off now, good and proper. I'd like to get to know you better – court you, if you want an old-fashioned expression – but with a particular end in view.' Andy felt the desperation of someone who's said something momentous, on which they can never go back. He went on instead. 'In the wilder moments of last night, and again this morning, I imagined myself asking you … I know it's crazy, a fantasy really, but I found myself wondering if I could ever ask you ... if you'd consider coming to live with me. Fuck it. Now I've said it.'

There was silence for a few long seconds, then, 'I hadn't done what I did last night before,' Nick said rather quietly. 'Go to bed with strange men, that is. And I'm not sure if it's a good jumping-off point for a serious relationship. I can understand how you may feel about it but that doesn't mean I automatically feel the same.'

'I accept all of that,' Andy said, momentarily looking at the carpet. He made a huge effort not to feel he'd been thrown against the ropes. He sprang back. 'I agree one-night stands don't necessarily make good starting points. But there are exceptions. Look at Borja and James. They spent one night together in a hostal in Madrid and it all started from there. So Borja told me.'

'James told me that too,' said Nick. 'They didn't have sex the first night. James more or less courted Borja by letter for six weeks before they went to bed together, and then set up home.'

'Well, if not having sex on the first night is a qualifying factor, it looks like we've already blown it,' said Andy, keeping a straight face. 'We could try not having sex on the second night, I suppose. Do you think that would do as a sort of second best alternative?'

Nick smiled.

'As for courting you for six weeks,' Andy said, risking the jocular tone a moment longer, 'I think I could manage that. Actually, I think I'd enjoy it more than anything. Only, do you think it would be OK if we slept together sometimes while I was doing it?'

Nick didn't laugh exactly, but Andy was relieved to see that he was far from frowning as he answered, 'You're great. You're crazy, but great too. Only I don't want to rush into something that might not… You go on about Borja and James, the perfect couple and all that. But…'

'But what?'

'Well, for one thing, I saw you kissing Borja when you'd come back from Casablanca. And then…'

Andy interrupted him. 'I know. Things happened between you and Borja. Between you and James, right? You can tell me.'

Nick answered slowly. 'Some things nearly happened…'

Andy stopped him, placed a hand on each of Nick's upper arms just below the shoulder. 'And might I hazard a guess that not all of the fault for that lay with James and Borja? Nobody is perfect, you know. No couple is the perfect couple. But sometimes things do work, if the people do a bit of the work too. Fancy giving it a try?'

Nick couldn't manage words. He just nodded.

Andy kissed him gently. 'Your jeans need stitching along the seam, I noticed,' he said. 'Is there some thread indoors? We need to get that fixed.'

That night there was no dissimulation. Nick and Andy said their good-nights and departed together to Nick's Chinese room, from which quarter they emerged together at breakfast time. And it was during breakfast that the registered letter from the airline came. Borja opened it with great agitation and read: … Taking all the circumstances together … series of systems failures … His eyes floundered back and forth among the words until … exonerated of any charge of… 'Hombre!' he called to James, 'I'm cleared! Reinstated!'

James seized the letter to see for himself. 'That's brilliant, man. Oh wait – oh hey – you're also a bloody captain!'

'No.' Borja grabbed the letter again himself; they both tried to take in all its news at once, James trying to hug and cuddle Borja at the same time. Then, both at once they remembered Andy, sitting at the table, staring and grey-faced. His own letter presumably awaited him in London. 'Isn't there a neighbour with a key,' James asked, 'who could read it to you over the phone?' But even as he uttered the words he realised how unattractive an idea that was.

Andy confirmed it for him: 'No-one I'd like to hear my future from.' He would have to drive down to Maida Vale, he said, and read the news for himself. He set off when the others left for work and promised Nick that he'd be back that night.

But it wasn't even lunchtime when Nick was called to the stage-door phone.

'I wanted to tell you first,' said Andy. 'Before telling Borja, before telling my parents. And I'm afraid the news isn't so great. I get moved sideways. Freight division. Flying cargo planes. A drop in pay.'

'It could be worse,' said Nick.

'You mean I might have lost the job altogether.'

'I mean you might not have anyone to share the cost of your flat with.'

There was a silence while Andy tried to work out what Nick was getting at. Then, tentatively, 'Is that … I mean, are you sort of saying yes?'

'I'd have said that even if you had been sacked,' Nick answered. 'I've made my mind up now. But listen, what I want to know is, how do I go about telling my parents? Borja made me realise that it wouldn't be as easy as all that.'

Andy laughed, simply with relief. 'You've thought as far as that already? Wow! But I might just as well ask you – what am I going to say to mine? It doesn't automatically get easier just because I'm older, you know. As far as mine are concerned I'm a divorced heterosexual man who'll presumably find another woman one day. They'll be a bit surprised to find I'm … making some sort of commitment to a bloke.'

'Oh,' said Nick. 'I hadn't thought of that.'

'I don't expect you had.' Andy had not expected the conversation to be going quite like this either. 'You're an extraordinary boy.'

'You too,' said Nick. But it wasn't the words themselves that went to Andy's heart.

'It's so unfair, so fucking unfair,' said Borja. The words came in the darkness as he lay, legs and arms entangled with James's, in the bed they shared. 'I've literally been given Andy's job. Through no merit of my own. I was as involved in the Casa mix-up as he was. It's simply that the company had it in for him. How can I accept promotion when it comes like that? I'd feel I was spitting in Andy's face.'

'But he doesn't see it like that,' said James. 'He told me when we were waiting for you and Nick to finish work. He said that finding Nick meant everything to him, that anything he might have lost didn't even weigh in the balance. And he sees you as the person who gave him Nick.'

'I'd found a friend in Andy,' Borja went on, ignoring James. 'The first one I'd made at the airline. The first real one anyway. Now we won't even be in the same division. I'm not sure I even want to go on being a pilot. I'm not sure I am one. Sometimes I feel I'm just a kid who's playing around with dangerous, expensive toys in the sky. I don't know if I could do what Rafael did: when the time came he traded in his life to give others a chance. That's what real grown men do.'

'Hey, Boyee,' James said gently. 'Do you think that Andy doesn't go through all that too sometimes? Don't you think that all pilots do – even the big macho he-men? Don't you remember what I told you two years ago when I sacked that old lady, Phoebe, in the box office, and six weeks later she was dead? Remember how I said I felt I had no business to be doing the job I did – that I was just a child with a Pollock's toy theatre? But Monday morning comes each week and we get up and get on with it. Last week you started a new job – as a stage manager. Next week you start again – again. Next Monday you're my captain.'

'Jamie, I can't. You must phone Equity. Tell them I want to join. I'll stay on as stage manager. Please.' Borja was holding on to James like a set of clamps.

James stroked his lover's hair. 'You know you don't want that. The new man's already lined up. What would I have to say to him?'

The unknowable, desirable, tantalisingly unreachable person your lover was before you knew him, James thought. Tonight he had the feeling of being nearer to that boy than ever before. Did their encounter with Nick, separately and together, have anything to do with that? Nick whose eyes were the mirrors of Borja's own. 'I'll tell you a story,' James said quietly. 'Remember once they let me up in the control tower at Luton when I was meeting you off a flight? And I watched the little pulsing blip of light that was your plane inching nearer, second by second across the dark screen? Later I could see it as a speck in the distant sky, then growing to the size of a toy as it touched the tarmac, expanding, when it reached the apron, into a whole world. A world of hardware, systems, cabins and cockpit and a stream of people pouring out: a world that was as big, as vast as my whole world – as big as everything – because it encompassed you.' He stopped, then went on, his voice almost a whisper. 'Sometimes you tell me, on a very clear day, when you've been heading up to Birmingham or Manchester, that you've seen Sevenscore from miles away…'

James felt rather than heard Borja remind him, 'And sometimes on the weather radar. Like you at Luton. Two tiny blips on the screen.'

And when it's clear...'

'Then the pavilions look like two salt-grains catching the light on a green cloth. So small…'

'And yet…'

James experienced Borja's nod of assent as a gentle rubbing of forehead against his temple and a small warm crackle of hair.

TWENTY-FOUR

It was nearly the end of the year when James and Borja paid their promised visit to Seville. They travelled via Salamanca. Borja visited his mother at the farm, but he made that particular pilgrimage on his own: James was unlikely to see the place until the matriarch had died. But he did meet Borja's brother Javier in a bar in the town and they got on just fine. To Borja's surprise Javier and Simón were making a good fist of running the farm together without falling out; it was only their mother who insisted on arguing with every decision they made, which was her way of coping with the loss of her beloved husband perhaps, but just maybe her interventions helped Javier and Simón to maintain their united front.

James met Marisa and her children, and Borja found himself confronting Rizo once again. But so much lay between the present moment and the patch of turbulence they'd gone through nearly a year ago that they faced each other as if across a chasm – the way that, in the theatre, the stage-left and stage-right crews faced each other, during a performance, across the unbridgeable chasm of light that was the stage. Rizo had grown a further inch or so, and his stub of a nose was beginning to develop into a strong straight one in emulation of his father's. He proudly introduced his new girlfriend.

In Seville they stayed for a couple of days in a small hotel while they attended and celebrated Mark and Alexa's wedding. After that, they moved into the house in Virgen de la Luz which had been briefly put at their disposal while its owners honeymooned in Italy. They chose to occupy the small cramped bedroom with the single bed, and late at night would sit on the roof terrace drinking a nightcap under the hanging stars.

In the daytime they took picnics into the gardens of the Alcázar. Skirting the cathedral where white-starred jasmine clambered over sun-cooked walls, they made their way through the familiar horseshoe arch into the palace grounds. Scrawny cats sunbathed and scratched beneath the palm trunks, and in the rough bark above them lizards scampered and peeped among the crevices. Through another archway in a wall where bougainvillea cascaded in a crimson petal fall, the whole vista filled with trees, lemon and orange, growing in a tidied luxuriance: dense gloss-green foliage from which their fruits blazed forth as if batteries had stored a summerful of sun.

They sat silently, contemplating the opulent gilded beauty that surrounded them. Even the ground was strewn with windfalls like balls of copper and gold. They had jokingly promised to take some back for Nick to make marmalade with. Nick and Andy were staying at the Court House in their absence. Since the summer they had divided their time between Sevenscore and London, where Nick was working part time, managing the English end of the Eulogio Pérez Cabrera Memorial Trust – thanks to one of Alexa's inspired ideas.

'I'm still rather amazed it's worked out so well between Nick and Andy,' James observed.

'They've only lasted six months,' said Borja.

'They've only known each other six months,' objected James. 'Don't be a damp fart. People used to say the same sort of thing about us. But I'm still surprised, aren't you? Andy's one thing – he might have been looking for someone like Nick for years. But Nick himself… It wasn't the same with us. We'd both had sex with men before, been romantically involved; we both knew we were gay, even if you didn't actually want to be. But Nick…'

'You're forgetting,' said Borja, 'that Nick and Andy had at least met each other once before, in London when we'd flown back from Casa.'

'Yes,' said James, 'but...' As he hesitated he heard Borja's intake of breath. He let him speak first.

'He did sort of seem to know what he was getting into,' Borja ventured cautiously. 'In a way.'

'Dancing with a man in front of six hundred people?' James said, with a hint of friendly mischief.

'Among other things, I suppose.' Disconcertingly a memory flashed: of a climb up to the grid, of the louvred shutters opening to reveal the roofscape of the city, magically sunset-lit...

'I suppose it may have had something to do with us,' James was saying, sounding part uncomfortable, part pleasantly surprised.

'Us together, do you mean?' queried Borja, 'or...?'

'Together and separately too, perhaps.' James found himself suddenly embarked on a torch-lit walk across the lawn to the ballroom pavilion; he heard the exuberant descending scale that climaxes the last Schubert Impromptu, heard its final echoing crash ring like a massive bell around the high walls and decorated ceiling; he thought it would resonate for ever now. He heard Borja say, musingly,

'I know that neither of us actually...'

'But all the same,' James said.

'It's as if the two of us were... You know what I mean by a STAR, don't you?'

'Woodcocks have STARs and pilots have them,' said James. 'Fixed but invisible ways...'

'I see,' said Borja, slightly thrown by hearing James quoting Nick, who'd obviously been quoting him. 'Well, it's almost as if we, you and I, I mean, were way-points along Nick's STAR.'

The idea pleased James, who smiled at it. 'Way-points along his STAR. Yes, I see...'

'OK, come on,' said Borja, peering down the sandy, fruit-overhung avenues that ran sunlit in all directions from where they sat. 'The gardeners aren't around. Let's get those oranges for him.'

'How many do you think we'll need?'

'A dozen or so, not more.'

'Maybe,' said James, 'we ought to make some for ourselves too.'

They got up and started to wander among the trees and the myrtle-hedged borders, avoiding the eye-lines of the gardeners, and feeling more like a pair of naughty schoolboys than one theatre manager and one airline captain, as they stooped to pick up the lemons and oranges that littered the sandy ground like fallen moons and suns.

****

Along the Stars is the second book in the **Seville Trilogy**. The first book is **Orange Bitter, Orange Sweet** and the third is **Woodcock Flight**.

About the Author

Anthony McDonald is the author of more than thirty books. He studied modern history at Durham University, then worked briefly as a musical instrument maker and as a farmhand before moving into the theatre, where he has worked in every capacity except director and electrician. He has also spent several years teaching English in Paris and London. He now lives in rural East Sussex.

Novels by Anthony McDonald

TENERIFE
THE DOG IN THE CHAPEL
TOM & CHRISTOPHER AND THEIR KIND
DOG ROSES
THE RAVEN AND THE JACKDAW
SILVER CITY
IVOR'S GHOSTS
ADAM
BLUE SKY ADAM
GETTING ORLANDO
ORANGE BITTER, ORANGE SWEET
ALONG THE STARS
WOODCOCK FLIGHT

Short stories

MATCHES IN THE DARK:
13 Tales of Gay Men

Along The Stars

Diary

RALPH: DIARY OF A GAY TEEN

Comedy

THE GULLIVER MOB

Gay Romance Series:

Sweet Nineteen
Gay Romance on Garda
Gay Romance in Majorca
Gay Tartan
Cocker and I
Cam Cox
The Paris Novel
The Van Gogh Window
Tibidabo
Spring Sonata
Touching Fifty
Romance on the Orient Express

And, writing as 'Adam Wye'

Boy Next Door
Love in Venice
Gay in Moscow

All titles are available as Kindle ebooks and as paperbacks from Amazon.

www.anthonymcdonald.co.uk

Made in the USA
Middletown, DE
12 April 2018